Death in Abundance

Frank Curtiss

Frank Curtiss

An Intellect Publishing Book

www.IntellectPublishing.com

Copyright 2022 Frank Curtiss

ISBN: 978-1-954693-71-5

First Edition: December 2022

FV-4

Inquiries to: info@IntellectPublishing.com

Contact the Author:

Frank Curtiss
11744 158th Ave. NE
Redmond, WA 98052
C: 425-269-3909

Email: curtissliterary@gmail.com
www.frankcurtiss.com

Dedication

This book is dedicated to Jenna Curtiss, the daughter who left us too soon. My heart will swell with joy on the day we are reunited in heaven.

Frank Curtiss

Death in Abundance

Frank Curtiss

~~~~ **TUESDAY, MARCH 3** ~~~~

Chapter One

Tuesday morning

What did I do? Antonio Cortese stared blankly through the concourse windows—coursing with rain—at the plane he was supposed to be boarding. *Is it too late to get on that plane?*

He watched the passengers boarding, several people wearing masks. Antonio wondered if they would soon become mandatory. It made it harder to read their faces, but their eyes told the story. Some were wide with nervousness. Others showed a huge sense of relief. The silver-haired woman glanced at him and her eyes gave a weak smile. A short time ago she was sitting next to him in the boarding area, wringing her hands. He'd watched the fear on her face as she desperately hoped that her stand-by opportunity would become reality … to escape Italy before it was shut down by the Covid-19 virus. Now he was her knight in shining armor, after they walked to the ticket counter and transferred his ticket to her.

When she asked him why, he'd told her about the phone call. She'd looked at him, cocked her head, and spoke, "A freedom fighter, huh? Well, go find whoever did that and give 'em hell!"

7

He'd made the decision the moment Gabriella called him. He hadn't taken the time to consider everything that was at stake. Now it felt rash. But Gabriella was the woman he had just become engaged to, and she needed him. Or so he told himself. Maybe it was the other way around. The problem was that he was also needed back home in Seattle.

Behind the silver-haired woman some people jostled in line. Tempers flared. It seemed stupid to Antonio since they all had assigned seats. But fear makes people crazy. And the pandemic was hitting Italy faster than any country in the world.

Second thoughts and feelings of irresponsibility kept overtaking him like a tidal wave. He might have called it *anguish of the soul,* a term he'd read in a book, but this was nothing compared to some of the hardships he'd faced in recent years.

C'mon, Antonio. Stop second-guessing yourself. You made your decision. Time to stick with it. It's what you do. Fighting evil was in his DNA, especially when it came against the people he loved.

The voice in his head was telling him the truth. At this time in his life, Antonio was a restaurateur. And he loved it. But he was a detective at heart. One who protects. It was what his father did. And his mother's younger brother, Nicolo. And that's how he'd spent twenty years of his career, until an injury forced his early retirement.

He felt his sense of purpose return, and that steely resolve in his gut. He took one last look at the jet plane, then pulled up the handle on his carry-on bag and headed toward the exit of Pisa's Galileo Galilei International Airport.

Chapter Two

Tuesday morning

Antonio forced aside the last vestiges of doubt as he sought shelter from the driving rain. He zipped up his coat against the chill. Still, the wind blew waves of moisture over him. He moved further back and huddled. Twenty minutes ago, he was heading back to Seattle, a newly engaged man, grudgingly leaving his fiancé behind to go home and set his life in order.

He still didn't know what their future together would look like. He couldn't imagine asking Gabriella to move to the States. Not only would she be giving up her career as Carabinieri Colonel, in charge of their investigative offices in Siena, but she had just taken custody of her niece, Serena, the daughter of her brother Andrea and his wife Bria, who lost their lives in a car accident. A move to the States would take Serena away from her extended family, a lot to ask of a twelve-year-old after such a loss.

Am I ready to move to Italy? he asked himself. It's not that he didn't love it here. His mother, Elena, was born and raised in Tuscany, and he had spent several weeks here every summer while growing up. His relationship with his Italian aunts, uncles and cousins was very close. But it meant leaving behind his stateside family, including his son, Jonathan, his wife, Leah and their five-month-old twins. The twins had brought him so much joy and healing after three years of grieving loss. He thought about how much he wanted to be part of their lives. *I suppose I could bring them to Italy every summer ... the way Mother did with us.* And then there was his restaurant to consider.

Antonio reached into his carry-on and pulled out the bottle of Tylenol. He took three to alleviate the throbbing pain in the broken knuckle of his right hand. He looked at his watch … 8:00 AM. He guessed it would be another fifteen minutes until Gabriella arrived back. It would be 11:00 PM in Seattle. Shane was a night owl. He hit his speed dial button.

"Antonio. *Come va?* What's up? I thought you'd be on the plane by now."

"I gave up my seat."

There was a long silence before Shane replied, "What's going on? Is everyone okay?"

"More or less. I just got a call from Gabriella … about an hour after she dropped me off. The *Polizia di Stato* detective who is investigating Andrea and Bria's accident called her. They concluded it was no accident. It was deliberate. Almost certainly premeditated."

"Whoa! But what does that have to do with you? I'm sure they'll be investigating it."

Antonio stated the only answer he could come up with, "She needs me, Shane. I could hear it in her voice."

"You realize the law enforcement people in Italy are probably getting sick of you sticking your nose into their business," Shane said, a sardonic smile in his voice.

"Yeah. I'm sure they are. But I need to do this." Antonio felt a twinge of guilt. He knew running the restaurant was putting Shane under a lot of stress. "I hope you understand."

"I do boss … sort of. I just hope you can make it back before they lock down Italy. I'm up to my eyeballs over here."

Antonio thought about the faces of the people boarding the plane. "I'm sure I can find a way. Just do the best you can until I get back. I'm going to owe you."

"Goes without saying. I'm really diggin' living in your house, though. If I had time, I'd finish remodeling your kitchen. It's kind of a pain with things all torn up."

"Why? You planning a dinner party?"

"I wish. Listen, have you talked to my mom yet?"

"No. I was going to ask you to give her a call."

"You don't want to face her yet, huh? I don't blame you. She's a mess."

Another wave of guilt hit Antonio as he thought about all that his sister Alessia was dealing with. "I imagine she's in bed by now."

"Yeah. Lucky for you. I'll call her in the morning. I'm sure you'll be hearing from her."

"Can't wait. How is *Nonna* Elena doing?" Antonio's eighty-year old mother, Elena, had just been released from the hospital—recovering from Covid-19. Her care had fallen to his sister, Alessia, who had too much on her plate already. Her husband, Matthew, had recently undergone surgery for a cancerous brain tumor. His radiation treatments were taking their toll on both of them.

"Getting stronger. You know what a fortress she is."

"I do," Antonio said, with a chuckle. He thought how his mother had beat cancer in her seventies. "Listen, I see Gabriella's car arriving. Gotta run. *Ciao!*"

"Before you hang up," Shane said, "I have one last thing to say. Be careful, *Zio* Antonio! Every time you help with an investigation over there you end up in the hospital. I'm worried that one of these days your luck's gonna run out."

"Don't worry, Shane. I'm done with Italian hospitals!" But just hearing Shane say it made him worry. Every time someone told him that, it turned out to be for good reason.

Chapter Three

Tuesday morning

Gabriella pulled up in her silver SUV, a first-generation Audi Q5. Antonio opened the rear hatch and tossed his bag in, getting even more soaked in the mere seconds it took. Serena gave him a quick hug as she moved to the back seat. Antonio climbed in the passenger side.

Gabriella drove like a rally car driver, as the windshield wipers slapped out their rhythm. She knew how to handle her vehicle. She didn't say a word for several minutes. He hardly recognized her with her brows furrowed and lips pressed tightly together. Finally, on a straight section of highway, she peeled her eyes from the road and glanced at him. "You don't need to do this."

"A bit late for that now."

"I shouldn't have called you. You might not be able to get home if you wait much longer."

Antonio stared at her. "Maybe I don't want to."

"I thought …" she glanced over, looking confused.

"I know, I know. I should … I need to. But you need me."

"Others need you, too. Aren't you worried about your restaurant?"

"Yes."

"And your mom and sister? Maybe you should try to schedule another flight."

"You tryin' to get rid of me?"

"No. But I can handle this."

Antonio didn't know what to say. This side of Gabriella was new to him. He knew she had a strong independent streak, and was used to looking out for herself. But it felt like she was pushing him away—like she had withdrawn her head into a tortoise shell.

"Tell me what you know," he finally said.

"It took forever for the forensic people to finish their analysis. They finally concluded that Andrea's car wasn't hit just once, but multiple times from the driver's side. Someone was clearly trying to force them off the road." She adjusted her rearview mirror to look at Serena. "I'll explain the rest later."

Serena leaned forward. "Don't try to hide this from me, *Zia!* I'm a big girl. I want to know what happened."

Gabriella stole another glance in the mirror, deciding how much to say. She moved over to the fast lane and passed a slow-moving truck before continuing. "They were forced off the road as they were coming onto a bridge. It had to be a large vehicle. Their car rolled several times … that's one reason it was hard to assess. The car ended up upside down in a shallow river, the Arbia. That's all they will tell me. I asked about the status of the investigation and she would not tell me anything. All she would say was that they were looking into it, but that they are undermanned right now with the pandemic. I get the feeling that she is a capable detective, but with too much on her plate."

Antonio glanced back at Serena. Her face was filled with disbelief and anger. "We can't let them get away with it!" she blurted out.

They rode silently for a few minutes. "I offered my assistance with the investigation," Gabriella said. "She turned me down. Said it was a conflict of interest, and I needed to stay the hell away from it."

"She's right."

Anger flared in Gabriella's dark brown eyes. "Whose side are you on?"

"Yours. I'm just …"

"You, of all people, should talk. The way you …"

"I know what you're going to say, Gabriella. The way I got involved with Nicolo when Giulia was in a coma. And when Raphael went missing. I'm not saying you should let this go. But the water is dangerous. We need to tread carefully."

She looked his way and her anger faded. "You are right. But I refuse to allow this to be moved to some back burner."

"I already knew that," he said, with a smile meant to disarm. "Start by telling me some information. I don't even know what Andrea did for a living. And why he and Bria went to Montepulciano."

"Andrea worked for the Italian Wine Commission as a fraud investigator. He told me he had some work to do in Montepulciano and that he and Bria were staying over an extra night for some personal time. She rarely accompanied him on a trip. God, I wish she hadn't this time."

Serena sat forward again. "They were having a hard time lately. Papà was under a lot of stress. They were fighting a lot. Mamà said it would be good for them to get away together."

She said it with such maturity, without the emotion Antonio would have expected. But then she turned and stared silently out the window. Antonio turned forward and saw they were nearing the town of Castellina in Chianti, which meant they were only a few kilometers from Gabriella's farmhouse.

"His job might explain what happened to them," Antonio said. "Maybe he discovered something that someone desperately wanted to keep secret."

"*Appunto!* Precisely what I was thinking."

Chapter Four

Tuesday, late morning

As they drove past Castellina's town coop, Italy's version of a grocery store, people were lined up under a sea of umbrellas that stretched for two blocks. Many were wearing masks, most of them makeshift. It dawned on Antonio that they were stocking up for the lockdown rumored to be coming. A chocolate-brown hound sat stoically on the stone steps, as if keeping guard.

Gabriella touched him on the shoulder and pointed. "The elderly couple there. Those are my in-laws, Renato's parents. Poor souls. I wonder how long they've been waiting in that line?"

Gabriella's first husband, Renato, a lieutenant in the Carabinieri, had died in a bomb blast while serving in Albania. Their daughter, Liliana, was just a baby when he was killed. Fifteen years later she died of leukemia. The loss of a spouse and daughter was something he and Gabriella had in common. A club neither wanted to be a part of.

The first time Antonio visited Gabriella's home, a two-hundred-year-old Tuscan farmhouse, she had told him the story of her in-laws. The house had been theirs. They bequeathed it to Renato and Gabriella when Liliana was born, and moved into a small house in Castellina. It was much less for them to take care of, and they could walk nearly everywhere they needed to go. After the death of Renato, they allowed Gabriella to keep the house. They treated her like their own daughter.

Gabriella found a place to park and turned to Antonio. "I would like to help them out. Do you mind? God knows how long they have been out here in this weather."

"Of course," Antonio replied. Gabriella pulled a large umbrella from the back. The three of them squeezed beneath it and walked two blocks to find them. The elderly couple smiled broadly when they saw them approaching. Antonio stood aside as they embraced the girls, commenting on how much Serena had grown since they last saw her.

Gabriella spoke. "Francesco, Gaia, I would like you to meet someone. This is my fiancé, Antonio Cortese."

"We've heard so much about you, Antonio," Gaia said, as she took his hands in hers. "You've been so good to our Gabriella. Congratulations on your engagement!" They were a fine-looking couple. The silver hair and deeply etched lines on their faces were worn with dignity. Antonio imagined that their son, Renato, must have been a handsome young man.

"How long have you been standing in line?" Gabriella asked.

"Over an hour," Francesco offered. "We probably have another hour to go. Everybody is stocking up. I hope there'll be something left when we get inside. *Grazie Dio*, we still have some food in our pantry from last year's garden!"

"Don't worry," Gabriella said. "We'll make sure you have enough. Whatever you can't get today, we'll find elsewhere."

Antonio glanced around. There was a coffee bar about fifty meters away across the street. "Listen, Gabriella, why don't I hold the place in line. You girls take Francesco and Gaia for coffee," he pointed. "I'll text you when I reach the front of the line."

"No, no. Completely unnecessary," Francesco said. But when he looked at his wife, she smiled and nodded.

"I insist," Antonio said.

"Can I stay with you, *Zio* Antonio?" Serena asked.

He scrutinized her face. This was the first time she had referred to him as uncle. "Absolutely. I'd love the company!"

*****

About forty minutes later, Antonio texted Gabriella. *Second in line.* People had been coming out loaded down like pack animals.

When they entered, he saw that Francesco and Gaia's fears were founded. The shelves were about three-quarters empty. They hurried through the aisles, grabbing this-and-that, with seemingly little thought. There was only a smattering of pasta remaining. Gaia grabbed three boxes and kept moving. A clerk was re-stocking the tomato products. Gaia placed a half dozen cans of whole-peeled tomatoes in her cart and some tomato puree. They bought cheeses, prosciutto, a salami, milk, flour, cream, coffee, lettuce, and a variety of winter fruit. When they got to the aisle where they should have found toilet paper it was empty.

Gaia turned to Francesco. "Time for you to install that bidet I've been pestering you about." He nodded, looking embarrassed.

As Francesco paid the clerk, who looked frazzled, Gaia turned to them. "*Grazie. Grazie mille!* Now, you're coming to our house for lunch. Just some panini sandwiches. But I will not take no for an answer."

"If you insist," Gabriella said. "But just for a short time. I have some important calls to make."

*****

They pulled down the long drive to Gabriella's farmhouse, shared by two other stone houses. The property sloped to the west, with a view of the valley below, a small stream overflowing its banks, and rolling hills beyond. A tiny hamlet occupied one of the hilltops. The hills were graced with vineyards, and groves of olive trees, interspersed with wooded areas. One thing Antonio admired about the Italians was their respect for the land. They always left a portion of the land in its natural state.

Antonio pulled out his cell phone and took a picture. The rain had stopped and the sky directly above was the deepest possible blue. But more stormy weather was headed their way. Above the hills to the west, dark purple cumulus clouds towered high into the sky.

They received an enthusiastic welcome from Gabriella's dogs. Serena knelt between them and wrapped one arm around each. "Lucia … Gia, I missed you girls!" They were beige and brown with hairy faces and ears. Antonio recalled that they were mother and daughter, Italian *Spinone*, a rare breed of hunting dogs.

Gabriella wasted little time. She led the way to one of her guest rooms and turned to him with a weak smile. "I hope you do not mind, Antonio. I know we are engaged, but I still …"

"It's fine," he said, with a reassuring smile. Gabriella had already explained that she intended to model her traditional values for Serena. He respected that. It made him all the more eager for their wedding night. He only wished he knew when that would be.

"I'm going to call Andrea's boss. I need to understand why he went to Montepulciano. Do you want to listen in?"

"That's the reason I'm here."

Chapter Five

Tuesday, early afternoon

Gabriella asked Serena to take the dogs for a walk, then feed and water them. She and Antonio took a seat at the kitchen table. She dialed, set the phone on speaker, and placed it on the table. It was answered on the second ring. *"Pronto."*

"Pronto. Arrivederci. Is this Agostino Leone?"

"Yes. How may I help you?"

"This is Gabriella Ferrara. My brother Andr …"

"Ah, yes, Gabriella. It's good to hear from you. I never got the opportunity to talk to you at the memorial."

"I'm sorry. I didn't realize you were …"

"No need to apologize. We … my wife and I … we arrived at the last minute. Heavy traffic leaving Roma. Afterward, there was such a crush of people wanting to give you and your family their condolences. And I knew you had never met us. I do hope you'll accept my apology for sneaking away without giving you our regards."

"Of course. Everything is a blur from that day anyway." She allowed an appropriate pause. "Listen, I hope you do not mind my intrusion. I am calling in an unofficial capacity. I was hoping you can tell me the reason Andrea had gone to Montepulciano. The *Polizia di Stato* will not give me any information."

The phone was silent for several seconds. "*Polizia?* Are you saying that this accident was intentional? I feared as much. I'm surprised the *Polizia* have not called me."

"I just got confirmation this morning, *Signore* Leone. The forensic team found it difficult to determine. Their car had rolled several times. But it appears that it was hit more than once and forced from the road by a heavier vehicle."

"*Madonna!* Listen, Gabriella, I know you are with the Carabinieri. But isn't it a conflict for you to be investigating this?"

"*Per favore, signore.* I understand your concern. I realize I am breaking protocol. But the *Polizia* are undermanned right now. They have a lot on their plate. If they are able to give it due attention, I will stand down and let them do their job. If not ..."

"I understand, *signora*. I'm sure I would feel the same."

"Then can you share the details with me? Was he investigating some kind of fraud? Something that could have motivated someone to kill them?"

"Alright. I will tell you what he was doing there. But if anyone asks, you tell them it was Andrea who shared the purpose of his trip with you. Do we have an understanding?"

"Yes. You and I never had this conversation."

"Do you recall the big controversy in 2008 regarding Brunello di Montalcino? The press called it Brunellogate."

"Of course. It was all over the news. There was a problem with production levels exceeding the harvest. It was thought that some wineries were adding illegal grapes into their wines. I heard much of the wine was declassified and sold for lower prices. Are you saying something similar is going on in Montepulciano?

"Possibly." Antonio stared at the phone in disbelief. His Aunt Chiara and Uncle Sylvio were producers of Vino Nobile di Montepulciano.

"I must ask that you keep that confidential," he added. "We have no proof of wrongdoing. We learned a great deal from the Brunello scandal. It was not handled well. Once the press got hold of it, the reputation of many fine wineries was sullied."

"I understand," Gabriella replied.

"We've been seeing increased production of Vino Nobile in the last few years, exceeding that of new vineyards coming into production, and the harvest reports do not support the increase. We were keeping an eye on it when the president of the *consorzio* came to us of his own volition. He had reason to be suspicious himself of a few of the wineries. He feared a possible scandal which could damage the reputation of the wine, which would hurt them all. He was being proactive."

"Andrea went to Montepulciano to investigate?"

"Yes. It was the first fact-finding trip. A general investigation. If I had any idea of the danger, I never would have let him take Bria with him."

"Do you know the details of who he was investigating? Who he spoke with, the wineries he visited?"

"Very little, I'm afraid. He did a good deal of research prior to his trip to narrow the scope of his investigation. There are over two hundred vineyards in the DOCG, the government-controlled wine region, which surrounds Montepulciano. He would have filed his finding when he returned, but of course, sadly, that never happened. It's the first time we have ever lost an investigator. If his death is related, he must have discovered something of importance."

"My thoughts exactly," Gabriella said. "Is there anything else that might help in the investigation?"

"The president of the *consorzio* may be of assistance. Andrea had a meeting scheduled with him. I believe he also visited four or five wineries which had sizeable production increases. He was supposed to deliver some wine samples to a wine chemist. With everything going on, I have yet to follow up to see if he made it."

"*Grazie, Signore* Leone. Can you give me the contact information for the chemist? I can contact him and let you know."

"Please, call me Agostino. Yes, I will look that up and text it to you. I wish I had more to tell you. Were you able to recover his personal effects? Andrea was fastidious. He always carried a small leather-bound journal in which he kept his notes. I'm sure there would be something there if it was recovered."

"We did receive some of his things … luggage and personal effects. My parents went through them. They said nothing about a journal, but I will look for it. *Grazie* again, Agostino. You have been enormously helpful."

"Feel free to call me anytime. And please, keep me in the loop on your findings. I would like to know if you discover who did such an evil thing."

"Certainly. I will."

A few minutes after hanging up, Gabriella received a text with the contact information for the wine chemist. She placed a call to him. It went directly to his voice mail. She sighed deeply and left a message.

Chapter Six

Tuesday evening

Antonio's teeth rattled as the house shook violently. Lightning lit up the night sky. Hail began to pound the red tile roof. Minutes later it turned to a torrential downpour. It was a good night to be curled up on the couch in front of a blazing fire, sharing a lap blanket with the girls. Twelve-year-old Serena leaned on his shoulder with her feet on Gabriella's lap. It seemed like just yesterday, and yet an eternity ago, when his own daughter would do the same thing. It put him in a melancholy mood.

When Gabriella first told him that she wanted to adopt Serena, he selfishly worried that it might disrupt their relationship … that raising her might cause Gabriella to put him on a back burner. Now it felt like they were becoming a family.

Dinner had been a simple affair. Gabriella's freezer was full of dishes brought by neighbors when they heard of Andrea and Bria's loss. Tonight, they warmed a casserole of Coniglio alla Cacciatore: rabbit, hunter's-style, in a sauce of tomatoes, red wine, onions, mushrooms and peppers. Antonio prepared a batch of creamy polenta, and they served the cacciatore over the top, with a side of broccoli raab, which Gabriella cooked with garlic and pine nuts. It had been the perfect meal for a night like this.

Serena, in her pink cotton nightgown, eventually wandered off to bed and Gabriella took her place, leaning against his chest. She stayed silent for a long time. The rain was like music on the roof. Every so often thunder rolled again and lightning lit the sky. It seemed to be moving farther off.

Antonio brushed his fingers through her hair. As they crossed her cheek, he felt warm tears. He wasn't aware she was crying. He leaned over and kissed her cheek. "Want to talk about it?

"Not really." She wiped her eyes with her sleeve. "I never thought I'd be investigating my own brother's murder. I do not know if I can do this." She went quiet again.

"I can handle it, if it's too hard. You can focus on Serena."

She sat up and locked eyes with him. "I have to do this. I'm glad you stayed, though. I don't think I could do it alone."

"What about the *Polizia*? It's certain to cause a problem if you cross swords with them."

"I'm going to call the detective first thing tomorrow. I'll tell her what we learned. I don't care if she gets angry. If I get the sense that she is devoting her time and resources, I'll back off."

"I'll support you. Whatever you decide."

She locked eyes with him again. "Thank you. I knew that. I'm going to go to bed, *cara mia*. Sleep well."

"I'm going to sit by the fire a while longer."

She nodded, then took his face in her hands, kissed him, and padded away toward her room. It took his last ounce of courage not to follow. He stood, put another log on the fire, opened another bottle of Chianti, and poured a glass. He sat down and put his feet up toward the fire. His body wanted to rest, but his mind had a lot of thinking to do.

*****

Antonio's life had turned out so differently than he thought it would. It didn't seem that long ago when Christina was Serena's age, and Jonathan was learning to drive. Antonio had loved his job as a detective in Newport Beach, California. He had fully expected to continue that career until he retired. Then came the night when he and his partner were trailing some drug dealers. One of them jumped him, causing them both to fall from the cliffs of Corona del Mar onto the rocks below. That split second in time changed the direction of his life, bringing his twenty-year career to an end.

Weeks in the hospital and an ensuing battle with opioids put him in a tailspin. Then his father, a detective in San Pedro, was killed on the job, only weeks before retiring. Not long after, his mother, Elena, was told she had breast cancer. He began to drink heavily and made a huge mistake, an affair with an ex-partner. It was short-lived, but the guilt followed him for years. He was still amazed and grateful that his wife, Randi—a woman of great faith—had given him a second chance. He still missed her every day.

When his sister, Alessia, got remarried to a great guy named Matthew, and moved to Medina, across the lake from Seattle, their mother moved up to live with them so Alessia could care for her. Looking for a fresh start, he and Randi followed. A year later they opened their Italian restaurant. The years that followed were challenging: his mother's cancer battle, establishing their business, raising teenagers, and rebuilding trust in his marriage. Things had come so far when they flew to France that summer to meet their daughter. Christina had spent a year in Paris attending music school. They were spending their last day in

France—preparing to fly on to Tuscany to visit family—when the unthinkable happened.

There are nightmares in life from which you never awake. That night in Nice was one of them—when a terrorist drove his large truck through the crowds, killing more than eighty, and injuring hundreds more. He could still feel the desperation he had as he searched for Randi and Christina. But he was too late. Three and a half years had passed. His mind had finally accepted that there was nothing he could have done, but his heart still wasn't buying it. He hadn't thought he would ever recover … or ever love another woman again.

He took a sip of wine as a thought invaded his psyche out of nowhere … *Time to stop looking at the world through that prism.* He set his glass down and stared at the fire. He'd never thought of it quite that way. *Where in the world did that come from?* He knew it was true. If only it were that easy.

Hindsight, of course, can be twenty-twenty. He was finally beginning to see how much healing had taken place … though in ways he had never expected. When he returned to Italy last year after a five-year absence—arriving as summer was giving way to autumn—he had hoped to find healing among the people and place he loved so dearly. On the day after his arrival, he and his young cousin, Giulia, were out cycling when they were intentionally run off the road, putting them both in the hospital. Giulia—not even the intended victim—ended up in a coma, and they faced the fear of losing her. In their manhunt to find the men who caused it, he had ended up in the hospital a second time. He would never forget the morning he woke up and Giulia was brought to his room. He thanked God every day for that miracle. She was like a daughter to him.

But it wasn't the only miracle that took place on that trip. The other was the morning Gabriella walked into his hospital room to investigate the cycling incident. He knew the moment he saw her that his life was about to change. What surprised him most was that their love had blossomed so quickly. Now they were engaged.

Antonio knew he should go to bed but poured another glass of wine and stared at the dancing flames, which mesmerized him. It occurred to him that it had been more than a week since he'd been plagued by his nightmares. He'd come to the understanding that he was dealing with PTSD. It wasn't his own life he was afraid of losing. It was the thought of losing others that he loved. Recently, in Firenze, when Gabriella was in harm's way, she'd found her way into his nightmares alongside Randi and Christina. The dreams were never quite the same, but there was one common element … his inability to protect those he loved, and the overwhelming feeling of helplessness.

He had begun to face these fears with the help of a man he greatly admired. Father Bruno was a Catholic priest who ran a rescue organization in Firenze that aided exploited women, especially those in the Nigerian refugee community who were forced into sex slavery. Father Bruno had been of great service in their search for Raphael. He and Antonio had become friends, and he had helped him to understand the root of his fears. He had also promised to pray for him. Antonio was beginning to think maybe God was listening.

A loud clap of thunder dragged his mind back to the present. He knew he should go to bed, but poured another glass of wine instead and watched the dying embers.

His mind picked up where it left off this morning, wrestling with second thoughts about his decision to stay, knowing how much he was needed at home. *C'mon, Antonio, stop second-guessing yourself. Time to stick with your decision. It's what you do. Fighting evil is in your DNA, especially when it comes against the people you love.*

That voice in his head was speaking the truth. Though he was a restaurateur at this time in his life—and he loved it—he was still a detective at heart. One who serves and protects. It was what his father did. And his *Zio* Nicolo. And it's how he'd spent twenty years of his life.

He felt his sense of purpose return, and that steely resolve in his gut.

~~~~ **WEDNESDAY, MARCH 4** ~~~~

Chapter Seven

Wednesday morning

T he early morning sun streaming in the window shone directly into Antonio's face. He squinted as he peeled his eyes open. If he'd gone to bed sober, he would have thought to close the blinds. His mind was foggy and his head throbbed. *Merda! Did I really need to drink the whole bottle?* It was out of character. His father had been a man who drank too much—his way of dealing with the stress of being a detective. Antonio had started to slide down that dark tunnel after his accident. He believed it was God's help, and Randi's forgiveness that helped him find his way back.

He dragged himself out of bed and stretched in front of the window. The last vestiges of the storm had moved on. There was hardly a cloud in the sky. A morning mist lay in the valley. Moisture clung to the branches of the barren vineyards, causing them to sparkle like diamonds in the sun. Some of the vines were beginning to bud, a few weeks earlier than normal. The world looked fresh and new.

Despite his muddled head, a peace seemed to settle over him. It felt foreign. He vaguely remembered some dreams from last night, but none that were nightmarish in nature.

He gulped down a glass of water like a man who'd spent a night in the desert. He showered, shaved, and headed for the kitchen. Gabriella was nowhere in sight but he was delighted when he saw there was fresh coffee. He poured a cup and walked over to the French doors. He caught sight of Serena with Lucia and Gia, racing each other after a well-chewed Frisbee. He would need to make sure she washed their muddy paws before they were allowed in the house.

He was wondering where Gabriella was when his phone rang. He looked at the caller ID and saw it was Alessia. *Oh boy! I'm in trouble now!*

"*Pronto, sorella.* I'm surprised you're up so late." It would be almost midnight in Seattle. "Are you calling to give me a piece of your mind?"

"I should be. But I heard what was going on. You'd be in big trouble if it was anybody other than Gabriella. I just wish all the troubles in Italy would get resolved so you could come home for a while."

"How are things … truthfully?"

"You asked." She paused and he pictured her taking a deep breath. "It's still really tough, both here and for Shane at the restaurant. I'm worried about him. He's under a lot of stress with the Covid-19 situation. He should be consulting you more than he is. He's making the best decisions that he can. But this is water nobody knows how to navigate."

Antonio's sense of peace flew out the window and guilt walked back in the door. "I'll need to stay in better touch with him. How about you? How are Mother and Matthew doing?"

"Mom's still exhausted most of the time. God, I hope she recovers fully. She seems older. Or her age, I suppose. She was so vibrant before. Covid took a lot out of her." Antonio thought of his eighty-year-old mother, and how hard she had worked to regain her strength after beating cancer.

Alessia continued, "Matthew is totally bald now. I shaved off the rest of his hair a few days ago. He's fatigued and has no appetite. I try to make him eat to keep up his strength, but he gets nauseous. He's lost so much weight. The doctors tell me all this is normal. He's going back to see them in a few days. They're hoping to reduce the radiation and be done with it soon."

"Is he still having memory problems?"

"Yes. That's what scares me more than anything. He was so healthy … so damn smart. It's tough to see him like this."

Antonio didn't know what to say. He wanted to comfort his sister, but knew his words were inadequate. *Damn, I should be there with her.* "I'm so sorry, sis. I can only imagine. I'm praying for him. And for you, too."

"Thanks. I don't know what I'd do without that. Sometimes I feel like I'm falling apart. But God is giving me the strength to put one foot in front of the other."

"I hope I can make it home soon. I may have to get creative, the way things are going."

"I know. I've heard how bad the virus is hitting Italy. I understand why you stayed. I probably would have, too. But be careful, Antonio."

"I will, sis. I will. I'll be damned if I'm going to end up in an Italian hospital again!"

*****

Gabriella walked into the room as he was hanging up. She saw the wine bottle on the counter where he'd left it, and held it up to the light. "Hmm," she murmured, with a sideways glance.

He held up the phone. "Alessia."

"How is she?"

"Not good."

"Antonio, should we call the airline and try to make a new reservation for you? Maybe you can catch an afternoon flight, or tomorrow morning."

"No."

She studied him intently, and decided not to press it. "I found something," she said, holding up a leather-bound journal. "Andrea's notes."

"Have you called the detective yet, to tell her what we've found?"

"Not yet. I want to go through this first. It might contain the answers we're looking for."

Chapter Eight

Wednesday morning

Antonio poured another cup of coffee. "I'm hungry. You?"

"No. *Grazie.* I don't usually eat much breakfast, if any. My appetite is gone. I can cook you up some eggs, though. Fresh from my neighbor. If you want bread, there is a loaf on the counter."

"Why don't I cook them myself? I know you want to dig into that journal. Should I make some for Serena?"

"No. She had a bowl of cereal. Her parents let her get hooked on that sugary American stuff. Ugh!"

"Ugh, is right. Maybe the stores will run out and she'll be forced to eat real food. There's a silver lining in every cloud."

Antonio began cooking breakfast while Gabriella began to pore over the journal. He found some mushrooms in the refrigerator and sliced three of them. He cracked two eggs into a bowl. Their bright orange yolks stood tall. He whisked them with salt and pepper, then pulled down a skillet from the rack above the range. He brushed it with olive oil, and warmed it over medium heat until the oil began to shimmer. He sautéed the mushrooms, pulled them aside, and then put the pan back onto the burner and reduced the heat. He poured the eggs into the skillet and swirled the pan, spreading the eggs evenly, then placed the mushrooms in the middle of the eggs. He let the eggs cook until the underside was set, then folded the two sides over the middle and let it cook a little longer. The key to a good omelet is not to overcook the eggs. He slid it onto a plate and broke off a hunk of the baguette. He joined Gabriella at the table. She was taking extensive notes.

"I want my own notes in case I have to turn this over to the detective," she said, without looking up.

"Why not just take pictures of the pages?"

She ignored him. He nodded to himself and watched her flip the pages and write in neat cursive. He wished his own writing was as legible as hers. He did his best to eat slow and savor every bite, battling his terrible habit of eating too fast. He saw her coffee cup was empty, so he refilled it. She took a sip without looking up. After about twenty minutes she closed the journal.

"What did you learn?" Antonio asked.

"A lot. I absorb better if I am writing it down," she explained. "I'm bewildered, though. He noted various suspicions. But they don't seem like the kind of thing someone would kill over. If someone from one of these wineries murdered them, then they must have thought that he discovered more than what is here. He visited five wineries and interviewed the owners. He made notes on production levels and his suspicions of who was being honest and who was lying."

"Did he come to any conclusions?"

"Nothing definitive. He still had unanswered questions about all of them, three more-so than the others. He took wine samples from all five, both from barrels and bottles. He also bought bottles of each at local wine shops, as a double check."

"What now?"

"I'm ready to call the detective."

*****

Gabriella looked up the number, hit the call button, and put the phone on speaker. It rang several times, then went to voice mail. "*Pronto*. You've reached the voice mail for Lieutenant Giovanna Zarella. Please leave your name, number, and a message." Gabriella left a message and hung up with a frown.

She pulled out a business card, found a second number for the station, and dialed it. A woman answered on the third ring, "*Polizia di Stato, Questura di Arezzo*." They had reached the local headquarters in the town of Arezzo. "How may I be of assistance?"

"I am trying to reach Lieutenant Giovanna Zarella."

"What is your business, *signora*?"

"I am calling about a case she is working on, regarding the murder of my brother and his wife."

"I am afraid the lieutenant is unavailable. She has taken leave. Her father, whom she lives with and cares for, has Covid-19. She is in quarantine with him."

Gabriella and Antonio locked eyes, both looking stunned.

"May I speak with the *Commissario*, please?"

"I will transfer you. What is your name, *signora*?"

"Colonel Gabriella Ferrara, with the Carabinieri."

They heard a click, followed by silence. Then a man came on the phone. "*Pronto*. This is Captain Dino D'Amici. How may I help you, Colonel Ferrara?"

"Thank you for taking my call. I am the sister of Andrea Marinelli." Antonio realized he had forgotten Gabriella's maiden name. He had only seen it once, on the program from the memorial service. "He and his wife, Bria, were killed a couple of weeks ago when their car was …"

"Yes. I am familiar with the case. Very tragic. Very. My condolences to you and your family. You know it was only yesterday that we got confirmation from forensics that it was not an accident. We had suspected as much. And now the case is weeks old. It will make it that much more difficult to find who did this."

The text notification on Antonio's own phone went off. He looked at the caller ID. It was his young cousin, Giulia. *How was your flight, Zio Antonio? I'm sorry I was not around to say goodbye.* Giulia always referred to him as uncle. Probably because he was thirty years older than her. He walked outside into the clear morning sun and called her. As the phone rang, he watched Serena sitting on the gravel, brushing the dogs next to a large tub of soapy water. She had washed them without being told. He smiled.

"I'm surprised you're calling me," she answered. "I figured you'd be in bed. Isn't it almost midnight in Seattle? I didn't expect to hear back until morning your time."

"I'm not in Seattle." It dawned on him that he hadn't told any of his Italian family, not even *Zio* Nicolo.

"Huh? Where are you?"

"About an hour from you, if you're at school." Giulia attended art school in Firenze.

"Did you miss your flight?"

"I gave up my seat ... to an older lady who was desperate to get out of Italy."

"Mighty chivalrous," Giulia said. "But aren't you worried about getting out yourself? I thought you needed to get home."

"I do. But I'm needed here more."

"What's going on?"

"The *Polizia di Stato* forensic team released their findings about Andrea and Bria's road incident. They determined it was intentional." He explained their findings.

"And you're going to play macho detective again? You know it's not your job to rescue everyone."

Antonio stayed silent for a minute. He'd heard this enough recently. "I know. But ..."

"You don't need to say it."

"Good." He told her about the call to Andrea's boss yesterday, about the journal, and about the detective being in quarantine. "Gabriella's on a call right now with the *Commissario* of the *Polizia di Stato*. He wasn't sounding that optimistic, so far. Hopefully, they have the manpower to continue the investigation. If not, Gabriella is determined to find the killers herself. My instincts told me that would happen. I should go. I want to see what she found out."

"Okay. Call me back and let me know. I'm just packing up my apartment."

"What? Why?"

"School's been shut down indefinitely. All of the schools."

"Wow! Okay, I'll keep you posted."

*****

41

Antonio walked back in the house. Gabriella sat at the table staring at her hands, with a look on her face that was difficult to read. It was somewhere between frustration, anger, sadness, disbelief, and determination.

"What did you find out?" he asked.

"They do not have the manpower to do much right now. They only have two detectives. With one out, they are overloaded. I filled the *Commissario* in on what we learned. He thanked me, and said he would do what he could himself, but he is stretched thin. He said most of his time is being taken up by the Covid-19 situation, which is changing by the minute. He said he spends half his time on conference calls with Roma."

"I'm not surprised."

"Neither am I. But he told me to leave it alone. The same old story about conflict of interest. He wouldn't tell me anything. He said they had a couple of leads but refused to give me details, not even the color of the paint of the vehicle that hit them!" She was getting more and more angry as she spoke.

"So, what's your plan?"

"I've got to make a couple more calls. Then I'm heading to Montepulciano in a few hours. Do you plan to join me?"

"That's why I'm here. But what about Serena?"

"I'm trying to figure that out. Maybe my neighbor, or Bria's parents. If neither of those work out, I can put her on a train to my parents in Marche. They'd love to have her."

"There's one other possibility," Antonio said.

Chapter Nine

Wednesday morning

I just got off the phone with Giulia," Antonio explained. "They closed her school … all of the schools. She's packing up her apartment now."

"Are you suggesting she look after Serena? She barely knows her."

"Just a thought. Listen, I need to do some laundry while you make your calls. Otherwise, you won't want to be around me. I only brought along my carry-on for the trip."

"Of course. Laundry soap is on the shelf above the machine. Run short cycles, though. I want to be on the road as soon as possible."

Antonio threw all of his clothes in together, and set the machine on its shortest cycle. He came back to pour another cup of coffee and thought he heard Gabriella say Chia's name. Chibuogo Umeh, nicknamed Chia, was a Carabinieri Major from Firenze of Nigerian descent. She had played a key role in the rescue of Raphael and taking down the Nigerian Mafia family who were trafficking young Nigerian girls in Firenze. Leonardo, Antonio's cousin, and the brother of Giulia and Raphael, had fallen for her in a big way and they were now in a relationship. When Gabriella requested leave, in order to spend time with Serena, Chia was assigned to fill in as lead detective in Siena in her absence.

"Chia?" asked Antonio when Gabriella ended the call.

"Yes. I've asked her to run a check on Andrea's credit card transactions and cell phone activity for the day he was killed. You know how good she is at that computer stuff."

"Great idea."

"I also called Major Marina Gallo." Gabriella was referring to the woman who headed up the Carabinieri Forensic unit in Firenze. She too had assisted on their case to locate Raphael. "I asked her if she could get us access to the forensic findings from the *Polizia*. She told me she is on friendly terms with their forensic captain, also a woman. She thinks she can go beyond getting us a copy of the report. She thinks she can get us into the yard where the car is being stored."

"What about Marcello? Isn't he going to be unhappy about you getting involved in this?" General Marcello Bianchi was Gabriella's boss, a very capable leader.

"I've asked them not to say anything."

"Are you sure you want to do that, Gabriella? You could get them both in trouble. Not to mention yourself. I really think you should call him." This was out of character for Gabriella. She had shown him nothing but integrity since the day he'd met her.

"And I think you should trust me!" she snapped.

Antonio decided it best not to answer that. He left the room before he responded in anger. He knew all too well what these situations could do to a person. He just didn't want her to do something that she'd regret. That seemed to be his main job of late, first with Nicolo, now with Gabriella.

He brushed his teeth, packed his toiletries kit, then moved his laundry to the dryer. He walked outside onto the terrazza to call Giulia as promised. Then he placed a second call. When he re-entered the room, Gabriella was talking to Serena, who wasn't happy.

"I don't want to stay with anybody else. I want to be with you guys! Please let me come. Please! I promise to stay out of the way."

"It might be dangerous, Serena."

"Then you shouldn't go … or Antonio! I don't want to lose you!" She bolted toward her room. Gabriella, unaware of Antonio, buried her face in her hands.

He took the seat beside her and put his hand on her shoulder. She shook it off. He stayed silent until she stopped sobbing, wiped her eyes and looked at him.

"Am I doing the right thing, Antonio?"

"That's not for me to judge."

"What would you do?"

He considered her question, "Probably the same thing you're doing."

"What should I do about Serena?"

"I just spoke with Giulia again. She has nothing to do with school out. She wants to come with us to help. I think we should let her. She can help with Serena. I also called Chiara and Sylvio. They said we can stay with them. It would be a safe place for Serena while we're doing our investigation."

Zia Chiara was the second oldest of the four siblings. His mother, Elena, was the oldest, the only one born before the war. Nicolo was the youngest, not many years older than Antonio. In addition to producing Vino Nobile di Montepulciano at their winery, Chiara made cheeses and taught cheese making classes. Like Antonio's own mother, she was a force to be reckoned with, a quality they inherited from their own mother, *Nonna* Valentina.

"Okay," Gabriella said. "I'll tell Serena she can come. How long until Giulia arrives?"

"Less than an hour."

Chapter Ten

Wednesday morning

G abriella tapped on Serena's door, opened it, and disappeared. She emerged a few minutes later and breathed a sigh of relief. "She's packing a bag. I'm going to do the same."

Antonio walked outside again to make one more call, this one to *Zio* Nicolo. He hit the button on speed dial. Nicolo was the *Commissario*, lead detective of the investigative unit of the *Polizia Municipale* in the medieval city of Siena. Antonio was closer to him than any man he knew. Nicolo had called upon him twice in the last year in times of crisis when a family member was in danger.

Now it was Antonio's turn to call on Nicolo to help. Problem was that Nicolo was recovering from a gunshot wound in his thigh. Antonio was with him when he was shot by a henchman for the Nigerian mob whom they'd been following—believing they had kidnapped Raphael.

"Antonio! Isn't it middle of the night in Seattle? Did your flight get delayed?"

"You could say that." He told him the whole story.

"Are you sure about this, Antonio? The whole country's going to be in lockdown any day now. I doubt you guys could solve this before that occurs. And I'd think twice before crossing swords with the *Polizia*. I know *Commissario* D'Amici. He could cause a lot of trouble for Gabriella."

"She won't listen, Nicolo. I tried."

"You should try harder."

"You, of all people, should understand how she feels."

Nicolo went silent for several seconds. "Of course, I do. And I wish I could help. I'm going stir crazy. I can't even get out to work the land, or go cycling on these beautiful days. Does Marcello know what she's up to?"

"No. She knows how he would react."

"Seems so out of character for her. I hope she doesn't ruin her career."

"I don't think she cares. She's thinking of retiring anyway. But you're right about it being out of character. I've never seen her in this state of mind."

"Watch her back, Antonio. And yours, too. Someone desperate enough to kill over whatever they believed Andrea discovered won't stop there if they feel threatened."

"I know that. By the way, are you aware that they closed the schools?"

"Yeah, I'm expecting to hear from Giulia. She broke up with her boyfriend the sculptor, so she's probably packing up to head home."

"About that, Nicolo."

"Don't tell me. *Merda.* Sofia's not going to be happy about this."

"Don't worry. She's only coming along to help with Serena. I already called Chiara. We're going to stay with them in Montepulciano. They'll be in good hands while we're investigating. Hey, I should go, Nicolo. I've got to pull my clothes out of the dryer and finish packing."

"Alright. Keep me posted. I'll share the news with Sofia. She went into Siena trying to find some more groceries and goods."

"I hope she's successful. It's *pazzesco* out there. Insanity has set in. *Ciao, ciao Zio.*"

*****

Antonio pulled his clothes from the dryer, carried them to his room, and threw them on the guest bed next to his carry-on bag. He began to fold them neatly and pack. He smelled Gabriella's scent before he saw her. She wrapped her arms around him from behind. He turned around and pulled her near.

"Thank you, Antonio. I know I've been a mess." She sat down on the bed and started matching his socks. "I just got a call back from Chia. That girl is efficient. Looks like Andrea and Bria took the southern scenic route from Montepulciano. He used his credit card in a pizzeria in Buonconvento, a tiny town on SR2. I also received the report from Marina Gallo. The pizzeria was just a few kilometers from where they were forced off the road where the highway crosses the Arbia River at Ponte d'Arbia. Chia called the pizzeria and they pulled their records. The card was run just after 1:00 PM on that Saturday. She's looking for CCTV footage that shows them on the road. If she can find them, she can probably find the vehicle that was following them."

"That would be huge. How good is the CCTV coverage on those roads?"

"Spotty. But there are usually cameras in the small towns, and strategic places along the highway."

They heard a door shut and heard voices. Seconds later Giulia stood in the bedroom doorway, with Serena behind her. "Don't tell me he's already got you doing his laundry," she grinned.

"Giulia! I'm so happy to see you!" Gabriella said. "It's sad that they closed your school."

"Yeah, well, a good excuse to go on another little detective adventure. Better than sitting home being bored out of my skull."

Antonio gave her a hug. "*Grazie, grazie* for being here to help us. Sorry to hear you broke up with your sculptor friend."

"His loss," she laughed. "And you were right, those sculptors get married to their work. Besides, someone has to watch your back. Maybe we can keep you out of the hospital this time. By the way, I need to make a quick stop at home to grab some clean clothes. I can head there now and come right back, unless you'd rather pick me up?"

"It's on our way," Gabriella said. "Go now and we'll be about fifteen minutes behind you."

"Can I go with her?" Serena asked, grabbing on to Giulia's arm, and looking at Gabriella. "I'm all packed."

Gabriella looked at her with surprise. "Fine with me."

As soon as they left, she looked at Antonio. "Looks like you were right."

"Wait? What did you say? Did you just admit that I was right and you were wrong?"

"Don't get used to it. I'm only wrong about twice a year."

Antonio just smiled.

Chapter Eleven

Wednesday morning

Antonio was rolling his carry-on bag toward the door when Gabriella stopped him. "Come with me. There is something else we need." She led the way into her bedroom, opened an armoire and unlocked the large safe inside. She swung open the heavy double doors. "We're not going unprepared," she said. "Or we might end up like Andrea and Bria. I'm glad Serena went with Giulia. I'd rather she not be aware of this."

Antonio looked inside the expansive gun safe. There were half a dozen handguns and a Beretta PMX Submachine gun mounted on clips. Below the safe in the armoire were several portable gun safes. She selected three, then removed a gun for herself, a Beretta 8000, the standard weapon for Carabinieri officers. She placed it in one of the portable safes. "Which gun would you prefer?" she asked.

He lifted out a Sig Sauer P226, a pistol used by the American Navy Seals. He had shot one at the range several times. He made sure the safety was on. It felt light in his hand. He checked the magazine. It was empty. *Good girl,* he thought. Rounds left in the magazine for lengthy periods can weaken the spring, causing a jam at the most inopportune time.

"I keep a single round in the chamber," she said, "for emergency." She handed him a box of shells.

"I hope to hell I don't need this," he said, as he placed it in one of the gun safes. He was not licensed to carry a gun in Italy.

She removed a third gun. "For Giulia." She saw his look of concern. "You are aware she's been going to the gun range with Raphael?" That was news to Antonio but he wasn't surprised. He didn't know how he felt about it.

"May I?" he asked, taking it from her with the barrel pointed down and away. It was a Beretta 92FS Vertec, an older model, perfect for Giulia's smaller hands. "I especially hope that Giulia doesn't need to use this one." He placed it in a portable safe.

"The combinations are all the same," she told him, "0572. The month and year I was born." It suddenly occurred to him that he hadn't even known her birthday. *What an idiot, Antonio,* he chided himself. *You still have so much to learn about this woman!*

She grabbed shells for their Berettas. They locked the safe and brought their luggage and the gun safes to the garage, where they loaded everything in Gabriella's Audi Q5 SUV. They placed their gun safes under their respective seats. Giulia's went under a hatch in the rear. Next to the Audi was Gabriella's Carabinieri vehicle, a black Alfa Romeo Giulia Quadrifoglio, which sported over five hundred horsepower. Antonio glanced at it longingly. He'd driven it home from Firenze just days ago while her arm was in a sling, the result of a bullet which had grazed her upper right arm. It was healing well. Gabriella saw his eyes on the car. "Sorry, Antonio. We are keeping this journey under the radar. Besides, my Audi has more room for the four of us."

Gabriella was turning on to the small local road to Castellina when her phone rang. She had the Bluetooth synced with her car. The screen announced *Pietro Landi, Wine Chemist*.

"Thank goodness," Gabriella said, as she hit the button to answer. "*Buongiorno, Signor* Landi. *Grazie* for returning my call."

"Of course. You said you are the sister of Andrea Marinelli. I'm afraid I have not heard from him. He was supposed to drop off some wine samples a couple of weeks ago. I tried to call him when he never showed. I left a message, but I never heard back from him."

"I'm afraid I have bad news. He and his wife were killed in an accident. I believe they were on their way to see you. *Accident* is the wrong word though, I am afraid. The *Polizia* determined that they were intentionally forced off the road." Antonio was surprised that Gabriella was able to deliver these facts with little emotion.

The phone was silent for a few moments before *Signor* Landi sputtered his reply, "*Dio mio!* I am so sorry, *Signora* Ferrara! I did not know. How can I be of assistance to you?" His voice had gone up an octave.

"You already answered my first question, as to whether or not the samples were delivered. I do not know where your lab is located, so I was uncertain if he made it to see you prior to the incident."

"Now I understand. I received a call from the president of the *consorzio* in Montepulciano … only two days ago. He knew your brother had taken samples. He was inquiring about the results. He sounded quite exasperated when I told him I never received them. You should let him know."

"I will," Gabriella answered. "May I ask where your lab is located?"

"Yes, we are on the outskirts of Siena, in Cerchiaia. Where were they run off the road?"

"Not far from you, on SR2, where the highway crosses the Arbia River."

"The president of the *consorzio* told me he will bring me bottles to do testing on. He did not think he could get barrel samples again … not without creating enmity with his fellow vintners. Apparently, some of them were quite angry about the investigation. My schedule is fairly wide open with everything going on. I believe I can have the results by Friday. Should I contact you?"

"Yes, please. And we are heading to Montepulciano to investigate my brother's death. I may be able to obtain barrel samples."

"Don't you think that should be left to the *Polizia, Signora?* It seems that could be very dangerous after what happened."

"My apologies, *Signor* Landi. I neglected to tell you. I am a Colonel in the Carabinieri. The *Polizia di Stato* began this case, but they have their hands full right now with the Covid-19 problems, so I am pushing the limits of protocol to investigate it myself. I'm sure you understand."

"Of course, *Signora*. I hope you find whoever did this, and bring the justice you and your family deserve."

Chapter Twelve

Wednesday, late morning

Approximately two kilometers before reaching the tiny hamlet of Fonterutoli, Gabriella turned onto the private drive leading to Nicolo and Sofia's house. The late morning sun cast shadows across the compact gravel from the Italian Cyprus trees. They saw that Giulia had pulled her car into the large garage, above which the family had built a two-bedroom apartment for their grown sons, Raphael and Leonardo. Both had lived with them until Raphael took his job as a policeman in Firenze. Giulia maintained a bedroom in the main house, and there were two additional guest rooms. The house had belonged to Antonio's grandparents until they passed. Now it was owned by Nicolo and Sofia, and was the natural gathering place for the extended family. The entire family felt as if it were part of them. It felt like a second home to Antonio. Below the garage and apartment, they had built a wine cellar for their amateur winemaking.

Antonio stepped from the car and breathed in his favourite view in the world. The hillside on which the house perched looked toward the southeast. The shallow slope opposite faced southwest, perfect exposure for the family vineyard, planted primarily with Sangiovese, with single rows of Cabernet, Merlot, Syrah and Canaiolo. The family made their own Chianti, and a Super-Tuscan style blend which had more of the Cabernet and Merlot than would be allowed in a Chianti, as well as a touch of the Syrah. The whole family participated in creating the blend each year, though the final decision always came down to Sofia, whose palate was highly regarded by her husband and children.

Past the vineyard the incline of the hill became steeper as it rose through a wooded area. Beyond that a large boulder crowned the hill, the perfect place to rest your legs and Antonio's favorite spot to take in the view. To the south you could see Fonterutoli, and beyond that, Siena, which crowned its hill like a golden tiara. But Antonio's favorite view was back toward the family home. It had been his inspiration when he remodeled an old house to become his restaurant in Woodinville, a little town in the wine country northeast of Seattle. He was proud of what he had created but it could never match this view.

Looking left, to the north of the vineyard, the land was terraced with stone walls built by *Nonno* Tommaso. The terraces were planted with olive and fruit trees, which were now beginning to flower. Nearer to the house he'd also built a stone wall to surround the vegetable garden, to keep out the deer and wild boar. Antonio smiled as he thought about the summer he helped *Nonno* place the stones. He was only ten years old at the time. When they finished the wall, they installed a solid wood gate to keep the rabbits out.

Antonio took a deep breath, inhaling the familiar aromas. He was just turning toward the house when a half dozen dogs, Bella and her full-bred *Bracco Italiano* pups, came tumbling toward him. Braccos have long ears like Basset hounds, and off-white fur with brown spots of various shades. But their legs are much longer than Bassets. They are highly intelligent and make superb hunting dogs.

He laughed as he knelt down. Bambina, the puppy that Nicolo and Sofia recently gifted to him, rolled over at his feet with her over-sized paws in the air. She was barely two weeks old. Antonio rubbed her tummy and she rolled over and jumped up on him. Her affection made him forget about his troubles for the moment. They'd had so little time together. She was noticeably bigger. Serena showed up at his side, and began to play with the other puppies. It would be another month, at least, before Bambina would be ready to take the plane trip to Seattle. He hoped the Covid-19 situation did not delay her from being sent. Sadly, he knew it probably would.

He rose to his feet, as he heard a familiar voice call to him from the apartment above the garage. It was Leonardo, Nicolo and Sofia's second oldest, standing on the tiny terrace off his room. "*Ciao, Ciao,* Antonio. I'm afraid I cannot come down to see you. I'm under quarantine."

"What happened? Do you have symptoms?"

"No, no, but my friend Luca does. I'm sure you remember him. We rode together a few days ago. Yesterday he began to show symptoms."

"Of course, I remember him … fondly. I'll pray he gets well quickly and that you don't get it. I hear it's rarely serious for the young and healthy." Antonio thought of Luca, who'd been a chef in a restaurant in Siena, unaware that it was owned by a Mafia family. He helped their investigation by placing a listening device in a mob family meeting, which was instrumental to bringing them down.

Giulia exited the house, pulling a large rolling bag which Antonio hefted into the rear of the SUV. It weighed a ton. "How long are you planning to be away?" he said, with a wry smile.

"You forget, Antonio. Girls need to be ready for any and all possibilities."

He turned back and saw Nicolo standing in the doorway, leaning on one crutch. "Sofia is making some panini," he said, "with mortadella and Fontina Val d'Aosta. Would you guys join us for a quick lunch before you go?"

Antonio looked at Gabriella who was standing with her car door open, leaning on the hood. She was the one in charge. He could tell she wanted to keep going. He nodded at her.

"I don't mean to be ungrateful," she said. "Is there a chance she could pack ours to go? We have a few stops to make on our way to Montepulciano." Antonio looked at her quizzically. She hadn't mentioned the stops.

"Of course," Nicolo said. "We suspected as much. Give us a few minutes."

While they waited, Gabriella knelt down to pet Bella, who was still fat with milk. He wished they had stayed, but he could see the tension and determination etched on her face. Bella wagged her tail, then snuggled close and licked her hand, as if she could sense her stress and it was her way of comforting her. *How is it,* he wondered, *that dogs have that sixth sense?* He watched some of the tension evaporate from Gabriella's body.

Chapter Thirteen

Wednesday, mid-day

W hy don't you let me drive so you can eat?" Antonio asked Gabriella.

"No. *Grazie*. I'm not hungry."

"I'm famished," Giulia said. "Do you mind?"

"Not at all," Gabriella answered.

Giulia opened the picnic basket. She held out sandwiches toward Serena and Antonio, and handed them each a bottle of mineral water. "She packed apples also, if you want one."

"I'll save mine for later," Antonio said distractedly. He looked at Gabriella, remembering that she had skipped breakfast. "Where are we headed? You said something about a couple of stops."

"To the impound lot to check out Andrea and Bria's vehicle. Marina came through for us. It's located on the eastern edge of Siena, near Acquedotto del Fiora, the water utility " There was an edge to her voice.

Antonio took a bite and considered this. *Why is she holding everything so close to the vest?* He was feeling like a third wheel. He recognized her emotional state so decided to cut her some slack, but in the back of his mind he was beginning to wonder if he knew her as well as he thought he did.

59

The roads were nearly void of traffic. It only took about twenty minutes to get to the impound lot. Gabriella asked Giulia to wait in the car with Serena. Gabriella and Antonio walked through an open gate where they found a small, stark office. A uniformed guard, appearing to be about thirty years of age, sat behind the counter, punching buttons on his cell phone with his thumbs. The bleeps told Antonio he was playing a game. He looked up, distractedly, then turned off his phone with a frown.

"Buongiorno. How may I assist you?"

"I believe you are expecting us," Gabriella said. "I am Carabinieri Colonel Gabriella Ferrara." She flipped open her badge case. "Major Marina Gallo from our Forensic unit in Firenze contacted you about us seeing a vehicle, the silver metallic Audi A3, which arrived here a couple of days ago."

"Yes. I am confused about that. We picked it up from the *Polizia di Stato* forensic site, then I received this call from the Carabinieri. Have they taken over the investigation?"

"Yes. The *Polizia di Stato* have their hands full with the Covid-19 situation." He gave her a skeptical look but invited them to follow him. They walked beyond cars of all makes and models, including some very expensive sports cars, Ferraris, Lamborghinis, and Porsches. Some were damaged, others looked to be in perfect condition.

They came to the Audi. "Poor souls," said the guard. "I heard the car ended up upside down in the river after rolling. They probably would have survived otherwise. These are well-made cars." Gabriella nodded, looking pale. Outwardly though, she remained stoic.

Antonio was struck by the extensive damage. The top was smashed in, though it never fully collapsed. One huge gouge appeared to have been caused by a jagged boulder. The windows on both sides were smashed, and both sides of the vehicle were severely dented. He could see why the forensic people had a difficult time assessing what happened.

Gabriella began her detailed examination. She circled the vehicle slowly. Antonio followed. In addition to the extensive beating the passenger side had taken from rolling, there was a long, horizontal scrape that appeared to be from the guard rail. When they reached the driver's side, Gabriella bent down and inched slowly from back to front, running her hand over the dents. She leaned in close to see them from different angles, nodding occasionally.

"Just like the forensic report," she said. "See these paint scrapings?" Antonio had to get just the right angle to see the white paint which was difficult to make out against the dented metallic silver. It could have been easily missed because of scrape marks from rocks and boulders, some of which had taken off the Audi's own paint. "There are several spots, beginning above the rear wheel well. Then here on the door, and there, just beyond the front wheel well."

The next thing she did was open the driver's door. It was jammed, and creaked loudly when she finally forced it open. It appeared the airbags had been removed by the forensic people in their search. The first thing Antonio noticed was dried blood on the remnants of the shattered glass of the side windows and console. A few strands of long golden-brown hair were imbedded in the glass on the passenger side. He cringed and watched a flicker of outrage cross Gabriella's face.

Suddenly they heard a gasp from behind them. They turned and saw Serena standing there with her mouth open and eyes wide. Hot tears streamed down her cheeks. She began to scream angrily, "How could they have done this!? How could they be so cruel?"

Giulia came running up from behind. "You were supposed to stay in the car!" Gabriella snapped. "Giulia, you were sup …"

"I know. I know. She needed to use the bathroom. Then she saw you and the car and bolted."

"Don't blame her!" Serena yelled. "And stop treating me like a child!" Judging by the look of determination on her face and the way she spoke, Antonio felt like he was watching a younger version of Gabriella.

Gabriella's face softened. "Trust me, Serena. You really do not want to see this."

Serena stood her ground as the tears kept flowing. Then she turned and ran back toward the car. "I'm so sorry," Giulia said. "I'll watch her more carefully."

"It's not your fault," Gabriella said, with tears in her own eyes. "Please, just go and be with her. We'll be there in a few minutes."

Gabriella turned away from Antonio. She didn't move for a long moment, as if frozen in time. Then she resolutely went back to her search. Antonio went around and opened the passenger door to search from that side, not really knowing what he was looking for. But that's usually the case until you find it.

After finishing the passenger side, Antonio went to the trunk. It was slightly askew and opened when he lifted it. The latch was broken and there was a dent on the bottom edge of the metal. It appeared someone had used a crowbar to pry it open. "Was there anything in the forensic report about the trunk latch?" he asked loudly. Gabriella was in the rear seat, looking under the seats.

"Not that I recall. Why?"

"The latch is broken. Someone pried it open. I don't think it was caused by the accident."

Gabriella crawled out of the car and came to where he was. "Look," he pointed. "See how the metal here is dented." She nodded.

"And look at these dark stains in the trunk," he said. "And I assume you can smell that aroma."

"Wine. It is mentioned in the forensic report," she said. "One or more of the bottles must have broken open. But there was no wine in the trunk when they found the car, and no sign of it in the vicinity where the car was found."

"You thinking what I'm thinking?" he asked."

"If you are thinking they pried open the trunk and took the wine. Yes."

"Exactly. It confirms our suspicions that someone from one of the wineries did this. They didn't want that wine to reach the wine chemist."

Chapter Fourteen

Wednesday afternoon

Seeing the car, the blood, the carnage, made it feel surreal. A slow burn began to churn in Antonio's gut ... a simmering boil. He tried to hide it.

"Are you sure you don't want me to drive so you can eat?" Antonio asked, as they headed toward the car. It was approaching 1:00 PM and she still had not eaten anything that he was aware of.

She stopped and gave him a look. "You really think I want to eat after seeing that?" He kicked himself for his lack of sensitivity. "But I will let you drive. I want to look over that forensic report again." She tossed him the keys.

He put his hand on her arm before she reached the car. "Something else occurred to me. Have you seen the autopsy report? Are we certain their death wasn't helped along?"

"No," she answered. "All I know is what the detective told me—that the cause of death was the accident—that they were unconscious and drowned when their vehicle was upside down in the water."

"Do you think Chia or Marina can get us a copy?"

"I'll text Chia."

They got in the car. Gabriella turned to look at Serena, whose eyes were red. She reached back and took hold of her hand. "Are you okay?" Serena nodded silently. Gabriella turned back, looking worried. "We have two more stops to make," she said. "First, at the incident site. It should be pretty obvious. Then the pizzeria. I want to see if anyone working that day saw anything." She picked up her phone to text Chia. It took her all of about ten seconds. It would have taken him ten times as long. She set it down and picked up the forensic report. She didn't say a word for the next fifteen minutes, glancing occasionally back toward Serena, who stared quietly out the window.

Gabriella's text notification went off. She set the forensic report aside and picked it up. "Chia was able to get a copy of the autopsy. She'll email it as a PDF. I don't think I'll be able to download it until I have Wi-Fi."

She switched to the Google Maps app on her phone. "We are only a few kilometers from the Ponte d'Arbia." Two minutes later they saw the spot. There was no way they could have missed it. The highway crews had not yet repaired the guardrail, which was sheared clear through, and one of the upright wood posts had been broken near its base, splintered wood protruded upward. Once across the bridge, Antonio pulled to the shoulder.

"I'm coming with you!" Serena said. Gabriella stared at her for a long moment, then nodded. "Okay. If you promise to listen to any instruction I give you."

All four of them got out of the car, crossed the highway, and walked the narrow shoulder to where the guard rail was broken. They peered over the edge. Antonio observed Serena as she clung tightly to Gabriella. They doubled back along the guardrail. Antonio found more damage, probably from Andrea and Bria's first collision with it. He and Gabriella examined it carefully. "This is all in the forensic report," she said. "I agree with their findings. Definitely caused by their Audi."

They continued back to the beginning of the bridge, to a spot where they could step over the guardrail and make their way down to the river. They picked their way through brush and over boulders embedded in the soil. Antonio could see evidence of where the car had rolled toward the river—pieces of broken stone, and shattered glass. He picked up a shard of red plastic, partly hidden under a rock. He thought back to the Audi, and the beating it took. He didn't recall seeing any broken taillights.

He knelt by the river's edge and immersed his hand in the water. It felt like snow melt. *This incident happened in February,* he thought, wondering if the roads had been icy. He stared at the moving water and tried to visualize the accident. He could almost see the terror on their faces and hear their screams and the screeching metal as their car was being pummeled. It would have taken severe force to drive it through the guardrail. It was violent and noisy. He pictured the Audi hurtling through the air, crashing into the bank above the river, rolling and landing upside-down, partially submerged in the river. He hoped they were unconscious by that point.

His mind returned to the scene in front of him. He saw what looked like dried blood on one of the rocks. He was surprised because of the rains. *Did they bypass this area?* he wondered. He didn't call attention to it, for Serena's sake. The simmering anger in his gut became a rolling boil. Again, he tried to hide it. It was becoming harder to do.

He didn't notice that Serena had made her way toward the bridge. "Look," she called out, pointing at something beneath a bush. Antonio, Gabriella, and Giulia walked over and spotted a scraped and dented hubcap, appearing to be from an older vehicle. Antonio drew near for a close-up look. It was weathered, and slightly rusted, but not very dusty. It did not appear to have been there very long.

Giulia came up beside him. "Definitely not from the Audi. Do you think it came from the vehicle that drove them off the road?"

"Possible," Gabriella said. "Look here," she pointed. "There is a track in the sand where it appears to have rolled. If it happened a long time ago, that would be gone. Let's leave everything exactly as is. I'm going to see if forensics is willing to take a look at it." She pulled out her phone and snapped photos of the hubcap and the track. "I'll send these to Marina. It might help her identify the type of vehicle."

Serena stood as still as a doe that sensed danger; her eyes glued to the hubcap. Antonio wondered what was going through her mind. Suddenly she blurted out, "I want you to catch them! I want you to punish the bad people that killed my parents!" Giulia, being near her side, placed her arms around her shoulder. Serena turned and buried her face in her chest.

When they arrived back to the road, Antonio pointed to a couple of buildings beyond the bridge. "Do we have any idea if the people here were interviewed?" he asked.

"No clue," said Gabriella, "since the *Polizia* refuse to give me their investigative notes." The buildings were only about a hundred meters away, so they walked. The first was a trattoria, which showed no sign of life. Antonio assumed they only opened for dinner but when they got closer, he saw a sign on the door: *Chiuso per quarantena.* Closed for quarantine.

The building across the road also appeared vacant. A closer look showed that there was a hostel, with a small market attached. The hanging sign in the window was flipped over to say *Chiuso*, with no further explanation. *Might be quarantine,* he thought. *Or maybe they just ran out of everything.*

"Let's head into Buonconvento," Gabriella said. "I'm hoping the pizzeria will be open."

Antonio looked at her. She had her cop face on—stoic, determined—but below the surface he could see her anger simmering, even more than his own—ready to boil over the moment they came face-to-face with whoever did this. *God, help us,* he thought.

Chapter Fifteen

Wednesday afternoon

Antonio pulled back onto SR2. There wasn't a car in sight. But he was surprised to see three cyclists pass them going the opposite direction. After a moment of envy, his mind returned again to the memory of the cycling road incident last September. He and Giulia had been riding the hilly backroads of Chianti when the black Ducati motorcycle came alongside and tried to force him into an oncoming Alfa Romeo Giulia, driven by a partner in their conspiracy. Antonio narrowly avoided a head-on collision. He had glanced off the side of the Alfa, throwing him from his bike. Giulia, in her effort to avoid it all, was forced from the road, and thrown headlong over her handlebars. It wasn't until the latter stages of their investigation that they discovered it was his *Zio* Nicolo they were really after. He had missed their ride—called away at the last minute for a murder investigation in Siena.

Antonio adjusted the rearview mirror, and saw Giulia with her arm around Serena. There had been no lingering effects from her head injury and coma. He recalled the feeling of anguish the day the doctor told them that she might live the rest of her life as a vegetable. They had felt helpless. All they could do was pray. The morning she awoke, lucid and smiling, had done much to restore Antonio's broken trust in God.

He smiled and turned his eyes back to the road.

*****

The pizzeria was located a few blocks off the highway in Buonconvento. It occupied a stucco building, sandwiched between two brick buildings, on a narrow pedestrian-only street. The Tuscan-gold paint on the exterior was beginning to peel. They parked around the corner and followed their noses. *The most wonderful aroma in the universe*, Antonio thought, wishing he hadn't eaten.

The interior exuded an eclectic old-world charm. None of the furnishings matched. Some walls were gold stucco, others brick. It wasn't until his vision adjusted to the dim light that he saw only one table was occupied—two old guys having a conversation with their hands about when to plant certain vegetables in their garden. The man with the deepest wrinkles said he was enlarging his garden this year because of food shortages. The other man responded with a tirade, claiming that Covid-19 was a conspiracy, foisted upon them by the Chinese.

A slender middle-aged man, wearing a long white waiter's apron, appeared from the kitchen. "I'm sorry," he said, "we are closed for the afternoon. We will re-open at 8:00."

"That's okay," Gabriella said, showing her Carabinieri badge. "We just have a few questions." The waiter glanced at Giulia and Serena, who had come in hoping to use the restroom. He narrowed his eyes, then answered, "How may I assist you, *signora?*"

Gabriella pulled out her phone and showed him a photograph of Andrea and Bria. "Do you recall seeing this couple in here a few weeks ago? They had lunch here on a Saturday."

"Did they do something wrong? They did not seem like the type. The *signora* was *molto bello*, with that wavy golden hair. Easy on the eyes." Antonio smiled from behind Gabriella. "They were very friendly ... not like these old curmudgeons I put up with," he said with a wry smile and a wave of his hand toward the occupied table. "And they spoke highly of my pizza. They said they were returning from Montepulciano." His eyes flickered toward the girls, and recognized their need. "Around the corner from the kitchen." He smiled as they disappeared.

"They did nothing wrong, *signor* ..."

"Muratori, Lodovico Muratori. I am the owner of this establishment. At least for now ... if we manage to weather this pandemic." Antonio felt empathy for the man. He shared the same worries. It reminded him of his need to return home to his own restaurant.

Gabriella had her note pad out, and jotted his name. "The reason we are inquiring, they were involved in an accident, not far ..."

"*O Madonna, Madonna!*" the owner erupted, "Yes, yes, I heard about it. I did not know it was them. But they say it was no accident. *Matre Santa!* What a waste. They had promised to return again soon. The man said he would be returning to Montepulciano in a couple of weeks. The lady wasn't sure if she could come with him." Antonio watched a light go off in his head. "Ahhh. Now I understand the phone call I received yesterday ... a Carabinieri Captain . a woman, asking me to pull up a credit card receipt. I didn't make the connection. We had many customers that day. Now as you can see," he waved his hand, "not so many."

It appeared he wanted to keep talking about this, but Gabriella interrupted, "Did you see anything or anyone else suspicious that day? We believe someone was following them."

Lodovico stared into space, rubbing his chin. Then his eyes lit up and he spoke rapidly, "*Si, si!* There were two men. They came in about the same time. I remember them because they left in a hurry. They tried to flag me down for their check, but when I didn't get it to them immediately, they threw a fifty-euro bill on the table and rushed out. I thought it odd because their tab was only half that."

"Can you describe them, *signor*?" Gabriella asked.

He rubbed his chin again. "There was little to distinguish them," he answered. "Italian, probably in their thirties. Average height. One had a neatly trimmed beard. He had intense eyes. The other … face as clean as a baby's bottom, and hair like Ignazio Boschetto." He saw Antonio's puzzled look. "The singer with Il Volo," he added with a smile.

Gabriella smiled as she scribbled in her pad, so Antonio asked the next question, knowing it was a long shot, "Did you happen to see what kind of vehicle they were driving?"

"No. No. *Mi dispiace*, I'm sorry. Cars are not allowed on the street by the pizzeria."

"Do you have a security camera?" Antonio asked.

"Yes. I put one in a few years ago." He pointed to a camera tucked away in a dark corner above the bar. "But it only holds a week, and then it records over it."

"*Grazie, Signor* Muratori. *Mille grazie!*" Gabriella said as the girls returned. "You have been extremely helpful. We appreciate your time." She handed him her business card.

"Please, if you think of anything else, give me a call. May I get your phone number in case we have more questions?"

"Yes." He walked to the counter and grabbed one of his business cards from the plastic stand. He pulled a pen from his pocket and wrote on the back. "My cell number. I hope you catch the *bastardi!*"

Chapter Sixteen

Wednesday afternoon

"Any more stops before we head for Chiara and Sylvio's place?" Antonio asked, as they followed the girls toward the car.

"No," Gabriella answered.

They still had a forty-minute drive ahead of them. The highway remained sparsely traveled as SR2 merged onto SR146. They skirted the town of Pienza, a UNESCO World Heritage site. A few minutes later, Antonio slowed and gave a wide berth as they passed a tractor, nearly as old as the farmer driving it. The girls rolled down their window and waved. The farmer raised his hat and a toothless smile crossed his face. Not long afterward they passed a grove of chestnut trees with gnarly trunks, which were probably around when the farmer was born. Chestnut trees could live hundreds of years. He thought about the stories his *Nonna* Valentina used to tell them, of how she had to bake most of her bread from chestnut flour during the great war—when wheat flour was nearly impossible to come by.

It had turned into a warm, sunny afternoon. The sky was a brilliant blue with a scattering of white cottony clouds. There was something unique about the Tuscan sky. People talked about it but he'd never known quite how to describe it. The land was alive and aromatic. The fruit trees were in flower. Among the deciduous trees, some remained bare, while others were budding fresh green leaves. This was an agricultural area and the rich landscape grew more and more abundant as they neared Montepulciano.

Antonio tried to talk Gabriella into eating her sandwich. She took a few bites to placate him before rewrapping the remainder. She drank her bottle of mineral water and stared at the passing landscape, all the while remaining aggressively silent. It was as if she had fallen down a dark well.

He began to wonder about their relationship. These last two days, she was a different woman from the Gabriella he thought he knew. *Be patient Antonio,* he told himself. *The road she's on is not an easy one. You of all people should know that.*

He wondered how much help he was being. He glanced in his rearview mirror and saw Serena's head on Giulia's shoulder. *I did one thing right,* he thought. Convincing Gabriella to bring Giulia along may have been his best contribution of all.

They rounded a curve and came into full view of the medieval town of Montepulciano, majestically perched atop the gentle rolling *monte*. Some called it the Pearl of the Renaissance. Its roots reached back to the Etruscans.

Antonio's mood lifted. It was one of his favorite towns with its stone-paved pedestrian streets that wound their way up the hill past shops, trattorias, coffee bars, and gelaterias until they reached the Piazza Grande at the top. The views from the high parts of town were his favorite, where every archway seemed to frame a patchwork quilt of vineyards and farms in the surrounding countryside. And then there was the wine. There were numerous tasting rooms and wine shops. Within many of them you could find steep stairways carved into the rock, descending into a labyrinth of wine caves and cellars, many of which interconnected. You could get lost if you didn't know where you were going.

Antonio was anxious to visit, but stuck to the highway which circumnavigated the town. He wanted to reach Chiara and Sylvio's. But when they came upon a gelateria on the outskirts of town, with its neon sign announcing *Aprire*, the temptation was too much to bear. He pulled into the tiny parking lot and turned to Gabriella. "Do you mind?"

Suddenly she awoke and returned to the land of the living. "I don't know how you can eat gelato every day and not get fat. And all those croissants and pizza!" She poked him in the shoulder. "I'm jealous."

Antonio wished it were true. He could stand to lose ten pounds. He was looking forward to the cycling season ahead, which always helped. "I'm buying!" he announced. Everyone piled out, even Gabriella.

A bell on the door announced their entry. His eyes feasted on the colorful display before he ordered his favorite, *Frutti di Bosco*, "fruits of the forest," made from a blend of fresh berries. Only one other flavor could compete for the top spot on his list … *Crema di Limone*. Just thinking about it made him salivate, with its creamy texture, and fresh lemon zest. There was only one gelateria he knew of that made it, located by the sea in Monterosso, in the Cinque Terre, where they held a lemon festival each spring.

He was pleased when Gabriella ordered a cup of *Gianduja*, chocolate-hazelnut. The girls ordered *Fragola*, fresh strawberry. They carried them outside and sat down at a wobbly table with a postcard view. Antonio was on his third bite when his nose picked up the intoxicating aroma of fresh-baked bread coming from next door. He wanted some. He fired off a text to Chiara.

Near the forno. Should we bring bread? Her reply came before he finished his gelato. *Si. Two loaves, per favore. Angelica and Umberto joining us.*

Antonio smiled. Angelica, their eldest of three daughters, was less than a year older than Antonio, closest in age of all his cousins. She was vivacious and fun loving. He'd had a crush on her when they were growing up. She was married to Umberto, a magistrate from Perugia, solid proof that opposites attract. He was a serious man.

Chapter Seventeen

Wednesday afternoon

They turned east on Via Antica Chiusina and drove eight or ten kilometers, then turned onto a private road shared by several small vineyards and an *agriturismo*—a working farm offering accommodations. Another two kilometers and the road ended at a wrought iron gate mounted on opposing brick columns. The faded wooden sign announced Fattoria Montieri. *Fattoria* meaning *farm,* and Montieri being Sylvio and Chiara's surname.

It would not be an easy place for a typical wine tourist to find, unless using a winery map. The limited traffic was perfectly fine with Chiara and Sylvio. They only offered wine tours or tasting by appointment. Chiara had her own side business. She taught cheese making classes and sold her cheeses in local specialty shops which catered to tourists. Antonio figured it would be some time before she was able to do either.

The gate stood open. They passed through and followed the gently curving drive uphill toward the house. The road was lined on both sides by Stone Pine trees, also known as Umbrella Pines, which formed a magical canopy over the drive. It had been at least a decade since Antonio had been here. The property was about four hectares, or just under ten acres on gentle hillsides which sloped away from the house, and then up a west facing hillside to the east. About half of the property was planted in vineyards, mostly Prugnolo Gentile—a superior clone of Sangiovese—known for its aroma of ripe plums. It is one of a myriad of Sangiovese clones, a grape which adapts itself to the various *terroirs* where it is grown.

Sylvio's father had bought the property during the days when Mussolini ruled Italy with an iron fist. He planted vineyards, but only to sell the grapes to others. There was little profit to be made with grapes in those days. Mussolini's vision was that wine should be as cheap as bread, so quality gave way to high yields and the price of grapes was cheap. When Sylvio came of age, he battled with his aging father to allow him to turn the property into a winery, with a focus on making quality wines. The vineyards were replanted or thinned out, and—against his father's better judgment—much fruit was removed from the vines so the energy would go into those that remained. It was risky, but over time the quality improved and demand grew. He and Chiara met and married in the early seventies when the winery was just getting on its feet. They had been reasonably successful for a winery of their size. Antonio believed that their wines were as good as any in the region.

They exited the canopy of the trees and parked in front of the centuries-old farmhouse. Antonio spotted Chiara and Sylvio in the vineyard. Sylvio was leaning on a crutch, wielding his pruning shears. He had recently sprained his ankle rather severely while working in the vineyard. Chiara was flailing her hands about in what appeared to be a family argument. A rather one-sided one from what Antonio could see.

Chiara spotted them and tromped their way, red in the face and spewing venom, "Stupid old man! He won't listen to me. He should be off that foot! I told him to hire someone to do the pruning. You think he'll listen to reason? No, the old fool! I hope he sprains the other ankle."

Antonio dared not show his amusement, fearing her wrath would turn on him. Chiara suddenly became aware of all eyes on her and composed herself rather quickly. She murmured a half-hearted apology, "*Mi dispiace*," then invited them into the house. Antonio glanced at Sylvio sympathetically and waved before following them inside. Sylvio waved back, pruning shears in hand.

It seemed Chiara had blown off her steam. She turned into a charming host, a natural talent she possessed. She had never met Serena, and the two of them took to one another immediately. Serena had a way of doing that to people.

Angelica and Umberto had not yet arrived. Antonio wondered if any of their children were coming with them. They had recently become grandparents by their oldest daughter, making Sylvio and Chiara proud great-grandparents.

Sylvio and Chiara's house was sizable, with two and a half levels. As their family had grown, they had thought ahead and remodeled years ago. In old farmhouses such as this—the lowest level of the house was often used as a barn area. They had converted that space to create two additional bedrooms with a bathroom, giving them a total of six bedrooms. Even that was not enough for all of their children and grandchildren to stay at once. Today they put Giulia and Serena in one, Gabriella in another, and Antonio took a room in the renovated area downstairs. He threw his carry-on bag on the bed and headed out to see Sylvio. He found him further down the row.

"Antonio!" Sylvio greeted him affectionately. "I hope Chiara didn't send you out here to give me hell. The woman's impossible! Treats me like an old man. I'm only seventy-four, two years older than her. But she treats me like I'm ninety. I'm healthy as a horse, aside from this ankle. I plan on living another thirty years."

"Maybe she has a point, Sylvio. Getting around on crutches in the vineyard. It has to be awkward. Aren't you supposed to keep that elevated?"

"These vines aren't going to prune themselves. I wasn't even halfway through the vineyard when I did this." He pointed at his right ankle.

"Why don't you hire some young men to help out?"

"Can't afford it." Sylvio turned away, not wanting to explain further.

Antonio lifted an eyebrow. "I thought the winery was doing well."

"It is, but yields were down on the vintage we released this year. And then my tractor broke down. It wasn't worth repairing anymore so I bought a new one. Last year, it was two new fermentation tanks. And those damn French barrels keep getting more expensive every year." He paused. "And who knows how this pandemonium ... or whatever they call it, is going to affect us?"

Antonio chuckled as he wondered the same. "Do you have another set of shears? You know *Nonno* Tommaso taught me how to prune when I was a teenager."

"The barn. Pegboard above the workbench. But I'll be knocking off soon to shower. Angelica and Umberto should be arriving around six."

Antonio went to retrieve the pruning shears. What Sylvio called the barn was a sizeable multi-purpose outbuilding of stone, built into the hillside. One section of it was an animal barn, with doors opening to an outdoor pen for their sheep and goats. Chiara used their fresh milk for her cheese making in a room next to it. The remaining area was farm storage, winemaking equipment. Behind it all, the wine cellar was built below ground level in the hillside. Within the cellar area Sylvio had walled off a small, rustic bedroom where he slept during fermentation, which required getting up in the middle of the night to punch down the wine to prevent it from bubbling over.

Antonio returned and started a few vines down from Sylvio. He eyeballed Sylvio's method to make sure he was consistent and began to prune. The pain in his hand, still healing from his broken and dislocated finger, forced him to adjust his grip. But he enjoyed the work. It relieved some of the stress he didn't even realize had been building inside him.

Sylvio used his crutch to leapfrog past Antonio and went back to his grumbling. "Chiara thinks we should sell the winery and move closer to one of our daughters. What would I do with myself then, huh? Sit around the piazza with the other old men? Get fat … grow old and die? I've got a lot of good years left in me. Your *nonno* worked in the vineyard until the day he died. What was he, ninety?"

"Yep." Antonio thought about how they found his grandfather's body in the vineyard. They'd gone searching for him when he didn't come home for lunch.

They worked for another half hour and Sylvio declared it a day. He handed his shears to Antonio. "*Per favore*, put these on the bench for me. I'll clean and sharpen them before we use them again."

*****

Sylvio hobbled into the kitchen using a cane, looking clean and fresh, his hair still damp and combed back. He came up behind Chiara and put his hand on her waist and whispered in her ear. She turned around. "Don't think you can sweet talk me into forgiving you that easily, old man." She tried to sound tough, but a half-smile showed she was done being angry. At least for now.

"What am I smelling?" he asked. "Smells heavenly." He looked at Antonio and winked.

"Lamb shanks, braised in your very own wine," Chiara answered. "Don't worry, I used the Rosso." Rosso di Montepulciano is a younger, less expensive version of Vino Nobile di Montepulciano, usually from younger vineyards. The best grapes go into the Vino Nobile, the 'Noble Wine.' There are various stories of how the wine got its name. Some say it was a favorite of one of the Popes and thus named by one of his attendants. Others claimed it was a favorite of the Tuscan nobility. It had gone through a resurgence in recent years, though most wine connoisseurs still showed a preference for the Brunello wines from nearby Montalcino, made from 100% Sangiovese Grosso. In Antonio's opinion, a well-made Vino Nobile—such as that made by Sylvio and Chiara—was just as good and a better value.

They heard car doors slam and the heavy front door squeaked open. Angelica breezed in, looking like a middle-aged fashion model. She headed straight toward Antonio. *"Cugino!"* She embraced him tightly. She pulled away and kissed him on both cheeks. "Oh God, I've missed you!" Over her shoulder, Antonio watched Gabriella looking on with a bemused smile. *Was that a flicker of jealousy I saw in her eyes?* Giulia leaned over and whispered something in Gabriella's ear, and they both laughed.

Angelica moved on to embrace Giulia, then Gabriella. "Congratulations on your engagement," she said, looking from her to Antonio. "I'm so happy for you!"

Gabriella introduced her to Serena, who looked a little overwhelmed by Angelica's passionate affection. A minute later, Umberto made it through the door, struggling with three pieces of luggage. Antonio hurried over to give him a hand. He was pretty sure that both of the largest pieces belonged to Angelica.

Chapter Eighteen

Wednesday evening

Chiara placed a board on the kitchen island, overflowing with her cheeses, olives, salumi, and grilled asparagus wrapped in prosciutto. "*Mangia, mangia*!" she said.

Sylvio opened two bottles of unlabeled white wines. "A young Malvasia," he announced. "We usually add a little to our Vino Nobile. Last year I decided to bottle some by itself. Tell me what you think." Antonio took a sip. It had a velvety mouthfeel and flavors of tropical fruit, nuts, and honey.

"It's excellent, Sylvio. You should sell it."

"Okay, everyone," Chiara interrupted, "gather around the island. We're having pici pasta with the tomato-red wine sauce that the lamb shanks are braising in. I made the pasta dough, but everyone has to help roll it out. I'm not doing all the work!" She looked at Sylvio. "Everyone but you, *amore mio*. Sit down and put that ankle up. Angelica, a pillow please." Angelica did as ordered. She placed it on a chair and lifted her father's leg on it. Chiara went to the freezer and pulled out a bag of frozen peas. "Here, put this on it. No argument!"

Sylvio hoisted his glass. "Aye, aye, *capitan*." Chiara thumped him on the head.

Chiara's plan for making pici was heartily embraced. Antonio took his place next to Serena. "Have you ever made pici?" She shook her head. "Easy. I'll show you." He cut off a strip of pasta with a quick swipe of a pizza cutter. "Some people start with a little ball of pasta, but if you cut a strip like this it is quicker. Then take it and roll it between your hands like this," he rolled it back and forth between his palms. "The idea is to make it long, like a big, fat worm."

"Ew! Worms are gross."

Antonio laughed. "I thought you loved animals?"

"Furry ones. Not slimy!" Now everyone laughed.

"Think of this as fat spaghetti then. Another way to do it, if it's easier for you, is to roll it on the counter like this." He placed his half-finished piece on the counter and rolled it back-and-forth with his hands. "But it will only work if you don't have too much flour. Otherwise, it slides around when you try to roll it." She watched him as he finished the one strand. "Your turn," he said, handing her the pizza cutter.

Serena cut off a strip and went to work. When she finished it, Angelica chimed in, "Look at that, you're already better than Antonio!" Serena beamed.

"Only because she had a masterful teacher!" Antonio said, feigning offense.

They were about halfway finished when Gabriella's phone rang. She glanced at the screen. "Marina Gallo," she said, looking at Antonio. "Excuse me." She walked from the room. Antonio wiped his hands and followed. When she saw him, she waved him away and turned her back. He rejoined the others.

Chiara read his face. "Everything okay?" she asked.

"I believe so. Marina Gallo is head of the forensic unit in Firenze. Gabriella contacted her for help. On our way here we stopped at the location of the accident. Our little detective here," he nodded toward Serena, "found something we believe was previously missed. An old, rounded hubcap that had rolled into the brush. It didn't appear to have been there long."

Gabriella returned as they were finishing the last of the pici. Chiara already had a huge pan of water simmering on the range. She added a good amount of salt and turned up the heat.

Gabriella had her cop face on. "Did you find out anything?" Giulia asked her.

"Yes. Major Gallo already went out to do her own search at the Ponte d'Arbia. I'll fill you in after dinner." Her eyes flicked to Serena.

*****

Dinner was *incredibile*, as the Italians would say. The lamb shanks had been made fork-tender by the long, slow cooking in the wine and tomatoes with onions, carrots, celery, and porcini mushrooms. The sauce, made from that braising stock, had deep, rich flavors. Chiara had added a little bit of tomato paste at the end to thicken it. Pairing it with the hearty pici pasta was brilliant.

As dinner was winding down, the family began to pepper them with questions. Antonio hadn't given much of an explanation when he had called Sylvio and Chiara to ask if they could stay with them.

"I still don't understand exactly why your investigation brought you here," Chiara said.

Antonio looked at Gabriella. She nodded for him to speak. "As I told you on the phone, the *Polizia* forensic unit determined that the road incident was intentional. Andrea and Bria's Audi was hit from the side more than once, with enough force to drive it off the bridge into the river. Clearly, it was a heavier vehicle. We stopped by the impound lot to examine the vehicle ourselves. We agree with their findings."

"Why not leave it to the *Polizia*?" Angelica asked.

"I would have," Gabriella answered. "But the detective assigned to the case is in quarantine, and they are so overwhelmed with this Covid pandemic that they do not have the manpower to do the investigation."

"You realize what you are doing goes against all protocol," Umberto said. "A magistrate wouldn't hesitate to toss out your evidence if you overstep your boundaries."

Gabriella looked at him and frowned. "I know. Trust me. I don't want to compromise the case and see their murderers go free. If we discover anything we'll have to be very careful how we approach it. But if we don't do the investigation, their killers may never be found."

He nodded thoughtfully. "What about talking to your commander? General Bianchi, isn't it?"

"He doesn't know I'm pursuing this. I'm on leave. If I tell him, I'm certain he'll try to stop me … tell me to wait until the *Polizia* can handle it."

"And he'd be right. I should stop you myself." Umberto stared hard into Gabriella's face, deciding on his options. Antonio saw her eyes imploring him. "But I won't if you promise to be careful. Contact me if you need direction, or if you discover evidence that we can confirm through other means. I'll do my best to cover your backside."

"I will," she said with a respectful nod. *"Grazie, Umberto. Mille grazie."*

"I still don't understand why someone would have targeted your brother and wife," Sylvio said.

"He worked for the Wine Commission," Gabriella answered. "They were investigating possible fraud of Vino Nobile wines. Similar to what happened in Montalcino in 2008."

"What? Brunellogate? Bah! I don't believe it!" Sylvio stared with his mouth hanging open.

"Oh, don't be naïve, Sylvio!" Chiara said. "We know most of the producers. Most are good people who would never cross that line. But with over seventy wineries, there's bound to be a bad egg or two." She turned to Gabriella. "Tell us what prompted the investigation."

Gabriella explained about her conversation with Andrea's boss, about Andrea's investigation, and journal notes, and Chia's findings about the pizzeria and how she was searching the CCTV camera footage. Antonio filled in their findings from today.

Umberto looked at her. "Doesn't sound like you've crossed any boundaries yet. What are you planning next?"

"I would like to re-interview the wineries that Andrea was taking a look at."

"Those interviews will have to be voluntary unless you have a warrant, which no magistrate would give you," Umberto added. "And don't go nosing about their premises without their permission."

Gabriella nodded. Antonio hoped she would heed his advice. He was glad Umberto was here to help ... to ensure she did not overstep any boundaries. He looked at Gabriella, "So what did you find out from Marina Gallo?"

Chiara interrupted, "Please, if you don't mind, lets clear the table and move to the living room. It's getting cold out. Antonio, Umberto, would you build us a fire while we ladies do the dishes?"

Gabriella picked up some dishes and turned to Serena. "Please clear your dishes, and then brush your teeth. It's late for you. We need to get you in bed."

"But …"

"No buts. You have a big day tomorrow. I was telling *Zia* Chiara how much you love animals. She asked if you would like to get up early to help her milk the sheep and goats?" Chiara added her affirmation.

Serena nodded, looking happy, sad, and pensive all at the same time. "Okay," she said. And went off to brush her teeth.

Chapter Nineteen

Wednesday night

Sylvio brought clean wine glasses and a small, unlabeled bottle of amber liquid, unmistakably Vin Santo—Holy Wine—that viscous sweet wine that Sylvio made from his Malvasia grapes, a long process. The grapes are hung in the barn for the winter to dry out. A type of mold, called botrytis, develops within the grapes, creating high sugars which ferment into alcohol. Come springtime, the grapes are crushed. The drying of the grapes creates low yields, so it can be quite expensive.

The girls joined them and they resumed the discussion. Chiara spoke first. "I knew you didn't want to talk about your phone call in front of Serena."

Gabriella nodded. "I appreciate your sensitivity. She saw more than she should have today. We didn't intend for her to see the car, but she pulled a fast one on Giulia." Giulia looked up, a guilty frown on her face. "It wasn't Giulia's fault. Actually, she has been a Godsend. Serena adores her. I am so glad Antonio talked me into bringing her along. Serena is a wonderful girl, but she can be pig-headed. A trait she got from her father."

"Right, from her father," … Antonio said with a smile in his voice. Gabriella elbowed him.

"What did you find out?" Giulia asked.

"She expanded the search area. She found a tire iron in the brush, a stone's throw away. There was dried blood on it. She's going to test the blood, and test for fingerprints. But she is pretty sure the perpetrator used it on them to make sure they were dead."

They heard a gasp, and turned toward the arched opening which led to the stairs. Serena peeked around the corner as everyone stared at her. She ran over and threw her arms around Gabriella. "Please don't be angry. I already know how they died. I saw the car! I saw their blood! I even saw the blood on the rocks in the river." She began to sob.

Gabriella held her close and stroked her hair. "You poor sweet thing. No young girl should ever have to go through what you have experienced."

"I'm not young. I'm practically a teenager! And I'm proud to be pig-headed! I want to be strong … like you, and like my father. I want us to find who did this!"

"I wish I were as strong as you think I am, Serena."

Giulia stood up and gently pried Serena away from Gabriella. "Let's put you back to bed, Serena. I'll stay with you a while. Maybe we can think of something cheerful to take our minds off all this."

Serena nodded and rubbed the sleeve of her pink nightgown across her eyes. They climbed the stairs hand-in-hand. Gabriella buried her face in her hands.

*****

Antonio held Gabriella close. There was nothing to be said as they stared at the fire. After a time, Chiara brought out a plate of cantucci, small almond biscotti, perfect for dipping, and

Sylvio poured the Vin Santo. Gabriella declined, then sat up straight, wiped her eyes with a tissue, and continued as if nothing had happened. She had a way of compartmentalizing her feelings, at least for a time.

"Marina believes we were correct about the hubcap Serena found. It came from a large, older model truck—a medium-duty delivery truck—what they call a class six. I called Chia to let her know, so she could narrow her search of the CCTV footage."

"Almost all of the larger wineries use those trucks," Sylvio said. "They can also be rented."

"But if it was rented they would have had to return a damaged vehicle," Chiara said.

"Unless they kept it long enough to have it repaired," Angelica chimed in. "Highly unlikely."

"Tell me more about this supposed wine fraud," Sylvio said. "I wouldn't have believed it but someone obviously has something they desperately want to hide if they're willing to kill to keep it secret."

"Exactly," Gabriella said. She went on to explain what they knew, and the wineries Andrea had been investigating. "What can you tell us about these wineries?" she asked.

"Before I get into that, you should know that the *consorzio* of Montepulciano wineries is having a meeting this Saturday—an emergency meeting to discuss the Covid-19 situation. Normally our annual meeting is in May, but they moved it up. They decided to have it outdoors. They think it will be safer to be outside with more distance between us. It's being held at Le Cascio wincry. They have a rather expansive outdoor area where they do special events. The weather is supposed to stay nice.

They'll be serving lunch, and a great deal of wine of course. You can come as my guests. I just need to let them know."

Gabriella thought for a moment. "Please, that might prove useful. Let me know any costs involved so we can pay you."

Sylvio waved off her last comment. "Now, as far as the wineries Andrea was investigating, I know some better than others. They are all among the larger wineries in the area. The first one you mentioned, Graziano, is the smallest of those, but still in the top ten as far as production. Most of their wine is made from their own vineyards. They've expanded over the years, buying new land as it becomes available. They buy some grapes from other vineyards in low production years … growers they trust. Maybe they're doing more of that now. That could explain increased production. It's owned by Enzo D'Angelo … a widower. He's a surly old guy. But I can't imagine him cheating the system. His grandfather started the winery, then his father doubled it in size. He is very old-fashioned … complains every time I see him about not having a son to pass it on to. He has three daughters. Personally, I think they are quite capable. They're making more and more of the decisions. Maybe they're buying more grapes and pushing up the production levels."

"That was what they told Andrea," Gabriella said. "He couldn't get many answers from Enzo, who he noted became very defensive when questioned. The oldest daughter stepped in and explained exactly what you said. She said most of the increase came from a vineyard that they've established a lease to own option on. Final payment is due to the heirs upon the owner's death."

"Ah yes, I know the vineyard they're referring to. Several hectares. Sounds legitimate. Will you investigate them further?" Sylvio asked.

"I've moved them to the bottom of my list. Andrea considered them the least likely to be cheating the system. If we don't find anything with the others, we can always do an interview just as a double check. Andrea did note that the youngest daughter seemed nervous. He wondered if she was hiding something."

"Hmmm. That would be Aria. She is an interesting one. That's not out of character for her."

Sylvio continued, "The second winery you mentioned, Fattoria Carrapaccio, is one of the oldest and largest in the region."

"Andrea's notes said they ranked third in production?" Gabriella said.

"Sounds right. The old man, Riccardo, is the fifth-generation owner. He's weathered and bent, but full of vigor. And quite affable. Still works every day. His son, Dante, manages things now. Dante has three children himself. They all play a role. And there are a bunch of great-grandchildren. I don't know Dante very well. He keeps to himself. I have no idea if he's capable of this kind of deception, but if he is, I doubt the old man knows about it."

Sylvio hobbled over and put another log on the fire. He poured more Vin Santo for anybody who was willing. Antonio put his hand over his glass. *I don't need another hangover.*

"The winery that surprises me most on his list," Sylvio continued, "is Villa Sant'Angelo. It's even larger and older than Carrapaccio. They've owned land and grown grapes since the 18th century. It may not remain in the family much longer though. The widow, Marianna Bellini, is a stately woman, and formidable, but her son has shown no interest in making wine.

If he decides not to take up the mantle, he may sell it. It would make him richer than Caesar."

Sylvio stared at the fire and rubbed his chin. "The one that I have the least knowledge of is Le Cascio, the winery where we are having Saturday's meeting. The winery's been around for over a hundred years but was purchased by a wealthy American several years ago, a man named Gerald Gregson. I hardly know him, other than he apparently made a lot of money in technology and has been buying up any land he can get his hands on. He's married to an Italian woman." He turned to Chiara, "What's her name, *cara mia?*"

"Gianna," she answered. "She seems very ambitious. She has three adult daughters from a prior marriage who are learning the business. None of them knew anything about winemaking. They paid top-dollar for a renowned winemaker; a man named Elio Pignatello."

"How many wineries are in the *consorzio?*" Antonio asked.

"About seventy that bottle wine. But there are another two hundred or so growers. Between them they account for about ninety percent of the vineyard land in the Montepulciano DOCG. The headquarters are located in the Piazza Grande."

"What about the last winery? Carpinteria?" Gabriella asked.

"That's the one I would look at most closely," Sylvio said. "When the owner, Emilio Fontana, died two years ago, it was taken over by a woman from Apulia … supposedly an illegitimate daughter. His wife had never been able to bear children. Her name is Alida. She changed her last name to Fontana. I believe her surname was Tarantino before that, like the movie director." He smiled at that reference.

"They are not the largest landowners, but they're growing at an unheard-of rate, almost thirty percent last year. They're expected to have the highest production this year. They buy a lot of grapes from the smaller vineyards. They've even tried to buy from me."

"And you were almost taken in by her charms, you old fool," Chiara said. "The woman is stunningly gorgeous. And an astute businesswoman, but shrewd. I don't trust her as far as I can throw her!"

"You're just jealous because she told me how handsome I was. She was just trying to butter me up because she knows how excellent our vineyards are. I was tempted. She was offering us top dollar."

Antonio had always thought that Sylvio was indeed handsome. He had aged like a fine Vino Nobile. Though weathered, his eyes were clear and piercing, and he had a strong chin. His hair was white on the temples, transitioning to streaks of silver and black on top. He didn't remember Chiara ever referring to him as an *old fool* so often as she had today. Maybe she was jealous. He didn't see the need though. She had the same beauty as her sisters, though hers was less cultivated. She wore little make-up, but her beauty still shined through.

Angelica, who'd been surprisingly quiet, chimed in. "Why did you say 'supposedly,' papà, when you called her his illegitimate daughter?"

"Just rumors. They say her family has a long history in Apulia. They own one of the largest wineries in the region. When Emilio died, people believed he had no heirs. Then she shows up out of nowhere."

"That can be settled easy enough with DNA testing," Umberto said.

"And rumor is," Sylvio said, "such results can be bought for a price."

~~~~ **THURSDAY, MARCH 5** ~~~~

Chapter Twenty

Thursday Morning

Antonio woke slowly. His mind was troubled by dark images, though he didn't think the nightmare had returned. The evening with family had been therapeutic, but when he awoke in the middle of the night, the anger welled up in him again, like it wanted to burn a hole in his gut. Whatever sleep he got after that hadn't done much to restore his body, or his normally optimistic outlook. It did not help that he had called Shane before going to bed. All he got was more bad news. On top of that, it got him thinking about the tax preparation that he'd yet to begin. It only added to his stress.

He dragged himself out of bed and threw open the curtains. The sun was out, and he could hear birds singing, and the sound of a tractor in the distance. He slipped on the clothes he'd worn yesterday, and stumbled barefoot to the kitchen, following his nose which told him someone had made coffee. *God bless the soul that did this,* he thought, as he poured himself a cup and wandered back down the stairs to his room.

The pain in his hand was bothering him less every day, so he decided to do some push-ups, keeping the pressure on the heel of the hand. The ache in his shoulders and elbows told him he needed to get back in the habit of doing them daily.

He took a hot shower, which he finished with a cold blast. That, in concert with the coffee, and he almost felt human again. His sour attitude began to improve. He put on clean clothes and climbed the stairs back to the main level. There was no life in the kitchen but he spotted Gabriella, drinking coffee on the terrazza, her face to the morning sun. He poured another cup and went out to join her. The light morning breeze carried a chill, but the sun was warm.

"*Buongiorno, cara mio.* How'd you sleep?" she asked.

"Like the dead," he lied, trying to be strong … a rock for her to lean on. "You?"

She looked him over doubtfully. "Better than yesterday. Are you sure you slept well?"

"I'll be okay." *Maybe after a third cup of coffee.*

"Look over there." He followed her eyes and saw Chiara, Serena, and Giulia coming out of the barn carrying pails of milk. Serena was chattering like a bird and practically skipping with joy.

"Chiara is going to serve a light breakfast in about an hour. It is too early to make my calls. Join me for a walk?"

"I'd love to." He took a swig of coffee, and gulped down some water.

They greeted the girls. Serena hugged them both as she excitedly explained how she had already mastered the art of milking the sheep and goats. She giggled as she told them about a baby goat that jumped up on her back when she was milking her mother. "Silly little goat!" she beamed, brightening everyone's mood.

"Follow me," Antonio said to Gabriella, his view of the world suddenly brighter. She took hold of his hand as they skirted the edge of the vineyard toward the hill. The vineyard went about three quarters of the way up, stopping short of a rocky outcrop. Antonio helped her over the rocks then turned and pointed. "Ever since I was a kid, I loved to come up here." Looking west you could see a vast panorama of rolling hills, with a patchwork of vineyards, wheat fields, olive groves, and woods. Beyond that, Montepulciano rose above it all, a fairy-tale city, pristine in the morning light.

They sat down on the rock. "I wasn't fun to be around yesterday," Gabriella said quietly, as she took it all in with a deep breath. There was a hint of wood smoke in the air.

"It's okay. I underst…"

"Stop! No, it's not! You are the last person I should be taking it out on. You stood by me when I pushed you away." They watched a hawk fly over their head in search of its next meal. "For some reason, I needed some space. Like him." She pointed at the hawk who suddenly dove after something, probably a small rodent.

"I wish you'd stop trying to carry the load all by yourself. It's lighter if you share it."

She didn't answer, just nodded and stared at the beautiful town on a hill. "How is it that evil lurks even in the most beautiful of places?"

It was a question Antonio had asked himself a million times. He had always found the paradox of good and evil in the world hard to grasp. There was so much beauty, so much goodness. Yet the battle between good and evil was real, even within his own soul. *How does a conscience get so seared that the good in a person gets lost?* he wondered.

"I wish I had an answer," he said, staring after the hawk as it flew away. "But I feel like hope and faith—or the lack thereof—have a lot to do with it."

"It occurred to me yesterday that you and I have never had any normal time together," Gabriella said. "We've been chasing monsters since the day we met. It troubled me. How well do we really know each other? Would we even know how to live an ordinary life together? Or would we get bored, and go looking for some injustice to battle?"

Antonio looked her in the eyes, wondering if she was right. "I heard a quote once," he said. *"From hardship comes enlightenment.* It stuck with me. Do you think that's true? We've been together through extreme pain and adversity. But I feel like it has shown me so much about you … your character … your strength. I can't picture myself ever getting bored with you. You're the most fascinating woman I've ever met. Personally, I can't wait to spend some days of peace and solitude together. I just hope we don't have to wait too long for that to happen."

"What about Serena?" she asked. "Are you ready to take that on? To go through the teenage years again?"

He pondered that for a moment. Raising teens is hard, even if they're not rebellious. "I believe so. She's an amazing young girl. I see now why you two have always been so close."

"Don't tell *her* she's young."

"Oh yeah," he laughed. "That went over well. At least I didn't call her pig-headed."

"That was a big oops!" She looked at him and laughed, then leaned over and gave him a soft kiss. She sat up and changed the subject. "Thank you for arranging for us to stay with Chiara and

Sylvio. They've been so helpful. And it's good to have Umberto to keep us honest. I don't want to mess this up."

"Me neither. During my years on the force, I've seen the guilty walk free when we didn't do our job right. It's the hardest thing in the world to see. Especially when it's as serious as murder."

"All we can do is hope that their justice comes someday, as God promised it would."

Antonio pondered that, then changed to a lighter subject. "It's fun watching Serena take to farm life."

"I think Chiara is loving it, too. I'm not so sure she had that with her daughters. At least, not the oldest. I can hardly imagine Angelica as a farm girl when she was growing up. She's beautiful, elegant, full of life." She elbowed him in the rib. "And she seems to like you."

Antonio hoped he wasn't blushing. "Do I detect jealousy, Ms. Ferrara? That's so unlike you! She's always been a flirtatious one. I'll admit I had a crush on her when I was like twelve."

She laughed. "See, my jealous streak is one of those things you don't know about me. We should head back. I need to call the wineries. I'm hoping we can visit two today, and the others tomorrow."

Antonio nodded and they started down the hill. "What's the game plan? Are you going to tell them we're investigating a murder?"

"Not on the phone. It would put them on the defensive. I will explain that the Carabinieri have been requested to do follow-up visits regarding the wine production issues that Andrea was investigating. Then we will drop it on them during the face-to-face interviews. Don't reveal any of that until I bring it up. But be ready to watch their reactions when I do. Remember the basics, we are looking for motive, means, and opportunity. Their body language can tell us a lot."

"Got it, Sherlock. This is going to be interesting."

Chapter Twenty-one

Thursday morning

Zia Chiara greeted them, "There you are. Just in time." Antonio's eyes and nose followed a colorful platter to the table. "A simple feast this morning; poached eggs atop ciabatta bread, topped with chopped prosciutto, tomatoes, shallots, and shavings of my aged pecorino." She also brought a plate of sliced blood oranges. Antonio often wondered when Chiara would ever slow down. She'd been like this as long as he'd known her. He poured another cup of coffee and placed one of the ciabattas on his plate, along with a generous portion of oranges, hoping the natural sugar would boost his lagging energy. Everyone except Angelica was at the table. Chiara mumbled something about "the princess sleeping in." Antonio saw a flicker of an amused smile cross Gabriella's face.

Sylvio spoke up. "I've been thinking. If someone were to use their own truck to force Andrea off the road, it would almost certainly be unmarked. The trucks I've seen from Carpinteria and Villa Sant'Angelo have their names on them. My first thought was that would rule them out. But I'm not so sure you should. Maybe they have additional trucks … or rented one. I still think Carpinteria should be looked at carefully."

"Good thinking, *Zio* Sylvio," Antonio said. "You should have been a detective."

"Who else would you most suspect, Sylvio?" Gabriella asked.

"I don't know really. Maybe Carrapaccio, only because I don't know Dante the son. He seems dark and moody at times. Or possibly Le Cascio. Not to say I don't trust Americans. It's the Italian wife that doesn't feel trustworthy to me. But I know so little about them, really."

Gabriella only ate half of her ciabatta with poached egg, then excused herself from the table. "I really need to start calling the wineries," she said. "I also need to contact the president of the *consorzio*. I don't even know his name. May I get his contact information, Sylvio?"

"Yes. Vito Crivello. Give me your number and I'll text it to you. I should have your number anyway." Gabriella gave it to him, and disappeared.

Antonio finished his ciabatta. It was so delicious he ate the rest of Gabriella's. He was helping to clear the plates when his phone rang. He was surprised to see the caller ID. "*Pronto*, Major Gallo," he answered. "I heard you were recently promoted from Captain. Congratulations!"

"Enough with the formalities," she interrupted. "It's Marina to you." Her voice rang with a sense of urgency. "I tried to call Gabriella, but she's been on the line. I decided to go and visit the impound lot to take another look at the Audi. You'll never guess what I found." She went silent but Antonio had no idea how to answer. "There was a GPS tracking device hidden underneath on the passenger side. I'd been wondering how a large truck could follow them all the way from Montepulciano without being obvious, especially since they made a lunch stop."

"Of course!" Antonio replied, kicking himself. "I should have thought of that. That's the second clue this morning that we had not considered." He told her about Sylvio's thoughts about them using unmarked trucks.

"That's why the team approach to investigations is so helpful. Most great detectives know this, except the fictional characters. One more thing," she added. "Did you notice that panel behind the rear window on the driver's side had a straight-lined indentation? That confirms what we surmised about it being a delivery vehicle. It was at just the right height for a class six delivery truck. By the way, I also tore out the carpet from the trunk, with the wine stains on it. I dropped it off to the wine chemist to see if he can discern anything from it. He said it was unlikely but he'd give it a shot."

"Good. By the way, can that tracking device be traced back to where it was purchased?"

"If the serial number is visible, possibly. This one was filed off."

"Of course it was. Still, it gives us a piece to the puzzle," Antonio mused out loud.

"Yes. It does. I'll let you know if I find any more pieces."

"You're amazing, Marina. *Grazie. Mille, mille grazie!*"

"*Prego.* By the way, General Marcello's been asking if I've spoken to Gabriella. I think he's suspicious that she's up to something."

Antonio thought it was funny that she used his first name with his title. "Thanks for the heads up. I'll tell the boss. *Ciao, ciao!*"

*****

Gabriella returned to the table. Angelica had made her appearance, looking like she was going to a photo shoot.

Umberto pulled a chair out for her. Antonio was starting to think he had misjudged the man who he had only known from large family gatherings. They had never really connected.

"We have two winery visits scheduled for today," Gabriella said. "Carrapaccio and Villa Sant'Angelo. Carpinteria is set up for tomorrow. I have been unable to reach the American, Mr. Gregson, owner of Le Cascio."

"Good luck," Sylvio said. "He's surely busy getting organized for the *consorzio* meeting Saturday. Were you able to reach the president, Vito Crivello?"

"Yes. He pushed hard for an explanation of why the Carabinieri were taking over the investigation. I had to swear him to secrecy. I don't want the word out yet. He was shocked when he heard about the murder. And, of course, he hopes like hell it was not one of the *consorzio* vintners."

"I bet he does," Sylvio said. "None of us want that kind of publicity. Our reputation is at stake."

Gabriella looked at Antonio. "We need to leave in thirty minutes."

He nodded, then said, "I got a call from Marina while you were on the phone. She tried to reach you but obviously your phone was tied up. She got a hunch and went to check out the Audi. Guess what she found?"

"I am in no mood for guessing games, Antonio."

"A GPS tracking device."

"*Merda!*" Gabriella said. "The possibility occurred to me after we visited the pizzeria. Then I forgot about it."

Antonio explained about Marina's other observations, confirming their theory about the type of truck used to force them off the road. "Have you talked to Chia about this yet?" he asked. "I know she was going to do a CCTV search. This could narrow it down for her."

"Not yet." She looked at the time on her phone. "I need to finish getting ready. I'll have you drive. I can call her en route. I forgot to mention, though. I checked my email for the autopsy report." She glanced around. Serena was on the far side of the terrazza, making friends with Chiara and Sylvio's Australian Shepherd, with its odd mix of grey, white, black, and brown splotches. She leaned forward and spoke quietly. "As we thought, it appears they were bludgeoned by something. Probably that tire iron. I hope they were already dead." She placed a hand over her face and shook her head.

Giulia had been listening in. She gave her a moment before asking, "Can I come with you guys? Serena would be fine here."

"Sorry, Giulia," Gabriella answered. "I think it would be hard to explain three of us. I don't want to make them any more ill at ease than they already are."

Giulia acquiesced, looking disappointed.

"Do you know how to find these wineries?" Sylvio asked.

"I was going to use Google Maps," Gabriella said.

"Not always dependable in the country. Here's a winery map the *consorzio* puts out," he handed it to Gabriella. "I circled the wineries for you."

"*Grazie*, Sylvio. You and Chiara ... I cannot thank you enough."

Chapter Twenty-two

Thursday morning

Carrapaccio winery was located in the southeast part of the DOCG. As Antonio drove the winding roads, Gabriella tried to call Chia. There was no answer, so she left a message. They turned onto a smaller road, barely wide enough for two cars to pass. It wound its way round a hill past well-manicured vineyards. There were rose bushes on the end of each row. A few were budding early.

The winery lay within a small hilltop compound surrounded by stone walls which enclosed about a dozen buildings capped with red tile roofs. Some of the buildings appeared to be centuries old. Others had obviously been built more recently. There was even a small chapel. On an archway above the gates a brass sign was mounted announcing Fattoria Carrapaccio. When they arrived, Antonio pushed a button on the post by the double wrought iron gate.

After about thirty seconds a woman's voice came over the intercom. "*Pronto*. May I inquire as to the purpose of your visit?" *Not very inviting,* Antonio thought. *But I don't imagine they're welcoming wine tourists these days.*

Gabriella leaned across Antonio and spoke clearly. "Colonel Ferrara to meet with Riccardo and Dante Carrapaccio, *per favore*. We have an appointment." With no reply, the wrought iron gates began to open. They drove forward and found a small parking area. Nearby, the heavy wooden double doors of a tall building stood open. A forklift was moving wine barrels.

As they stepped from the car, an aged man hurried toward them from inside the barrel room. "*Arrivederci*, Colonel Ferrara. I am Riccardo Carrapaccio."

"*Piacere!* Pleased to meet you. This is my partner, Antonio Cortese," she replied, as they shook hands. Riccardo had the rough, cracked hands of a farmer. The sun had engraved deep wrinkles on his weathered face. He was wiry, and his back was permanently hunched below the neck, likely from thousands of hours in the vineyards. Still, he exuded life, and vigor, with eyes that sparkled when he spoke. His wavy hair was pure white. Antonio decided immediately that he liked the man.

"My son, Dante, is occupied at the moment. He should be with us in a few minutes. May I show you around?"

"That would be lovely," Gabriella answered. "Briefly, though. We have a limited amount of time to conduct our interview."

"*Si, si, signora.* I understand." He led them around the grounds, explaining which buildings were part of the winery operation, which were family houses, and which were guest houses. Next to those a large swimming pool sparkled in the late morning sun. Circling back, they crossed paths with three of Riccardo's great-grandsons, kicking a soccer ball around a small, graveled piazza. When the ball came toward Riccardo, he stepped up and kicked it briskly to the youngest. He beamed as he explained, "I take a little time to play with them every day," he said "when the weather permits. Their parents are always too busy. It keeps me young." Walking back, he explained that the winery was started by his great-great grandfather in the late nineteenth century.

Arriving where they began, Antonio noticed a white delivery truck, a class six, the same type of vehicle they believed was involved in the accident. The driver's side was undamaged. He circled it to get a look at the passenger side, which was where any damage would have occurred. There was none, and four hubcaps were in place.

A few moments later a man in his late fifties walked up to them. He was clearly Riccardo's son, with the same wiry build, but his eyes lacked the spark of life that made his father such a pleasure to be around. His father introduced them, but Dante did not offer his hand.

They entered an office attached to the barrel room. They passed through the reception area and into a small conference room, with a large picture window which perfectly framed the view of the vineyards. On one wall was also a poster-sized photo of Riccardo holding his rifle upright as he knelt next to a huge wild boar. Against another wall was a glass-fronted gun cabinet, with a half dozen hunting rifles on display.

"Please, please have a seat," Riccardo said. "May we offer you some wine?"

"*No, grazie*," Gabriella said. "This is a working visit. As I explained on the phone, we have been requested to do some follow up on the previous visit by the Wine Commission."

Dante leaned forward and slammed his hand on the table. "Why the Carabinieri now? We have no time for this nonsense! We've done nothing wrong. The inspector who came took wine samples. He seemed satisfied. I'm certain they proved we are making our wine according to the DOCG regulations."

"Please, Dante," his father intoned. "These people have a job to …"

Dante turned to his father. "Don't you see, Father? This is harassment. And the timing! We have enough on our plates with this plague!"

"Please, may I speak?" Gabriella said, with measured calmness. "I am afraid the wine samples did not make it to the chemist. There was an accident, you see …"

"That's not our problem!" Dante said, with eyes that practically bulged from their sockets.

"Wait," Riccardo said, holding his hand up toward his son. "An accident? This man, Andrea …?"

"Marinelli," Gabriella answered.

"Is he okay?" he sputtered.

"I'm afraid not," Gabriella said. Antonio could see she didn't want to answer yet, but felt she had to. "He and his wife were driven off the road into the Arbia River on their way to see the wine chemist."

Her voice was displaying emotion. Antonio knew it was time to step in. "Their car was hit multiple times from the side by a large delivery truck, the same kind of truck you have outside here."

Dante turned red in the face. "Are you accusing us of …"

His father held up his hand again. "Enough! A man and woman are dead! Show some respect! Let these people do their job."

"But …"

Riccardo spoke over his son, "Please, forgive my son. He forgets his manners. Ask us whatever questions you need to. And we would be happy to provide more samples."

"Thank you," Gabriella said, having regained her composure. "It appears that *Signor* Marinelli must have rattled some cages during his investigation. Someone had something to hide, something incriminating enough that they felt they had to take drastic action to prevent it being found out. All of the wine samples disappeared."

"I don't believe it," the old man mumbled, looking troubled.

Gabriella looked at Antonio. He took the cue. "Please don't take this personally. Under such circumstances we are required to question all parties involved. With your cooperation we can rule you out as suspects."

Riccardo nodded sadly. Dante was seething beneath the surface like an angry teenager. "Can you tell us, how many of these trucks do you have?"

"Two." Riccardo answered. Dante put his hand on his father's arm. Riccardo shook it off. "I've been told the other is in the shop getting repaired." He glared at his son. Antonio caught a flicker of anger cross Gabriella's face.

"It is," Dante said. "It was having a problem with the carburetor. You saw it before it went in, Father. I just took it in on Monday. The shop is just outside of Orvieto … Vendetti's Truck Repair."

Gabriella made a note, then spoke. "The road incident took place nearly three weeks ago, on Saturday, the 15th of February. Do you know what you were doing on that day?"

Dante thought for a moment, then pulled out his phone and touched a button, presumably his calendar app. "I was here all day. We were pruning the south vineyards."

"And did anyone else have access to your trucks that day?" Antonio asked. "Is it possible any were unaccounted for?"

Dante glanced at his calendar again. "The truck you saw outside. It was picking up a load of French barrels from the Port of Livorno. My son, Giorgo, is in charge of all transportation. If you want, I can get you a copy of the bill of lading."

"Can you please take a picture of it and text it to me? My number is on my card here." She handed him a business card. He nodded.

"And the other truck?" Antonio asked.

"We were not using the other truck because it was idling rough. I hope that is all the questions you have. I can assure you, we had nothing to do with the death of the Wine Commission inspector." He stared unflinchingly at Antonio as he spoke. "Now if you will excuse me, I have a winery to run." He started to rise.

"Not yet!" Gabriella said firmly. "Please sit down. I have some additional questions about your wine production."

"I already told you; we closely follow all of the DOCG regulations. We would never risk our reputation by mixing in unauthorized grapes."

Gabriella leaned forward and locked eyes with him. "Then you won't mind answering our questions."

Dante crossed his arms across his chest. "Ask away."

"You have made it abundantly clear that you follow all of the DOCG regulations. Are you aware of any wineries that do not?"

Dante looked at his father. Something unspoken passed between them. "No," Riccardo said. "And if we did, such things are better taken care of in-house." Antonio saw a brief flicker of his eyes toward his gun cabinet. "Otherwise, they could ruin the reputation of us all."

Gabriella pressed, asking a series of questions, which Dante answered begrudgingly, under the hawk-like stare of his father. Finally satisfied, Gabriella concluded, "Thank you for your cooperation. The only thing we need now are barrel samples, and bottles of your most recent vintages. We will pay for those of course. Can you please show us to your barrel room?"

"That's not possible right now. I'm afraid it's too dangerous. You saw the forklifts at work. They are bringing in the new barrels and re-racking. I will pull the barrel samples for you. My father can get the bottles you requested."

Antonio remembered Umberto's instructions that they were not to go where they were not invited. He watched Gabriella to see how she responded. She glanced at him, then back at Dante. "That will be fine, *Signor* Carrapaccio. *Grazie* for your time!

Chapter Twenty-three

Thursday, mid-day

A ntonio asked to use a restroom. There was one attached to the barrel room. When he came out, Dante walked up and handed him a small, unlabeled bottle. "Your barrel sample," he said. He turned and walked away without another word.

Gabriella was waiting by the car. As he drove down the hill toward the main road, he asked for her observations. She just shook her head. "Hurry. We're supposed to be there in ten minutes." Gabriella put the next winery in her Google Maps app, then pulled out the winery map, to double-check. Her phone said the winery was 11 kilometers away. But it appeared to be half that as the crow flies. "Turn north," she said. He did so and accelerated quickly, pushing the limit on the winding road. The car handled well. He heard the text notification sound on Gabriella's phone.

"Chia," she said. "Asking if I'm available to talk." Gabriella dialed the number. The call came up on Blue Tooth speakers. "*Pronto*, Chia. Do you have something? I only have a few minutes."

"I wanted to let you know. I think I found the truck on the CCTV footage. A class six delivery truck was behind them as they approached the bridge, but then goes out of camera view.

All I got was a front view. It was an older model, white, no logos. The plates were removed. I figured they would be. I need to research body styles on the internet to see if I can identify the model."

"Can you see how many people were in the cab?"

"Two. Both males. Both wore caps which made it hard to get a look at their faces. One appeared to have a beard. But these cameras are not high def so the images are not going to be much help."

"Can you get me still photos of the best images you have and send them to me anyway? One of the truck, and the best close up you have of the men."

"Of course. I knew you'd ask. I'll text them as soon as we hang up."

"One more thing. Can you call Marina Gallo and coordinate with her? She has a hubcap which may have come from the truck. It could be one more clue to help you figure it out."

"Got it. Be careful out there, Gabriella."

"We will. *Grazie,* Chia. *Mille grazie!*"

Moments later she was studying the two grainy, blurred photographs.

*****

A sign beside the road announced their arrival at Villa Sant'Angelo. The grand wrought iron gates stood wide open to welcome visitors. He doubted there would be any today. Maybe it was just for them. Tall Italian Cyprus trees lined the long, straight drive, which sloped gently upwards, ending in front of the palatial villa. The exterior was stucco of a pale orange-coral hue which reminded Antonio of the rind of Valle d'Aosta

Fontina cheese, one of his favorites. The grounds were immaculate, with formal gardens. Fish swam among lily pads in a rectangular, man-made pool, fed by a small waterfall pouring from the mouth of a lion. Along the garden pathways statues of women and angels alternated with oversized Italian urns overflowing with early spring flowers.

Stepping from the car, they were greeted by two small, white balls of fur, residing calmly on the steps, heads cocked sideways. Moments later the front door opened and a finely aged woman with perfect posture emerged. Her short hair was silver, and pulled behind her ear on one side. She ran her fingers through it to make sure not a hair was out of place. The pale, teal-colored pants suit she wore could have come from Armani, as far as Antonio knew.

"Ah, I see you've made acquaintance with my boys." Her voice was well-mannered, yet playful. "Please, please, come in. I was hoping you might join me for a light lunch. It's so quiet around here these days. I must admit, I've been lonely for some interaction … of the human type," she said, motioning toward her dogs who eagerly took to their feet.

Antonio looked at Gabriella. She nodded imperceptibly and spoke. "It would be an honor to join you. But first, please tell me, what breed are these adorable little guys? I've never seen them."

"It is a breed known as Bolognese … like the pasta," she laughed elegantly. "They originated in Bologna in the eleventh century. A toy bichon breed, quite popular with the nobility at one time, but nearly disappeared as the nobility did. My family was given a pair by Cosimo de Medici in the seventeenth century. These boys are descendants. They do make excellent companions for a widow like myself."

She turned, and the dogs, as well as Gabriella and Antonio, followed her up the grand steps which converged towards the ornately carved door. Crossing the threshold, Antonio felt like he stepped into a different world, one he had only seen in movies, representing the glory of days gone by. It was breathtakingly beautiful, yet he could not imagine living in such a place, which made him feel very small. He felt underdressed in his blue jeans, button-down shirt, and crew neck sweater.

From the marble tiled foyer, they followed her down a corridor to a large dining room with a long table, topped with a cut-crystal vase full of fresh flowers. She suddenly wheeled around, looking dismayed. "Where are my manners? I never introduced myself, or even found out the name of this gentleman. Marianna Bellini," she said, holding out her hand toward Antonio. "But please, call me Marianna."

For a half-second he thought he should kiss her hand but reached out and shook it instead. "Antonio Cortese," he said.

"You're American," she said, matter-of-factly, staring at him, somewhat surprised.

He was trying to think of an explanation but she turned to Gabriella. "And Colonel Ferrara, I presume. It is nice to meet a woman who has advanced in the ranks. I must say, you've managed to maintain your beauty and femininity in the process. And yet I see a strength in your eyes."

"Please," her tone seemed humble. "Call me Gabriella."

Marianna nodded. "And these are my ancestors," she said, waving her hand around the room at the dozen or so formal portraits which adorned the wall. "They're not very good company, I'm afraid. I rarely dine in here, unless I'm having a grand dinner party. I do that less and less these days. Many of my friends are dead or dying. Follow me. If you think you'll be warm enough, we'll dine on the small terrazza off the kitchen. It's where I prefer to take my meals when the weather allows."

They walked through the kitchen, which made Antonio jealous. It was three times the size of the kitchen in his restaurant. They passed through a pair of French doors onto the intimate terrazza. The landscaping on either end gave it a sense of privacy, but it opened to a breathtaking view of the vineyards which seemed to go on forever. They took a seat at the round table with inlaid tiles. Marianna pulled a chilled bottle of Vermentino from a wine bucket and poured them a glass without asking. It had their Villa Sant'Angelo label on it, which featured a drawing of the villa. Antonio recalled it was the second largest winery in the region.

Antonio expected a servant to serve them but Marianna disappeared and returned a few minutes later with a platter of salad made of white cannellini beans, arugula, crispy pancetta, marinated asparagus, and shaved pecorino. She disappeared again and returned with a basket of warm crostini made from a rosemary bread.

Perfetto! Antonio thought, enchanted by the incredible setting, and a delightful spring lunch. It made him uneasy though. Typically, you want to interview suspects on your turf, not theirs. He knew that wasn't practical here, but all this pampering put Marianna in the driver's seat, and she seemed to take immediate advantage of it. Or maybe he'd just grown too cynical in his years as a detective.

As they dished out the salad, Marianna launched her own line of questioning. "Gabriella, you said on the phone you were following up on the investigation by the wine commissioner. I was of the impression that the gentleman inspector was completely satisfied when he left here. I don't even understand why we were chosen to be looked at in the first place. We have eleven generations of fine winemaking. We certainly wouldn't jeopardize such a long-standing reputation. Yes, we have had some notable increases in production the past few years, but for good reason. If you look at our history over the last decade, our yields dropped off for a few years as we replanted many of the older vineyards. As those vines matured, the production levels naturally increased."

This made sense to Antonio. And he could not imagine this woman being a stone-cold killer. If he wasn't enjoying himself so much, he would consider this a waste of time. Yet he recalled that Andrea, in his notes, indicated that he felt she was hiding something. He'd seen no signs of it so far.

"If that is the case, we should be able to put these concerns to bed rather quickly," Gabriella said. "I just have a few questions."

"Of course." Marianna lifted her glass, swirled, stuck her nose deep within and inhaled. She took a sip. "It's so sad," she said. "My husband was so happy when our son was born. It was very hard for me to get pregnant. We were afraid we'd have no heirs to pass the winery to. Now it appears to have made no difference. Our son, Jacopo, has no interest in running the winery. He fancies himself a movie producer, though he's had little success. Probably because he spends most of his time running around the Riviera with budding actresses half his age."

"May I ask when you lost your husband?" Gabriella asked.

"He died of lung cancer twelve years ago. He was only sixty. I tried to get him to stop smoking. He wouldn't listen."

"And you've been managing the winery by yourself ever since?"

"Yes. With help of course. Two years ago, my estate manager passed away. His father had managed the estate before him. We were very close." A subtle smile came and went as she paused to reflect a moment. Antonio wondered about their relationship. "Not long afterward, my winemaker of thirty-seven years retired, due to declining health. My son, though he rarely even visits, talked me into hiring a friend of his to manage the estate. He, in turn, chose the new winemaker ... with my blessing, of course. They are younger men. Both quite capable. But I feel a bit lost without my old friends. I'm rarely consulted these days—except for when they need me to open my purse strings, of course." A melancholy seemed to settle over her as she spoke. Antonio was beginning to understand her loneliness.

"Would it be possible to speak with them?" Gabriella asked.

"Not today, I'm afraid," Marianna said. She quickly picked up her glass to take a drink as her eyes flicked toward the vineyard. Antonio got the impression she was trying to think of an excuse. "I gave them a few days off before we get into the busy season."

"You didn't want them to attend the *consorzio* meeting Saturday?"

"No. I told them I would be attending and report back to them." Antonio thought that was odd. "Are you aware that it will be held at the winery owned by the Amer ..."

"Yes. We are aware," Gabriella interrupted. "Another question I need to ask. Does your winery own any large delivery trucks? Specifically white ones?"

"Yes. Of course. Why do you ask?"

Antonio studied Marianna's face as Gabriella explained the events which led to the death of Andrea and Bria. She listened with horror in her eyes, and he caught sight of a tremor in her hands before she moved them to her lap.

"What a terrible thing!" she said, shaking her head. "Now I understand why you were called in. And why you are asking about the trucks. We own three such vehicles. I can show them to you."

"Yes, please," Gabriella said, then asked, "Do you know your fellow winemakers well? What I'm asking is, do you have any idea who might do such a thing?"

Marianna's eyes narrowed and stared far off. "I haven't a clue," she finally answered. Antonio suspected otherwise.

"And with your permission we would also like to obtain more barrel samples and purchase bottles of your most recent vintages of Vino Nobile."

"Of course. The truck garages are a short distance from the barrel room. As soon as we finish lunch, we can take a walk."

Chapter Twenty-four

Thursday afternoon

Antonio glanced at Gabriella as he pulled from the driveway onto the highway. He was anxious to discuss his observations but she had retreated into her cocoon again. He could almost see the cogs turning inside her head. They rounded a curve in the road and Montepulciano came into view, framed by tall, white cumulus clouds coming in from the sea. She suddenly perked up. "I could use an espresso. Shall we go into town?"

"You read my mind."

They arrived at the parking lot on the south end of town near the Porta San Donato. It was nearly vacant. Antonio parked and they climbed the steps past Fortezza Medicea, a Renaissance castle, then past the adjacent gardens—Giardino Don Marcello del Balio. Gabriella, still quiet, reached out and took his hand. *That's something,* he thought, as they began the gentle ascent up Via Fiorenzuola Vecchia, keeping to the sunny side of the street. There were few people on the street and many of the eating establishments and wine tasting rooms were closed. Antonio saw a number of people on their balconies. Covid-19 had sent many into hibernation. He saw a wispy-haired gentleman, dressed in a rumpled suit, leaning on his rail watching the street life below. The voice of an Italian tenor, Antonio thought it might be Pavarotti, wafted from behind him, singing his rendition of *Nessun Dorma*, which seemed to fit the mood.

They continued upward past the Teatro Poliziano and the Cattedrale di Santa Maria Assunta, Montepulciano's principal place of worship. Two elderly women in black dresses and scarves climbed the steps and entered through the heavy doors.

Antonio and Gabriella arrived in the Piazza Grande, the highest point in Montepulciano and its main piazza. In front of them was the Palazzo Comunale, the town hall with its clock tower, an almost exact replica of the Palazzo Vecchio in Firenze. Near it was a well with small pillars supporting a cross piece on which sat gryphon*s*, those legendary creatures with the body, tail and hind legs of a lion, and the head and wings of an eagle.

"Have you ever been to Caffe Poliziano?" he asked.

"Years ago. I came here for the Bravo delle Botti, the barrel races they hold in August. Have you been?"

"Once, when I was a teen. I spent a week with Chiara and Sylvio and they brought me. Quite exciting watching those teams roll their barrels up the hilly street."

"And was Angelica with you?"

Antonio turned red in the face and nodded.

"I knew it." She elbowed him and laughed. "Do you remember how to find the Caffe?"

"I do. It's near, but we have to take a round-about route." He led her across to the northwest corner of the piazza onto Via Ricci. They walked a few blocks on the gentle downhill slope, then took a soft right onto Via del Poggiolo, the *street of the balcony*. When they reached Via dell'Erbe, the *street of herbs*, they made a sharp right toward the south. A couple of blocks later, they found it open.

Caffe Poliziano looks ordinary on the outside, but through those doors you enter a world that is refined and elegant, with an art nouveau atmosphere. There is dining on two floors, one mostly coffee and pastries, the other a dining room. Both floor areas open onto outdoor patios providing sweeping views of the surrounding valley. They stepped up to the long coffee bar and ordered two double espressos and took a table with a view. There was only one other person in the place.

Gabriella finally spoke, "So, what do you think?"

"I assume you mean the winery visits. Shall I start with Carrapaccio?"

She nodded, then took a sip of her espresso.

"Not guilty of murder in my opinion. Dante's a piece of work. His defensiveness could lead one to believe he's guilty of something. I see it the opposite way. If I did something like that, I'd be going out of my way to act like I had nothing to hide instead of being rude and stubborn. What a contrast between him and his father. But I assume you'll want to follow up on the other truck which they claimed to be in the garage for repairs?"

"I already did ... while you were using their restroom. The mechanic confirmed that the truck is there and says there is no damage to the body."

"That's what I expected. But I think they may know, or at least suspect, one of their fellow wineries of blending illegal grapes into their wine. You saw how Riccardo reacted to that question. I worry he might take things into his own hands. But something else seemed fishy, too. That was a lame excuse for not allowing us to accompany him to the barrel room."

"I agree. Dante is a piece of work, as you call it, but I didn't see any body language to indicate he was lying. As far as the samples, we also have the bottles … both the ones we bought from the winery and the ones delivered by the president of the *consorzio*. So, unless it's a brand-new practice, we'll know."

"Aren't we supposed to get the results from the bottles the president dropped off soon?"

"Yes. *Signor* Landi thought he would have them by tomorrow," Gabriella said. "What did you think about Marianna?"

"Sad and lonely."

"And charming."

"That, too. Quite disarming. But I think she's lost control of what's going on. It appears that her son—who claims to want nothing to do with the winery—has quietly taken the reins by putting his own people in there. They could be cheating the system and she'd never know it."

"I disagree. She's too smart for that. She's been drinking her own wine all of her life. If they began to mix in other grapes, she would taste it in a heartbeat."

Antonio nodded. "You're right. But as far as murder, she's the least likely candidate I can think of. What would her motive be? Her explanation of rising yields from the newer vineyards makes complete sense. And I don't see the means or opportunity … unless her relationship with her manager is far different than what she told us. Besides, all of their trucks had logos painted on them. The only red flag I saw was her reaction when she talked about her son and the new manager and winemaker he brought on board. Something didn't feel right. I don't think she trusts her own son."

"Agreed." Gabriella's phone began to ring. She answered, "*Pronto, Signor* Gregson. Thank you for calling." She listened, nodding her head. "*Perfetto.* Would 10:00 be okay?" She listened, then replied. "*Si, grazie!* We'll see you tomorrow. *Arrivederci.*"

She hung up and looked at Antonio. "The American … from Le Cascio."

"I got to thinking about something. Maybe we should be calling all of the truck shops or body shops in the area … to see if any trucks were brought in for damage repair?"

"Good thinking. I could …"

Antonio interrupted. "Why not ask Giulia to do it? She's anxious to help out."

Gabriella pondered the idea. "Okay, give her a call. Have her start with a twenty-kilometer radius and work her way out."

Antonio called her. She was eager to do so. "If they ask," he added, "tell them you're with the Carabinieri," he said. "You can give them Gabriella's name and position if they press you." Gabriella gave him a glaring look. "But only if they ask," he added before hanging up.

"I don't think that's a good …"

"Got any better ideas? You approved her making the calls."

She gave him a look and downed the last of her espresso in one gulp. "I'm ready to head back."

"One more stop," Antonio said. She read his mischievous look.

"You and your gelato!"

"How else is a man supposed to survive the long stretch between lunch and these late Italian dinners!"

She gave him an elbow. "Okay, but you're buying again."

Chapter Twenty-five

Thursday afternoon-evening

T he sun ducked behind the cumulus clouds, now rising thousands of feet into the sky, and a chill breeze kicked up as they drove the highway back toward Sylvio and Chiara's. The road wound past vineyards, olive groves, and fields of winter wheat. Passing a farm, Antonio saw a herd of pigs—two-toned—dark, with a broad white band around the middle. He slowed down and pointed.

"*Cinta Senese,*" she said. "*Cinta* means belt, referring to the white belt around their middle. They were almost extinct a few decades ago. Now they are considered a Heritage Breed. Their meat is leaner than other breeds. It is the best pork in the world."

Shortly after passing the farm, Antonio saw a white delivery truck appear in his rearview mirror. He wasn't sure where it came from. His hands tightened on the steering wheel when he noticed the front grill was damaged. It accelerated quickly until it was just a few car lengths behind them. Two men rode in the cab. He alerted Gabriella. She lowered her visor to look in the mirror, then turned to view it in the passenger side mirror. "I don't think it's anything to be concerned about," she said, as she calmly reached under the seat, pulled out her gun safe, and retrieved her Beretta 8000. "But we're not taking any chances." Antonio sped up as she pulled out her phone to look at something. The truck stayed with them. He was beginning to get nervous. When it made a turn he took a deep breath.

"Should we follow it?" he asked.

"I don't think so. Neither of the men had a beard, and the truck looked different to me than the one in the photo Chia sent." She held up the photo on her phone. Antonio agreed.

Ten minutes later they turned onto the stone pine canopied drive leading to their temporary residence at Fattoria Montieri. When they pulled up in front of the house, Sylvio came limping toward them from the barn, wearing a large straw hat, looking weathered. They climbed from the car and greeted him. "*Ciao, ciao,* Sylvio. How is the pruning coming along?"

"Very well," he replied. "I had help most of the day. Umberto in the morning. Then he said he had some business to tend to. I don't think he's used to the manual labor," he smiled knowingly. "Then Giulia helped me for a few hours after lunch. She knocked off about an hour ago … said something about making some calls for you. She's quite good with the pruning shears. Says she helps with the pruning at home. We finished the east vineyard. Tomorrow we'll finish the north side."

"And that's all?"

"That's it. I was very grateful for the help. It kept Chiara off my back. Speaking of which, she and Serena are making some Pecorino cheese right now." He turned his thumb toward the cheese making room off the barn. "Those two have become inseparable."

Gabriella smiled. "I'm so thankful for that. Seems everyone has been busy today. Do you guys need help making dinner? I can't imagine you or Chiara having the energy after the day you've put in."

"True, true, but I believe it's under control. Angelica has made herself useful. She's been in the kitchen for the better part of the afternoon. I have no idea what she's cooking up."

They entered the house, which smelled fabulous. Umberto was wearing an apron, working alongside Angelica, stirring something in a large pot.

"What smells like heaven?" Antonio asked."

"*Cugino!*" Angelica said, as she gave him a kiss on the cheek and pinched his bottom. Antonio thought he was probably beet red as he looked at Gabriella. She just laughed.

"You'll see. Dinner will be early tonight … around 8:00. Save your appetite."

Antonio looked at his watch. It was 6:40. He was glad they'd found an open gelato bar.

"Do you need help?" Gabriella asked.

"*No, no, grazie!* Wait, actually there is one thing you can do. Open two bottles of the 2010 Vino Nobile Riserva and decant them, *per favore*. *Papà* can show you where to find them. And the two bottles of Orvieto that are in the refrigerator. We brought those from one of our favorite Umbrian wineries. You're such a dear. *Tante grazie!*"

Antonio smiled to himself as he quietly left the room. He wanted to check in with Shane. It would be 9:40 in the morning in Seattle.

*****

"Hey, Uncle," Shane said. "What's going on in Tuscany? Have you guys found your killers yet"

Antonio didn't think the question sounded very sincere. "We're working on it."

132

"I'm still worried that you won't make it home, boss. Or that you'll get Covid. I keep hearing on the news that Italy's having the most serious outbreak of anywhere."

"I'll make it."

"How do you know? *Merda!* I can't handle this much longer without you. I hate making some of the decisions I'm having to make … cutting hours … I had to lay off two of our newest service people. I'm afraid that's just the beginning. Dine-in business is getting worse by the day."

Antonio could hear the stress in Shane's voice, and felt his own blood pressure rising. He took a deep breath. "Just do the best you can. I'll make it home soon. I promise."

"Yeah, well hopefully you'll have a restaurant to come home to."

"Listen, if it comes down to laying off any long-term employees get ahold of me. I've got some cash reserves we can dig into to give them a separation bonus. It will take time until they can get their unemployment. I'll check our bank balances and move some funds in preparation."

"Will do. I've just been trying hard not to bother you."

"Bother me, Shane! You shouldn't have to carry this weight all on your own shoulders."

"Okay. Okay. I will."

"Now tell me how your *Nonna* Elena is doing … and your mom and Matthew."

*****

Gabriella looked at Antonio. "You look worried."

"I called Shane."

"Is everything okay at home?"

"Not really."

"Talk to me, *cara mio*."

"You've got enough on your plate."

"Just this morning you told me to stop trying to carry the load all by myself. It's lighter if you share it, you said. It is your turn."

"It's just that things are really tough for Shane right now. And Alessia is still under a lot of stress with Matthew."

"I really think you should go home, Antonio. They need you."

"I knew you'd react that way. That's why I didn't want to tell you."

"You wonder why I've been quiet at times. That's one of the reasons. I'm feeling guilty, too … keeping you here when you need to be at home."

"That was my choice."

"I can handle myself, Antonio! I have been a detective longer than you, remember?"

"And you're off on your own. No backup … no partner if I leave. Hell, you're not even supposed to be doing this. You're risking your life, your career. And for what? What do you want, Gabriella? Revenge?"

Her eyes glared at him. "You know me better than that!"

"I'm not going to let you play Lone Ranger! What if something happens to you? What about Serena? I know she's like a daughter to you. She needs you!" he took a deep breath. "I need you, too."

Gabriella's eyes looked over his shoulder. He turned and saw Serena staring at them. Gabriella turned and wrapped her in her arms and broke down in tears.

*****

Dinner was amazing, but the tension was thick enough that you could cut it with a knife. The whole family had heard their argument. Angelica showed a different side of herself, taking the seat next to Gabriella. Antonio watched her place her hand atop Gabriella's and give a gentle squeeze. Serena sat on her other side, leaning into her. Antonio sat opposite.

Umberto brought the first of Angelica's creations, a tureen of Ribollita, a twice-boiled soup of bread, black cabbage, and white beans. Sylvio poured the straw-colored Orvieto and raised his glass. "*Salute!*" he said. "To your health."

"*Salute!*" they all replied, rather subdued.

Antonio could not tear his mind away from his conversations with Shane and Gabriella. He felt like he was being torn in half. He was needed in two places at once. Part of him wanted to get on a plane bound for home. The other part felt strongly compelled to stay. *I lose either way,* he thought. But in the end, he knew what he had to do. *God help me,* he prayed. *Help me to do what's right.*

The next course was Braciole di Vitello, thin cutlets of veal, rolled and stuffed with spinach and prosciutto and cooked in tomato sauce. It was served over polenta, which is what Umberto had been stirring in that large pot. They served broccoli raab as a *verdura*, quickly blanched then sautéed with olive oil and shallots, and sprinkled with Chiara's aged pecorino. To go with the course, Sylvio poured the 2010 Vino Nobile Riserva. "An amazing vintage," he proclaimed. "I believe it is my favorite wine we've ever made." No one was going to argue the point. It had just enough age to pair perfectly with Angelica's Braciole.

At the end, Angelica brought out a platter of cheese and fruit. Antonio ate little, his appetite fully satiated. Finally, it was Umberto who broke the ice. "Tell us what you learned today." Antonio let Gabriella do the explaining. When she finished, while the others retired to a fire in the living room, Antonio excused himself and dragged himself off to bed.

He pulled out his phone and checked flights from Pisa to London's Heathrow Airport.

~~~~ FRIDAY, MARCH 6 ~~~~

Chapter Twenty-six
Friday Morning

A ntonio awoke with a parched throat, runny nose, and itchy eyes. For a brief moment the thought of Covid-19 passed through his head. Reality was that spring was simply having its usual effects on him. His hay fever seemed to get worse every year. He looked at the clock. It was nearly eight. Though he'd gone to bed early, sleep had evaded him for hours, as he rolled things over and over in his mind. He scheduled a flight to London for tomorrow, then cancelled it before making the purchase final.

He downed the glass of water by his bed and opened the curtains. The clouds were gone and he could hear the cheerful sound of birds singing. At least his mood had improved somewhat overnight. On his way to the shower, he glanced in the mirror. *Ugh!* His eyes were bloodshot, and he was badly in need of a haircut. He wondered if the salons would even be open by the time he got back to Seattle.

After his shower and eye drops, he looked marginally better. Hoping that coffee would take him to the next level, he went searching. He was surprised when he found Angelica in the kitchen squeezing oranges. He smelled a delightful aroma coming from the oven. "*Buongiorno, cugino!*" she said, a little too cheerfully, with a peck on his cheek. "Better this morning?"

"Was I that bad?"

"No ... well … maybe. I'm just used to you being the eternal peacemaker and optimist."

"What's gotten into you? That amazing dinner and now you're cooking breakfast?"

"I've no idea," she laughed. "Something about being here. But I'm not really cooking. I'm just warming some *cornetto* that we picked up yesterday afternoon. We better enjoy them. The owner of the *forno* said they're shutting down indefinitely." She poured him some fresh squeezed orange juice. "I can make you a couple of eggs, if you'd like."

"That would be awesome, *grazie!*" He headed for the coffee, which smelled fresh, and poured his first cup. His ears picked up some cheerful voices and laughter, then Chiara entered the kitchen from outdoors with Serena and Giulia in tow. "*Buongiorno!*" Chiara said. "How are you feeling? Better I hope." These questions were beginning to give him a complex.

By the time he'd received hugs and kisses from the girls and sat down to eat, with a glass of fresh orange juice, his attitude had come around. He was just beginning to wonder about Gabriella when she walked into the room and took a seat beside him. Before he could say good morning, she spoke rather hurriedly, "Antonio, I just got off the phone with Chia. There was a fire! It destroyed the wine lab. The chemist, Pietro Landi ... he was shot, and the fire was set to cover it up. Chia just arrived, shortly after the fire department, she is heading up the investigation. I asked her to call in Marina Gallo."

Antonio stared at her dumbfounded. He knew for certain now that his decision to cancel his flight was the right one. "I assume they were trying to destroy any evidence about wine fraud," he said. "We should call the president of the *consorzio*. Find out if he was given results yet. My guess is no."

Gabriella pulled out her phone, dialed, and put it on speakerphone. "*Pronto*," he answered.

"*Signor* Crivello? This is Colonel Ferrara. We spoke two days ago."

"*Si, si!* Do you have news about the wine samples?"

"I was hoping you did. I just received a call from my colleague in Siena, Chia Umeh. She is at the wine lab now. There was a fire last night. The lab was completely gutted. Almost certainly arson. And the chemist, *Signor* Landi … I'm sorry to say he is dead. His body is badly burned but it appears he was shot."

The line went silent for several heartbeats. "*Dio mio!*" he finally said in a quiet voice. "He seemed like a good man. He was going to call me today. Tomorrow, we are having our meeting of the *consorzio*. I was hoping to know something. Not that I would have made the results public."

"*Signor*, Crivello. I have to ask. Do you have any idea … any idea at all who could be behind this?"

"No, no. I wish I did. The reputation of our fine wine is at stake. Not to mention the lives taken."

"Let me put it this way," Gabriella said. "If you were investigating this. Where would you begin?" The line went silent again. "Please, *Signor* Crivello. We need to get to the bottom of this before more people die."

He cleared his throat. "All I can tell you is rumors and speculation."

"Please. Anything would be useful."

"You did not hear any of this from me."

"Of course."

"Some people suspect our newcomers. Possibly the Americans. Or the long-lost daughter who came from Apulia."

"Is it just because they are outsiders? Or are there more concrete reasons?" she pressed.

"Probably both. The American, *Signor* Gregson ... he's very ambitious. Most blame his Italian wife. She was a fashion model in Milan." The way he said that last line made it sound as if that explained everything.

"And the woman from Apulia, Alida Fontana?"

"Some people suspect there are mob ties."

"Why would they suspect that?" Gabriella asked.

"Personally, I think it's simply speculation because she comes from the south." A few moments later he added, "And she seems to have unending resources."

"*Grazie* for your time, *Signor* Crivello. We'll keep you in the loop if we learn anything. *Arrivederci*."

After she hung up, Antonio asked some questions. "I assume Chia checked for security cameras? Anything inside would probably be destroyed. He may have had outside cameras."

"She said there were none on his building. But she's going to check to see if the complex has any. The lab was located in a business park."

"What about his computer? It was probably destroyed in the fire. On rare occasions a good tech can still get something from the hard drive, even if it's damaged."

"I neglected to tell you that part. The computer case was charred but open. The hard drive removed."

"These guys knew what they were doing," Antonio said.

He sat quietly and relished his coffee. It was beginning to clear the fog from his mind. "You know, most computer files are backed up onto the Cloud nowadays."

"I hadn't thought of that. No wonder I kept you around!" she said lightheartedly, obviously trying to make amends. "I'll call Chia. She's the computer geek." She dialed and they spoke briefly. "Chia will follow up on that. She said to tell you that you're brilliant."

He stood up. "I'll be even more brilliant after another cup of coffee. Can I get you some?"

"Please." She took his hand before he walked away. "Thank you, Antonio … for staying. You were right, you know. I do need a partner."

He didn't tell her how close he came to leaving.

Chapter Twenty-seven

Friday, mid-morning

The morning drive on the winding road to Le Cascio took them to the western edge of the Vino Nobile viticulture area. They passed a herd of *Chianina* cattle grazing on the hills. These unusual looking cows, with their white coat, and a bump at the base of the neck are known for their exceptional beef. It is the largest breed of cattle in the world, standing nearly six feet tall, and one of the oldest, with roots dating to Roman times. It is also the only breed used for the famous Bistecca alla Fiorentina.

As they drove, Gabriella updated him with Andrea's journal open on her lap. He sensed that she was done hiding within herself, at least for now. "Our American winemaker, Gerald Gregson, bought the winery seven years ago, but it had been in operation for a hundred and fifty years before that. He has poured a lot of money into it to modernize production. He came from the Silicon Valley where he made a small fortune. He met his wife at a fashion show while vacationing in New York. It must have been love at first sight because they married two weeks later. She had three teenage daughters, who are now in their late twenties. They all reside on the estate and have various roles. One of them spends much of her time in New York managing their stateside import business. It is the fourth largest winery in land size but second in production."

"You found all that in Andrea's notes?"

"Some. I did additional research on Google. I wanted to know more about his background."

They arrived at the Le Cascio property, which undulated over a wide area of rolling hills. It had the least amount of natural wooded areas of any property that Antonio had seen in the area.

"I'm guessing they've cleared some forest land since purchasing the winery," Antonio said, "and added more vineyards. It seems like almost every square foot is planted."

As they parked, it became obvious why this place was chosen to have the meeting of the *consorzio*. It had a large parking area. From there, stone steps led to an impressive array of buildings, a fusion of old-world and modern. An expansive stone building, which appeared to be the original winery, housed a tasting room, gift shop, and restaurant. Across from that a sleek, contemporary winery of steel and glass was built into the hillside. A spacious *terrazza* lay between the two, much of it covered by a pergola with grape vines growing on it. It made for an inviting atmosphere. Everything was designed to optimize the tourist draw. What appeared to be a small compound of homes, probably where the family resided, perched on a nearby hillside overlooking it all, and the city of Montepulciano beyond.

As soon as they climbed the steps, Gerald Gregson was there to greet them. He was a tall, handsome man of great charm and charisma. He wore neatly pressed linen slacks and a blue shirt with a beige sport coat. Antonio guessed him to be early fifties. He greeted them with familiarity, though he had met neither. "*Ciao, ciao, signora!* You must be Colonel Gabriella Ferrara. What a delight! You are not at all what I envisioned. Even the Carabinieri are beautiful here in Italy. Please, please, this way. Such a lovely day. We must enjoy the terrazza." He put his hand on her elbow and led her toward a table. "And who is this gentleman accompanying you?"

Gabriella appeared unfazed by his charms. "This is my associate, Detective Antonio Cortese."

He shook Antonio's hand. "A pleasure to meet you. Call me Gerry. Please, have a seat, my wife will be down to join us shortly." As soon as they sat a young waiter of African descent showed up with bottles of mineral water, glasses, and a bowl of marinated olives and peppers.

"Thank you for being patient with my schedule," he said. "So much to prepare for tomorrow. How can I be of assistance?" Antonio could see the preparations underway. In addition to the twenty or so tables already on the terrazza, there was a stack of folding tables against one wall, and a dolly stacked with chairs.

"As you know," Gabriella said, "there were concerns by the Italian Wine Commission of irregularities in the wine production into which they were looking. Someone has been going to great lengths to interfere with that investigation, so we have stepped in to continue where they left off."

Two women were just making their way down a path from the houses on the hill. Both were extremely beautiful and dressed to kill in chic dresses cut above their knees and open-toed shoes making them three inches taller. Antonio guessed one to be Gerald's wife, though neither looked old enough. Gerald stood to greet them. Antonio and Gabriella rose, too.

"My dear," Gerald said, "please meet Colonel Ferrara, and *Signor* Cortese of the Carabinieri. And this is my eternally young wife, Celestina, and her eldest daughter, Charis … goes by Charlie." He pulled out their chairs.

Charlie sat next to Antonio. She put her hand on his for a moment and gave him a flirtatious smile. Gabriella did not appear appreciative. Gerald pointed toward Gabriella and Antonio, "They are here to continue the investigation of wine production. They were just telling me someone was interfering with the investigation, so the Carabinieri have taken over."

"Interfering? In what way?" asked Celestina, her smile fading. "And what would that have to do with us? We've done nothing out of sorts."

"I'll explain in a moment," Gabriella said. "But first, may I ask … does your winery own any class six delivery vehicles?"

"Yes. Of course," Gerald answered. "Any winery of good size has at least one. We own three. Why do you ask?"

"Are they white?"

"Yes. That's pretty standard."

"And do your trucks have your winery name or logo painted on them?"

"Actually, no. We've never gotten around to that. Not a bad idea, though."

"And what model and age are the trucks?"

"These are strange questions. Two are older, they came with the winery. One is made by Hino. I don't recall the other. I'll have to look. The third truck was purchased about two years ago to handle the growing demand. It is a Freightliner."

"Have any of the trucks been damaged recently, say from an accident?"

Gerald cast a nervous glance at his wife. "No. We can have a look at them, but not that I'm aware. But please, you still haven't explained yourself. Why this line of questioning?"

"The wine inspector, *Signor* Marinelli …. and his wife were forced off a bridge and killed by two men driving a class six delivery truck."

"And you know for certain it was intentional?"

"Yes. Two forensic teams have come to the same conclusion."

"But there are so many of those trucks on the road," Gerald Gregson said. "Why are you investigating it as if it was one of us? Isn't that a reach?"

"It happened on their return trip from his investigation here. And the wine samples were removed from their trunk." Gabriella paused and watched their reaction. "There is one other thing which we believe confirms it—a second murder—someone shot the wine chemist last night and burned down his lab in an effort to hide it."

Gerald sat back, looking stunned. Celestina and Charlie remained impassive. Then Celestina leaned forward. "Surely you don't believe that people like ourselves—of upstanding reputation—would stoop to such depths?"

Gabriella locked eyes with her, and spoke with an edge to her voice, bordering on anger. "I'm afraid we do not know you, *signora*. And all of the wineries under investigation have stellar reputations. But someone has a lot to hide. Something important enough that they are willing to murder three people. Surely you understand that we must look at each winery that was under investigation."

"It's certainly not us!" Celestina said forcefully, as she rose from her chair. "I'm afraid our hospitality here has run out. Gerry?" She turned to leave. When he did not get up, she stormed away.

"You must forgive her," Gerald said. "She is used to getting her way. I assume you would still like to see those trucks?"

"Yes, please. And we need to purchase some more wine samples. Both barrel and bottle if possible. Everything obtained so far has been destroyed."

"I understand. Please walk with me."

Charlie, looking troubled, excused herself and followed her mother up the hill.

Chapter Twenty-eight

Friday, late morning

As soon as Gabriella pulled her car door shut, she boiled over. "Those people! They think they can turn on the charm and we'll be placated. I'm sick of everyone telling me about their stellar reputations. They care more about their precious reputation than they do the loss of innocent lives! I hope to God we catch whoever did this!"

Antonio chose to keep quiet and let her blow off steam. To defend anyone would surely not end well. Gerald had actually been quite cooperative in the end. He just hoped she could keep her emotions in check. He suspected the next winery would be no easier.

They drove east, back toward Montepulciano. After a few minutes of silence, Gabriella started to fill him in on the next winery. She'd found a way to clamp a lid on her emotions for the moment. But he sensed the volcano could erupt again with the smallest tremor.

"Carpinteria," she said. "Should be fascinating. A few years ago, they barely cracked the top ten in production. Now, after two years under Alida Fontana, they are forecast to be number one in production this year. Thirty percent growth in two years. That sounds like something worth protecting. Hold on, you just missed the turn."

Antonio pulled a U-turn and doubled back a hundred meters and turned south, putting Montepulciano in his rearview mirror.

"The story on Alida Fontana—nee Tarantino—is that she grew up in Apulia. Her father, or the man who raised her as his own child, owns one of the largest wineries there. They produce Negroamaro, Primitivo, and the white Greco Bianco. Have you ever been to Apulia?"

"I've always wanted to go."

"I have a cousin there … a year older than me. I used to go and stay with her when I was a teenager. The beaches are stunning."

Antonio conjured up an image of Gabriella and her cousin in bikinis, frolicking in the crystal-clear waters, with the boys ogling them. He shared it with her and she laughed.

"Not too far off," she said. "Anyway, word is Ms. Fontana-Tarantino is quite the assertive businesswoman. She is a widow with two sons. There," she pointed. Antonio made the turn. This was the nearest winery they had visited to the town of Montepulciano. Though the town was probably about five kilometers distant it felt as if it sat on top of them. This winery sat in a valley, with their furthest vineyards climbing hills to the north, providing south-facing vineyards.

The entrance road, lined with Italian Cyprus trees, seemed to go on forever, ending at a castle-like villa surrounded by a tiny hamlet. They could see the swimming pool with lounge chairs and umbrellas surrounding it. In a circle which came near the grand entrance to the villa sat a red Ferrari. Antonio, with his love of Italian sports cars, recognized it as a F8 Tributo, sporting over 700 horsepower. He imagined himself driving the winding roads of Tuscany in it, then pushed his envy aside.

There was no sign of life except for two large black dogs which approached and circled Gabriella's car when they parked. Antonio thought they looked rather intimidating with short tails and upright ears. They reminded him of Rottweilers.

"Cane Corso," Gabriella said. "Excellent guard dogs. The name roughly translates from Latin as *bodyguard dog*." Antonio was nervous to exit the car but Gabriella stepped out, knelt down and put her hand out. The nearest one smelled her hand then sat down. She rubbed his neck and they became immediate friends. The second dog came and sat next to the first.

"I see you've met the lads." The loud, feminine voice came from somewhere behind Antonio. He turned and saw a statuesque woman walking toward him, dressed in skin-tight designer jeans, torn at the knees, and an equally skin-tight V-neck blouse showing off her attributes. "I assume you are Colonel Ferrara," she said as she approached with her hand extended toward Gabriella. "Alida Fontana." She rounded the car and shook Antonio's hand firmly. "And you are?"

"Detective Antonio Cortese."

"*Piacere di conoscerti*. Pleased to meet you. Do I detect the hint of an American accent?"

"I've spent more time there than in Italy," Antonio said, telling a half-truth for Gabriella's sake. He had an aversion to lying.

"*Benvenuto!* Welcome to Carpinteria. Would you like a brief tour?"

Gabriella assented and they followed Alida as she showed them the production facility. It was in an old stone building, but inside it was fully modernized with all the latest winemaking equipment. Then she showed them the tasting room, gift shop, and breakfast room for their guests, all of which were closed. Passing by the two buildings nearest the pool, she explained that they housed six guest rooms. "And those two buildings nearest the villa are the homes of my two sons," she pointed. They circled back. "And this, this is my home," she said proudly, as she led them toward the tall villa, painted a pale Tuscan gold. Nowhere on the tour had Antonio seen any delivery trucks.

"Your Ferrari?" Antonio asked.

"Yes. A gift from my *papà* … the man I believed was my father until I found out my real father was Emilio Fontana. I never met the man. My mother hid it from me all those years. I didn't believe it until we had my DNA tested. Emilio's wife was never able to bear children, so he left the estate to me in his will. I still think of Lorenzo Tarantino as my true father, though."

A very generous one, Antonio thought.

She invited them into the villa. The floorplan was shaped like a squared off C. The circular drive, which came near the front door, encircled a bubbling fountain. The dogs followed as they entered, their sharp nails clicking on the shiny marble floor. The grand size of the rooms was overwhelming. But the décor was gaudy and overdone for Antonio's taste. The furniture appeared to be French Provincial, but the artwork on the walls was modern-contemporary. *An odd mix,* he thought.

She led them into a more intimate study and offered for them to sit in the black leather chairs. "Would you care for some coffee or tea, or possibly mineral water?" she asked.

"Water would be nice, *grazie,*" Gabriella answered. The dogs took seats on either side of Gabriella's chair. It seemed they had taken a liking to her.

Alida picked up her phone and typed something. "Forgive me," she said, when she looked up. "I'm asking my sons to join us." Then she stood and disappeared for a minute, returning with an ice bucket with bottles of mineral water and crystal glasses to drink from. She poured them each a glass, then sat across from them.

As they waited for the sons, she explained how she had learned the winery business from her father in Apulia, and was modernizing production with the goal of becoming the largest winery in Montepulciano.

When the sons arrived, they were older than Antonio had anticipated. He guessed early thirties, though Alida did not appear a day over forty.

"Please, these are my sons, Rocco and Donato," she said. She introduced Gabriella and Antonio as they rose to shake their hands.

It took Antonio mere moments to see that the two brothers were polar opposites. Rocco, who appeared to be the older of the two, was wearing hunting clothes. His complexion was dark and ruddy, with about a ten-day stubble on his chin. Antonio wondered if he had shaved a beard and was re-growing it. He had arrived carrying a shotgun, which he placed against the wall in the corner of the room. Alida looked at his muddy boots and frowned. He was intensely serious and stared at Antonio and Gabriella with disdain in his eyes. Donato, on the other hand, was clean-faced, handsome in a delicate sort of way. He smiled with effusive charm.

Alida began the conversation. "I understand you have picked up the investigation begun by the Wine Commission. There must be a reason. How can we help you, Colonel Ferrara?"

"Let me get straight to the point," Gabriella said, catching Antonio off guard. He immediately became alert to watching their body language. "Someone has taken to extreme violence, almost certainly to protect themselves and some improprieties they do not want known. Not a very smart tactic. They are about to bring the wrath of the Carabinieri and Italian government down on their heads."

"Extreme violence? What kind of ...?" Alida acted shocked. Antonio wasn't sure he was buying it.

"The murder of three people. And before you put on an air of innocence, explaining how you would never put your reputation at risk, let me tell you that you and your sons are suspects."

Antonio was stunned by Gabriella's direct approach. She hadn't warned him in advance of her tactics. Alida appeared to be caught off guard but quickly recovered. Antonio looked at the two sons. Rocco had an angry scowl as he expected he would. Donato looked amused. Antonio didn't know what to make of that.

"Please explain how these murders came about. Isn't it possible they were unrelated?"

Gabriella's eyes bored into Alida's as she explained about the road incident and the murder of the wine chemist. "So, as you can see, we'll be needing new wine samples. And also, to examine your trucks."

Antonio watched Rocco's eyes flicker toward his shotgun in the corner. He was ready to tackle him if he made a move. He wished they were carrying their handguns. He would have insisted on it if he'd known Gabriella was going to go after them with both barrels blazing.

"Since you've made it abundantly clear that we are suspects," Alida said calmly, "there will be no further cooperation without our lawyers present."

Antonio watched her carefully. Her hands lay calmly in her lap, but the slightest spark of fear or anger had sparked in her eyes.

"If you have nothing to hide," Antonio said, speaking for the first time since introducing himself, "then the wine samples and seeing your trucks could help clear your name." He glanced from Alida, to Rocco, to Donato. Rocco stared back with cold eyes. Donato still appeared to be amused by the interactions.

"I'm sorry. But I feel you've given us no choice in the matter," Alida said, "coming in here with these preposterous allegations as you did. Perhaps we could arrange to have our attorney join us and talk next week."

"How convenient that you would stall," Gabriella said, "when there are rumors of Italy going into complete lockdown at any moment. I suppose we'll have to get a search warrant and return for what we need."

"*Buona fortuna* with that," Alida said. "It has been a genuine pleasure having you today." Her lips smiled but her eyes did not. "Donato, can you please see them to their vehicle."

"*Si, Madre.*"

"I have one last question," Gabriella said, before rising. "I understand that your guardian, Lorenzo Tarantino, who grew up in Taranto, has ties to the *Sacro Corona Unita?*" Antonio stared at her. *The United Sacred Crown?* He'd heard of this mafia clan, referred to by some as the Fourth Mafia. *Merda! Is she trying to provoke them?* He checked Rocco's position again in relation to his shotgun.

154

"I'm afraid you heard wrong," Rocco said, speaking for the first time, his voice deep and threatening. He nodded to his younger brother.

Donato, taking his cue, rose and held his hand toward the door. Gabriella stood, speaking as she did, "Yes, it has truly been a pleasure, *Signora* Tarantino. We'll see ourselves out." She headed toward the door, with Antonio behind, and Donato following.

As they approached the car, Antonio saw Rocco coming out the front door, carrying his shotgun. His stomach knotted, but Rocco turned toward the hillside. He suddenly became aware that Donato was speaking. "You won't find anything, you know. There's nothing to be found." Then he turned back toward the house, where he greeted his mother as she headed for her Ferrari.

Chapter Twenty-nine

Friday afternoon

What was that all about?" Antonio asked, wiping the sweat from his brow.

"I am tired of playing games. I decided to play hardball. I think that's what you Americans call it?"

"Yeah, a baseball reference. But, next time, can you warn me ahead of time? I'd have felt a whole lot better if I'd had a gun on my person."

"You really think they would do that in their own home? They're smarter than that. They'd have to assume that someone knew we were there."

"I'm not so sure Rocco thinks with his brain."

She looked at him and laughed. "Made you nervous, huh?"

"Not funny, Gabriella! If these guys killed Andrea, Bria, and the chemist, they obviously don't think much of the value of human life. What was that about the mob … the *Sacro Corona Unita*. Do you know something I don't?"

"Just a wild hare. I wanted to see what kind of reaction I got."

"You might have hit the nail on the head. You think they're guilty?"

"They seem like the most likely candidates to me," she answered. "By the way, I'd like to go into Montepulciano to find some bottles of their wine."

"Chiara said they want to take us to dinner in town tonight. We could pick them up then. Apparently their favorite trattoria is closing after Saturday. Not enough business to remain open."

"Not surprised. But I doubt the wine shops will be open that late. We have time now. I will buy you a gelato."

He turned to her and grinned. "You do know the way to a man's heart."

"You're such a pushover."

They came to a roundabout and took the road leading to Montepulciano. "You think there's any chance of us getting a search warrant?" he asked.

"I'll ask Umberto when we get back."

"Your hardball tactics might have been effective. It kept us from getting barrel samples though, and from finding out about their trucks. I didn't see any trucks on the grounds during our tour."

"Neither did I. But I saw a building that appeared to be a garage. The doors were closed, though."

"Let's hope we can get that search warrant. But I think it's a long shot. Unless Italian magistrates are easier than American judges. That reminds me. What did you make of that comment that Donato made?"

"The one about not finding anything? Personally, I do not think he was proclaiming their innocence. I think he was saying there was no way we would find any evidence. He thinks they are smarter than us."

"My thoughts exactly," Antonio said. They drove on for a few minutes, each deep in thought until Antonio broke the silence. "A lot of the wine shops were already closed when we were in town. Why don't you call Sylvio and ask if he knows of any shops that are open and likely to carry their wines?"

"I do not have his number. I should probably get it."

"Here, call from my phone." He handed it to her.

"An android? I'm not sure how …"

"Swipe the phone, enter my passcode, 1-0-2-8, then hit the phone icon and the contacts button at the bottom. He'll show up on the Favorites list."

She followed his instructions and put the call on speaker. "*Ciao,* Antonio," Sylvio answered.

"It's Gabriella," she replied. "We're heading into Montepulciano. We need to find a wine shop that would carry wines from Carpinteria. Do you have a suggestion? Many of the shops have already shuttered up due to the pandemic."

"I believe my friend, Roberto Marinetto, is still open. Let me call him. I'll call you right back." He hung up. Antonio was just parking when his phone rang. "*Si.* You're in luck. His shop is located one block from the Piazza Grande. It's called Vino Amore." He gave them directions.

"*Grazie*, Sylvio. *Mille grazie!* We'll be heading back as soon as we're done there."

"You mean after you stop for gelato," he laughed. "Don't be too long, we finished pruning the north side. I'm going to spoil myself with a hot bath to soak this ankle. Then I'm looking forward to a hearty Bistecca Fiorentina to celebrate."

"You know Antonio all too well," Gabriella laughed. "Enjoy your bath. *Ciao, ciao!*"

*****

Vino Amore had a narrow storefront which opened up to an expansive interior. Every wall was lined with wooden wine racks, and there were more islands full of wine throughout the middle. His inventory had to be thousands of bottles. *I hope for his sake the quarantine is short,* Antonio thought.

"May I assist you in your selection?" A handsome white-haired gentleman asked. He appeared to be about seventy.

"Yes, are you Roberto Marinetto?" Antonio asked. "My uncle, Sylvio Montieri, suggested your shop to us. We're looking for some wines from a specific winery, Carpinteria."

"Hmmm. Curious. Why that particular winery? Good wines, but your uncle's are better."

Antonio was trying to think of an answer when Gabriella spoke up. "It is for an associate of mine. They requested wines from a few specific wineries. We were able to purchase the others at the wineries but did not obtain any of this one."

Roberto appeared less than satisfied with her answer. "Yes, I have their 2015 Riserva, and the 2017 standard Vino Nobile. Emilio Fontana bottled both before he passed. You might be aware that his daughter from Apulia has taken over. Nobody even knew he had a daughter until the reading of his will."

"And how is the wine faring under her?" Antonio asked.

"Too early to say. Her first vintages will arrive on the market next year. She's now buying a lot more fruit from other growers to increase her production. Most are quite reputable. The wine will change because of the varying *terroir,* but it should still be good. I know she has invested a lot in the latest gravity flow equipment."

"What does that mean?" Gabriella said.

"A gravity flow winery is set up on two or more floors. No pumps are used to move the wine. Gravity is used to crush the grapes, then the juice flows downward to the fermentation tanks. It's a gentler, less interventional approach to winemaking."

Antonio looked around the shop. "You certainly have a lot of inventory. You must be worried about the country going into quarantine."

"You're only seeing a portion of it. Follow me." He led them to a narrow brick stairway which spiraled downward. They went down a level and he turned on the lights, illuminating an expansive cave-like room with thousands of bottles. "This is where I store the higher end stuff. It is easier to maintain a consistently cool temperature and humidity down here."

"Wow!" Antonio said. "Can you afford to be shut down for months, if that's what it comes to?"

"It's going to require moving into a new era of distribution. My nephew is a computer whiz. He's working on setting up an online store. As soon as we're able to begin shipping, I hope to start shipping wine all over. We'll focus on Europe and America. In the meanwhile, I've been running deep discounts to move a lot of the wine that might age-out if this drags on."

Roberto turned to Gabriella, "Have you ever explored any of underground Montepulciano?"

"No. But I am afraid we must be going."

"Just a few minutes of your time to get a feel," he said. "Follow me." He led them down a corridor which opened into another room with high ceilings. Its walls had a patchwork of stone carvings. "There is a vast network of tunnels under the city. Many of the tunnels were built to connect the grand palaces. You can only imagine some of the ways that was used." He winked at Gabriella. "They were also used as escape routes and hiding places during times of war. When they were building some of them, they discovered that someone had beat them to it. The early Etruscans built tombs down here, like this. Many items have been moved to an Etruscan Museum. But you can see, their artistic skills were quite impressive."

Antonio studied the wall. There were dozens of stone blocks depicting a variety of scenes. Some were of people—women or warriors. Others were carved with words or artistic designs. Still others depicted mythical creatures such as centaurs—half horse, half man creatures. "Amazing," he said breathlessly.

"One of our neighboring wine shops has an agricultural museum, a selection of fossils, and a fascinating collection of rare torture instruments," Roberto added. "Others have cellars with vaulted ceilings reminiscent of Gothic Cathedrals. You must come back to explore when things return to normalcy."

"I certainly will," Gabriella promised. "*Grazie, Signor* Marinetto."

"Enough of the formalities. It's Roberto to you." He paused for a moment to gather his courage. "But, *signora*. I must say, your explanation about the wine purchase seemed … how shall I say? … incomplete. I feel like there is more to it. Does this have anything to do with the wine fraud investigation?"

"If it did, Roberto, would you have any information to assist us?"

"Only speculation, my dear. Only speculation."

Chapter Thirty

Friday Evening

Antonio could feel the anxiety in the air when they walked in the house. Sylvio muttered something under his breath that sounded like, "The woman is impossible," and stormed out the door, limping toward his workshop.

"Look at him," Chiara said. "He should still be using a crutch, or at least his cane. But he refuses. Stubborn old man!" Antonio decided it best to keep his mouth shut. He gave her a hug and a kiss on the cheek.

"How was your investigation?" she asked.

"Interesting," Antonio answered. "Why don't we explain it all over dinner so we don't need to tell the story over and over. Will Angelica and Umberto be joining us? We need to consult with Umberto."

"Yes. He's taking a nap. He and Giulia helped Sylvio with the pruning. Angelica even helped for a while. Can you believe it?"

Antonio laughed then heard the sound of the door opening. Giulia and Serena entered, carrying pails of milk. Serena plopped hers down. She ran and threw her arms around Gabriella, then gave Antonio a kiss on the cheek. She began to rattle on about how Chiara let them do the afternoon milking all by themselves, and the other adventures of their day. Antonio took it all in and smiled. Seeing her happy after everything she'd been through melted away his stress.

*****

It was dark as the eight of them climbed the quiet street of Montepulciano. Warm light shone out from the homes above the street. A few of the French doors were open despite the evening chill. Antonio heard the sound of a television newscast from one home and Italian pop coming from another.

Sylvio, looking dapper in a sport coat, was using his cane in an effort to keep the peace. Chiara walked on his good side, with her arm linked in his, smiling victoriously. Antonio was glad to see the fireworks were over for now. All of the ladies were wearing dresses, and Umberto also wore a sports coat. The best Antonio had been able to do was a Merino wool sweater. He was thinking he should have added a coat. Serena took hold of his hand. His mind traveled back to when his own daughter would do the same. He looked down at Serena and thought how good it felt to have her in his life. The good feeling disappeared as quickly as it had come, though, when he thought about his pending return to Seattle, not knowing when he'd be able to return.

The smell of roasting meat gave notice that they were approaching the trattoria. Antonio opened the heavy wood door for the ladies. When he did so he noticed a lone man who he thought had been behind them all the way up the hill. When he looked, the man stopped and turned away. He got a weird feeling in his gut. *Stop being paranoid,* he told himself.

Angelica pinched his cheek and gave him a flirtatious smile as she entered. He knew better than to make anything of it. It was just who she was. Sylvio saw tables pulled together and led them there like he owned the place. There was only one other party, a middle-aged couple seated in a quiet corner. Sylvio and Chiara walked over to greet them. When they returned, Sylvio pulled out the chair for Chiara and helped her off with her coat. Antonio found himself with Serena on one side, Gabriella on the other, and Giulia next to Serena. He decided to forget about leaving, and make the most of being with these women he loved.

The owner arrived to greet them. He was a jovial man of about fifty. Sylvio stood. "Everyone, please meet *mi amico,* Luciano." He introduced him around. Luciano took an interest in Antonio when Sylvio explained that he owned an Italian café and pizzeria.

"I hope you won't get hit as hard as Italy by this pandemic," Luciano said. "Tomorrow night will be our last until who knows when. Maybe forever."

"Don't talk that way, Luciano," Chiara said. "When this is over, people will be dying to get out and eat."

"Better than dying from this awful disease," he said. "I already lost an aunt in Orvieto. She was elderly, seventy-seven, but her health was good."

"I'm so sorry!" Chiara said. "I used a poor choice of words." She put her hand over her mouth.

"*Grazie.* No worries. She was so cantankerous I'm surprised she didn't kick it in the teeth!" He laughed, then a sadness crossed his face and he returned to business. He cast his eyes around the table. "I will be serving you this evening. I already laid off all my waiters. A difficult thing. I've only kept on my chef and his helper for now. Our menu is more limited. We are trying to use up our food. But Sylvio told me to feed you whatever we were serving, family style, so long as it included

Bistecca Fiorentina. I'll be back shortly with wine and antipasti."

Luciano returned a few minutes later with a white Vermentino. Sylvio took the bottle, as another couple entered the front door. "I'll pour," he said. "You have other guests to attend to." Luciano thanked him and rushed toward the door. Sylvio reached around the table and poured, then sat back and raised his glass. *"Cin cin!* May God protect each of us and the people we love during these difficult days."

Luciano sat the other party. He disappeared, then returned a few minutes later with antipasti; white asparagus wrapped in prosciutto and grilled, a young pecorino cheese and salami, and crostini topped with warm sautéed greens and pine nuts. *"Buon appetito!"* he announced with a bow.

Chiara inquired again about their day. Antonio looked at Gabriella, who nodded. "It was quite an interesting one," he said. "I must say Le Cascio is quite a beautiful place. I can see why they chose it for tomorrow's meeting. We met with Gerald Gregson, and were joined by his wife Celestina, and her eldest daughter … goes by Charlie. At first it seemed they were trying to distract us with their charms. But Celestina became angry and stormed off when Gabriella began to ask questions about the murders. Gerald was reasonably cooperative, despite his wife's defensive behavior."

"Temper tantrum, you mean," Gabriella said, still clearly angry "She seems far more concerned about their precious reputation than about people being murdered!"

"But we found nothing to implicate them," Antonio added. "I got the feeling they were hiding something, but have no idea what. I can't imagine it would be murder."

"Tell us about Carpinteria," Chiara said. It was clearly the one which intrigued her the most.

Antonio looked at Gabriella and laughed nervously. "Quite a story there. We met with Alida Tarantino-Fontana and her two sons … total opposites from one another. It appeared Rocco had just returned from hunting. He placed his shotgun in the corner of the study, just a few feet from where he was sitting. Gabriella went at them hard … she as much as accused them of the killings and of being connected to the *Sacro Corona Unita* mafia clan." He looked at her. "I have mixed feelings about whether that was the right tact. It shut down their cooperation. Alida said any future interviews would have to be done with their lawyer present. But their response was somewhat telling. They refused to let us see their trucks or provide wine samples."

"They were not going to tell us anything anyway," Gabriella said. "And I just recalled something from Andrea's notes. They refused to give him samples as well … or allow him access to their cellar."

Sylvio was leaning in, rubbing his chin. "You think they could be your killers?"

"Yes," Gabriella said. "They are at the top of my suspect list. I believe they had motive, means, and opportunity. The problem is I can't prove any of it yet." She turned to Umberto. "What would it take for us to get a search warrant for their property?"

"A lot more than what you have so far," he said. "Which is almost entirely speculation, unless I'm missing something."

Gabriella nodded. She'd been expecting that answer. "We're working on it."

"Enough detective talk for now!" Sylvio said. "Let's take time to enjoy our meal."

As if on cue, Luciano arrived with the primi course. "Tortelli do patate al sugo di anatra." Potato tortelli with duck sauce. They stayed with the white Vermentino for this course. As they ate, they talked about the Covid-19 pandemic. Gabriella turned to Serena. "I'm afraid you won't be starting school for quite a while." Serena nodded pensively.

"She's welcome to stay with us anytime, if you need to return to work," Chiara said. "She's an eager farmhand, a joy to have around the farm."

When they were finished with the primi course, Luciana brought clean plates. A few minutes later Antonio smelled the aroma of grilled beef as the main course came their way—two huge Bistecca Fiorentina sizzling on cast iron platters. Each weighed at least two pounds. Sylvio carved the meat off the T-bones, sliced it thin, and passed it around. The meat was rare and juicy—the only way the Tuscans will serve it—and perfect to Antonio's liking. Luciano returned with a platter of white beans cooked with onions, garlic and greens, along with a loaf of warm bread.

Sylvio asked Antonio to open the red wine. "I thought we'd have something different tonight," he announced, "a Taurasi Riserva, from Campania, made with Aglianico grapes, the noble varietal of the south. We've been drinking enough Sangiovese. Aglianico is one of my favorites." It was one of Antonio's favorites as well. He carried one at his restaurant but sold little. Few Americans were familiar with it.

The talk at the table turned to family. Angelica and Umberto told them about their children and grandchild. Then Chiara and Sylvio began to pepper Antonio with questions about what had transpired in Firenze recently, with the disappearance of Raphael, and Nicolo's gunshot wound. They had only known the basics of the story.

It was quite some time before they saw Luciano again. Three other parties had arrived. When he made his appearance, looking more and more frazzled, Sylvio held up his hands. "*Favoloso*, Luciano. *Favoloso!* But we can't take any more! Chiara has dessert for us at home, an orange marmalade tart. You can please bring me the check, whenever you have time."

"I'm afraid I cannot, *mi amico*. Someone has already taken care of it." Luciano nodded toward Antonio. Sylvio blustered but gave up after Antonio refused to back down.

"You've been very generous to us," Antonio said. "Just my way of saying *grazie, mille grazie!*"

Tipping is uncommon in European restaurants, but Antonio added a generous gratuity with a note of thanks. He was pleased when everyone else added generous amounts of cash on the table as well. As they stepped outside into the cool night air, Luciano followed them out. Moved to tears he hugged each one and fled back through the door.

Halfway down the dimly lit street, Antonio caught the glow of a cigarette in his peripheral vision. He turned and spotted a man huddled alone in the deep shadows. He was certain it was the same man he'd seen earlier. The hair on the back of his neck stood to attention.

Chapter Thirty-one

Friday, late evening

It was approaching eleven o'clock when they arrived back to Chiara and Silvio's. Gabriella asked Serena to change into her pajamas. Giulia followed her. Moments later, a piercing scream sent them all rushing toward their bedroom. When they entered, Giulia stood holding a piece of paper with trembling hands. Her eyes were wide with fear. She held it out. Gabriella snatched it from her hands.

"They were here!" she said breathlessly.

"Who was here? What ...?" Antonio stammered, as everyone started to talk at once.

She handed the paper to Antonio. In hand-written Italian it said, *Time to drop your investigation ... if you care about the people you love.*

"Where did you find this?" Gabriella asked Giulia.

"Serena found it. On her pillow!"

Serena was sitting on her bed with her arms wrapped around herself. She appeared more angry than scared. Gabriella took a seat on one side of her, Antonio the other. Gabriella embraced her tightly. "It's okay," she whispered. "We won't let anything happen to you."

"It's you I'm scared for!" she said hoarsely, then threw her arms around Gabriella's neck.

"Now, now." She patted her on the back. "It's alright. Nothing is going to happen to me … to any of us. I promise!"

Antonio wished she hadn't said those last two words. None of us know our fate. Especially in the face of danger. "That's why I'm here, too," he said. "To help protect you both."

Serena looked up at him and smiled weakly. "Why did they do this!?"

"They are just trying to scare us," Gabriella said. "Before we find out what bad things they have done and arrest them."

"But who?"

"That's what we are trying to find out," Gabriella said, making eye contact with Antonio. He nodded.

Chiara had moved close to Giulia, who was still shaking, and enfolded her in an embrace. Umberto took the note from Antonio's hand and looked at it. He pulled out his phone and snapped a picture. "We need to get this to a forensic team as soon as possible," he said. "First thing tomorrow."

"I'll call Marina Gallo," Gabriella said, pulling out her phone.

"Hold on a moment," Antonio said. "We need to get Serena to a safe place. You too, Giulia." He turned to her. She began to object but then looked at Serena and relented. "I'll call Nicolo and Sofia to see if they can pick them up in the morning. I'll stand guard tonight. We can send the note with them. Marina can pick it up there. It's much closer to her."

Gabriella nodded, and Antonio made the call. Nicolo agreed to come first thing in the morning. Sofia would drive. With that settled, Gabriella dialed Marina, though it was after 11:00. Marina didn't hesitate. She asked to have Nicolo text her when they were on their way back. She would begin the analysis right away.

Antonio went to the car and retrieved the gun safes. He beckoned Gabriella and Giulia from the bedroom and gave them their guns. Giulia was surprised, but took the gun and handled it confidently. She made sure the safety was on and checked the magazine. "Keep it under your pillow tonight," Antonio said. "I'll be standing guard … it's just a precaution."

"I'll stand guard with you," Sylvio added. He had returned with his shotgun. "Or better yet, we should take shifts."

"I knew we should have installed security cameras!" Chiara said. "There have been incidences at some of the farms in recent months."

"What kind of incidences?" Antonio asked.

"Just a few break-ins. House robberies and the like."

"Let me call Chia," Gabriella said. "We have extra surveillance cameras at the station which we can install temporarily, until you can order your own. Nicolo can pick them up in the morning." She placed the call and it was all arranged.

No one felt like going to bed with the adrenaline flowing through their veins. Umberto built a fire while Chiara dished up the orange marmalade tart, made even more remarkable by a touch of Cointreau orange liqueur added to the whipped cream.

Sylvio rambled on and on about someone having violated their home. He figured out they had picked the lock on the French door which entered the kitchen from the terrazza. Antonio found him at the dining room table, drinking strong coffee and cleaning his shotgun. Every light in the room was on.

Antonio saw that the outdoor lights were on as well. "Bastards!" he said. "I hope they come back."

"No," Antonio said. "You don't. Because if they do, either you'll be dead, or they will. You don't want that on your conscience. Trust me."

Sylvio stared intently at him. "Sounds like you've had to do that."

Antonio remained silent for a few beats. "My first year as a detective. A drug dealer. He raised a gun at me. He was only nineteen." Antonio's voice cracked.

Sylvio held eye contact and nodded, but said nothing. "I've got the first shift. I can cover the whole night if you want. I doubt I'll be able to sleep anyway."

"There will come a time—when the adrenaline abandons you—and it is almost impossible not to. I'll take over around 2:30 or 3:00."

Sylvio nodded and took a drink of coffee. He held up the cup. "I'll warm some of this up for you when you take my place."

"Smells strong enough to kill me," Antonio said with a laugh. "Where's the best place to set up?"

"I was thinking right here in a kitchen chair," Sylvio said. "I can see the French doors, as well as the corridor to their room. The front door has a deadbolt. Besides, I don't want a comfortable chair. I might fall asleep."

"Too exposed," Antonio said. "They'd see you before you saw them unless you sit in the dark. That makes it too difficult to stay awake." They talked about the options and decided upon a place around the corner, near the front entrance. All they'd have to do is lean their head back to see the French doors.

Antonio found Gabriella on the couch by the fire, doing her best to remain calm for Serena. Serena was stretched out on the couch with her head on Gabriella's lap. A half hour later she fell asleep. One by one, the others wandered off to bed as the embers died away. Around midnight Antonio carried Serena to bed, and Giulia followed. Antonio double-checked the lock on the window. He pulled the curtains together so not even a crack was open. They'd have to break the glass to come in this way. He was pretty certain the intruders would not return, but they were ready if they did.

He rejoined Gabriella. He decided to add another log to the fire and sleep on the couch. He sat down next to her. She took her lap blanket and threw half of it over him, then spoke, "There is obviously something more to this than wine fraud. That is not enough reason for them to go to such lengths. Three murders. Now this."

"I agree," Antonio said. "I think the wine fraud, if it even exists, is just the tip of the iceberg. There's definitely something bigger that someone is desperate to hide."

"What could it be?"

"I haven't a clue. If you're right about Alida Tarantino—or whatever her last name is—and her sons, I sure would like to get a look at their trucks. With Alida's stepfather being in Apulia, and if your instincts are right—a possible link to the *Sacro Corona Unita*—we should see what kinds of things that mob is up to. Maybe this is a pipeline for drugs or something being moved up north. Possibly even human trafficking like we saw with the Nigerians in Firenze."

She sat up straight and looked at him. "You may be right. I'll do some research in the morning. And I would also like to see their trucks."

"Too risky," Antonio said. "Those dogs alone are enough to scare me, not to mention Rocco and his shotgun."

"Those dogs are my friends now," she smiled slyly. "You think it was an accident that I bonded with them?"

Antonio smiled then turned serious. "But remember, we still don't have a warrant, and no evidence yet to justify one."

Gabrielle nodded. But her mind was somewhere else now.

"You should go to bed," Antonio said. "I'm going to sleep here … or try anyway. I'll be taking over for Sylvio in a couple of hours."

"Nice try," she said. "Which end of the couch do you want?"

~~~~ SATURDAY, MARCH 7 ~~~~

Chapter Thirty-two
Saturday Morning

Antonio awoke with a start. His bed was disheveled, soaked with sweat, and his mood darkened by images from his dream. He had managed to stay awake for his watch, despite only a couple of hours of fitful sleep on the couch. Around dawn Chiara showed her face, and he headed off to his bedroom to try and get a few more hours sleep. It had been more than two weeks since the nightmare had haunted him—the longest stretch he could remember since the loss of Randi and Christina. He knew it was the threat to the girls that triggered it.

The dream consisted of bizarre images of past traumas: that terrible night on the promenade in Nice … the fall from the cliff in Corona del Mar that ended his detective career … and the road incident in Chianti that put him and Giulia in the hospital. The way these events presented themselves were never the same, but bizarre twists of the original events which morphed in unexplainable ways as dreams do. The worst part of the dreams was his inability to protect the people he loved. Someone had suggested it was survivor's guilt. He thought it made sense.

During their investigation in Firenze, Gabriella had begun to show up in his dreams, always with someone trying to take her life. It almost came true. Now, that part of the dream had returned.

He pulled the sheets off the bed and piled them on the floor. He dragged himself into the shower—attempting to restore life to his body. After washing away the sweat, he turned the water to cold and stood under it as long as he could stand.

His adrenaline began to flow again, fueled by last night's events. He decided to do his morning pushups. The pain in his broken hand was becoming more manageable. He pushed himself until he collapsed. He dressed and made his way to the kitchen, fearful that the coffee would be the stuff Sylvio made last night. Someone had made fresh. He was rejoicing in that small thing when Gabriella shuffled into the room with her hair all tussled. He'd never seen her looking so bleary-eyed. She poured a cup of coffee, mumbled "*'giorno,*" and disappeared. He knew she'd look beautiful next time he saw her.

Antonio took a seat at the kitchen table and watched the household begin to rouse itself. Umberto appeared next, poured some coffee, and said he was planning to make breakfast after he showered. Then Giulia walked in the room, stifling a yawn. She poured herself a cup and sat down next to him. "You get any sleep?" she asked.

"Not much. You?"

"Some. I'd finally fallen asleep when I heard Serena having a nightmare. I woke her up and we talked for a while. She's still sleeping."

Hearing that was like a punch in the gut. He was thinking how much she had been through when his text notification went off. It was Nicolo. *We'll arrive about 8:30.* He looked at the time. That would be about ninety minutes from now. He showed Giulia.

"I don't want to leave," she said firmly.

He searched her eyes. They were resolute. "It would be really helpful if you were with Serena. The two of you have really connected. She could really use your support. We don't really have a need for you here."

"Thanks a lot!" she said with a glare.

"That's not what I meant, Giulia. You know we love having you around. But this is getting dangerous. You'd be one more person for me to worry about."

"You know you can be such a chauvinist sometimes."

"So, I've heard. But cut me some slack. I'm not in the mood."

She stared at him and nodded. "Okay. But I'm afraid I won't see you for a long time after this is over."

"I'll be sure to say goodbye before I head home. And I promise I'll return as soon as I can. There is a wedding in my future after all."

One-by-one the rest of the family found their way to the kitchen. Everyone except Serena. Giulia went to wake her so she could be ready when Nicolo and Sofia arrived. Angelica, still looking sleepy herself, barred her mother from the kitchen and went to work alongside Umberto making breakfast. They prepared two large frittatas with prosciutto, a soft, young pecorino, sun-dried tomatoes, and fresh spinach from Chiara's garden, with fruit on the side. It was just coming out from under the broiler when Nicolo and Sofia arrived.

The family went outside to greet them, shielding their eyes from the bright morning sun. Nicolo got out of the car—walking with a cane. He opened the rear car door and Bella bounded out. Then Nicolo helped Bambina down to the ground. She headed straight for Serena, which made Antonio smile. She needed her affection more than he did.

A few minutes later they surrounded the table. As they ate, Nicolo had a hundred questions about their investigation and last night's home invasion. "What's your plan now?" he asked.

Antonio looked at Gabriella. "I spent most of the night thinking about it," she said. "Chia texted. She wants me to call her so she can give me an update. I'll do that after you leave. She and Marina have been investigating the chemist's lab. Later today, we are attending the meeting of the *consorzio* with Sylvio and Chiara. We will make the rounds ... keeping our ears open. We might pick up some clues. I am not especially hopeful but we maybe we will get lucky." She glanced at Antonio. "I did some online research about the *Sacro Corona Unita* while Antonio was sleeping. We think it is possible Carpinteria winery has a connection to them. As we suspected, they move drugs and are involved in human trafficking. I cannot see the latter going through here, though. But there is another possibility. They are heavily involved in arms trafficking, mainly small arms. My instincts tell me they are trucking either drugs or small arms here, storing them at the winery, and then sending them out with wine shipments to the northern half of the country."

"Interesting hypothesis," Nicolo said. "But no way to confirm it without a search warrant."

Gabriella nodded toward Umberto. "Yes. Umberto has been guiding us on such matters. We know we need more." She turned to Antonio again. "I think we should begin a stake-out at the Carpinteria winery. Maybe we'll get lucky. Unless you have any better ideas?"

"I wish I did. A late-night stake-out means more sleepless nights. But count me in, unless we find some other leads."

"I can stay and help!" Giulia said.

Antonio glared at her. "We've had this discussion, Giulia. Serena needs you to be with her."

"No, I don't!" Serena said. "I'll be fine. She should stay if she can help."

Gabriella looked at Serena, then Giulia, then at Sofia. Sofia spoke up. "We've got plenty to keep Serena busy. She can help me care for the litter of puppies and help me with my ceramics painting. I'm going to take advantage of this Covid quarantine to build up my inventory. Do you like to paint, Serena?"

Serena nodded enthusiastically.

"Sounds like it's settled," Gabriella said.

Antonio frowned. He had little choice but to surrender.

Chapter Thirty-three

Saturday Afternoon

There was little joy in the air despite the gorgeous spring weather, as the winemakers and growers arrived for the meeting of the *consorzio* set to begin at noon. The tables were set up in the shade of the grape arbor and vintners wandered among the tables searching for their name cards. Sylvio had reserved spots for the entire family.

Guests were invited to go through the buffet line as soon as they found their table. It was a colorful spread of antipasti, fruits, ciabatta and other breads, and Pasta Bolognese. Old friends greeted one another as they moved through the line. Only a few wore masks. Antonio paid attention to their conversations which seemed to focus on two subjects: One was whether or not the government was going to force everyone into quarantine. The other was the wine fraud investigation and the death of the Wine Commission investigator and his wife, and the wine chemist. Word had spread quickly.

Beyond the buffet, additional tables had been set up where a number of the *consorzio* wineries were pouring their wines which flowed abundantly. Gabriella and Antonio kept wine in their glass but made a pact to drink little. They wanted their wits about them, suspecting that the flow of wine might create loose lips. It appeared they were correct.

People wandered from table to table, seeking out friends. Antonio stuck by Sylvio's side, and Gabriella and Giulia stayed near to Chiara as they mingled. Sylvio introduced Antonio as his nephew, but many eyed him with curiosity or suspicion, guessing his purpose for being there. Antonio quickly realized that there were few secrets in this tight-knit community. He hoped it might work to their advantage. Sylvio had told a friend about the break-in at their home, and word was traveling like wildfire. Nearly everyone he encountered expressed concern.

At a table near the front, Antonio noticed an empty seat at the place set for Marianna Bellini. Her place settings appeared to be untouched. He decided to inquire. "*Mi scusi*," he said to the others at the table. "Has anyone seen *Signora* Bellini? I hoped to give her my regards."

"No," the man next to her spot answered. "I had been looking forward to seeing her myself. Perhaps at her age the idea of being around all these people during this epidemic was too much for her." Antonio thanked them, but alarm bells were going off in his head. She had expressed no such concern two days ago, and had told them she would see them today.

After they wandered for about fifteen minutes, the president of the *consorzio* stepped up to the microphone and asked everyone to find their seats. Antonio found his. He leaned in close to Gabriella and whispered, "Lots of interesting discussion going on. I heard bits of speculation regarding the death of Andrea and Bria, and the wine chemist. Nothing solid though."

"Same here," she said. "But I did hear some whispers that make me think we are not the only ones who have put Alida and her sons at the top of our suspect list. It appears they are not widely trusted among this crowd."

Antonio searched around for Alida and her sons, whom he had not seen yet. He spotted them sitting at a table near the back, their heads together in whispered conversation.

*****

Vito Crivello, the president of the *consorzio*, cleared his throat, took a drink of water, and called the meeting to order. "*Grazie, amici. Mille grazie,* for coming today! I was worried that many of you would choose to stay home. No one would blame you. These are trying days. I know that, like me, many of you are worried about your livelihood and you have many questions: Will the government be shutting down the country, and if so, will we still be able to distribute our wine? Obviously, people will need to buy food, and I suspect that wine will be in high demand. *Merda*, what else will people have to do if they are stuck in their homes except to eat, drink, and watch television!"

A bit of laughter filtered among the tables, followed by low-level conversation.

"I'm afraid I have few answers to those questions. In preparation for our meeting, I've made every effort to get answers from our local government officials for the commune, as well as the regional Tuscan government body in Firenze. No one knows for certain what our national government will do. The prime minister and his aides are keeping their decision-making close to the vest."

"Then what are we supposed to do?" Someone spoke from a table near the front. It was followed by a wave of murmuring through the crowd.

"*Per favore*, please!" Vito said. "I want answers as badly as you do. This one thing I would advise. Take advantage of whatever time remains to move your product to market. I believe it is more than speculation that all of Italy will be shut down any day now." More murmuring followed.

Vito opened the floor up for questions, which was a poorly calculated move, considering he had few answers. After about ten minutes, he moved to the next item on the agenda. "Now, we have something else we need to discuss. As you all know, the Italian Wine Commission launched an investigation into some possible wine fraud, specifically the possible use of unapproved grapes in the making of Vino Nobile. I know you are all aware that they track harvest yields and production levels to ensure that DOCG regulations are being followed. That statistical information showed some anomalies, and a preliminary investigation was launched. Thankfully, this was not leaked to the press as it was in Montalcino, which as you know, brought a great deal of harm to their reputation before any wrongdoing was even proven."

Another voice called out from the crowd, "This investigation has no merit! None of us would stoop so low as to add in other grapes. Why would we? The rules allow adequate flexibility."

"I agree with you, Domenico," Vito Crivello said, "that our DOCG guidelines are quite workable. They allow for a certain amount of flexibility, while upholding the integrity of our wine. But the Wine Commission came to me first. I saw the numbers that created the concern. I agreed it was enough to warrant a quiet investigation."

Those gathered did not like his answer. A great buzzing of table-talk ensued. Then another voice spoke angrily, "We heard you supported this investigation, Vito. How could you betray us like that? You question the integrity of the very people who elected you as our president?"

"*Per favore* everyone, maintain order!" Vito said with exasperation. "If you have something to say, please stand and be acknowledged." He went quiet for a few beats, as he considered how to answer. Then proceeded slowly and deliberately. "If you have an issue with my presidency, I am happy to resign. I never asked for this thankless job anyway! Like many of you, I have been a winemaker here my whole life, as was my father before me, and his father before him. During that time, our growing reputation for making exceptional wines has benefitted us all. Any and every decision I make is only to protect you and me, and that reputation."

He paused to let that sink in. People were at least listening. "I firmly believe that the majority of winemakers here would never do anything to damage that reputation. But I must say … based on the events of the last few weeks, it appears someone has something to hide. The murder of …"

"Nobody here would commit murder!" a voice cried out. "And even if they did, it would only have been to protect themselves from these unfounded accusations!"

Gabriella gave a start and her face turned redder than the wine in her glass. Antonio put a hand on her arm. Heads swiveled, and tempers flared. The voice had come from behind them. Antonio didn't see who spoke but thought he recognized Rocco's voice.

"I am shocked that you would justify murder, *Signor* Tarantino, under any circumstances." Vito stared at him for long moments, then glanced around the crowd. "It is my strong position that the investigation be allowed to continue unhindered, and that all of us should give the Carabinieri our fullest cooperation. The sooner we can put this ugly matter behind us, the better. If it were not for Covid-19 dominating the news, and the quiet way in which the investigators have gone about their work," he nodded toward Gabriella and Antonio, "it might have made national headline news by now."

"Now, before we proceed to more mundane business, I would like to know if I should continue to chair this meeting, or if you would like to elect a new president. If any of you would like us to conduct a new presidential ballot, please raise your hand."

Not a single hand went up.

"Okay then," Vito Crivello said, with a humble nod. "Let's take a fifteen-minute break before we move on to our other matters."

Chapter Thirty-four

Saturday Evening

The meeting of the *consorzio* was winding down when Gabriella's phone rang. It was Chia. Gabriella hung up and texted. *I'll call you back.* She got up and walked away from the table. Antonio followed. They found a quiet spot away from prying ears. Antonio turned and caught sight of Giulia following. She huddled with them. Gabriella dialed and put it on speakerphone.

"*Pronto,* Gabriella," Chia answered. "Sorry I was unable to talk when you called me this morning. I was involved in a case. Nothing major."

"I've got Antonio and Giulia here with me. We have you on speakerphone."

"Good. I just got an update from Marina Gallo on her findings from the lab fire. She also told me about the note found at the house. That's *pazzo!* Someone is trying to scare you off. I hope you're being careful. Any idea who it is?"

"I was hoping the forensics on the letter might tell us something. We have our suspicions, but nothing to prove it by and not enough for a search warrant."

"And you're running out of time, I'm afraid."

"That too. Please give us something useful."

"Well, we have various bits of information, but like with most cases it will help more on the rear end of the case than the front." Antonio knew what she was talking about. Often, forensic evidence does more to help confirm a case against a perpetrator, than solve it on the front end.

"First of all, regarding your note," Chia continued. "No fingerprints. No DNA. The handwriting would only be useful if we had something else that person had written for comparison. We can tell you it appeared to be a man's writing, written with a gel pen on paper designed for laser printers. That's it."

"Okay. What about the lab? What do you have?"

"Let's start with ballistics. The chemist, Pietro Landi, was shot twice in the chest with 9-millimeter Parabellum rounds. As I'm sure you know, that is a wide range of handguns: Glock 17s, 19s, Beretta 92s, SIG-Sauer P226s and 229s ... even Uzi submachine guns, to name a few. If we got our hands on the gun, we could confirm it."

"What about the fire?" Gabriella asked.

"Started with regular old gasoline. No fancy accelerants or anything traceable. We couldn't find any evidence that someone broke in. No broken windows or locks. Either the doors were unlocked or Pietro let them in. Possible it was someone he knew. No fingerprints or DNA at the scene."

"What about witnesses or CCTV evidence?" Antonio asked.

"Nothing. Everyone else in the business park had gone home for the day. But it looks like we were wrong about him not having cameras. We found a bent mounting bracket among the rubble but no camera. Either he had taken it down or they stole it. Likely the latter. It was probably synced to his own computer.

Remember that they removed that hard drive. Find that, and you've probably found your killer."

"Without a search warrant, our odds of finding evidence such as the gun or hard drive are nil," Gabriella said. "And so far, we've found no trucks which match the one that ran Andrea and Bria off the bridge. One winery refused to allow us to see theirs. We're planning a stake-out there to see if we get lucky."

"Good luck with that," Chia said in a sardonic tone.

"And as far as CCTV footage on nearby roads, there was nothing suspicious. Whoever did this probably wasn't driving that same delivery truck. I do have one interesting thing to tell you, though. I managed to find Pietro Landi's lab files on the Cloud as you suggested. Took me two days of on-and-off searching. The last files he uploaded were the results of the wine analysis he did for the president of the *consorzio*. I wish it was more helpful. He found nothing out of line. But all of those wines were three to five years old. So, either nothing was going on or it's a more recent crime."

"But no video files from his camera?"

"No. If it was active, it's possible it was only going to his hard drive."

"*Grazie. Grazie mille*, Chia, for spending so much time on this. I owe you."

"Not really. I love this stuff. Besides, with Leonardo in quarantine I've got nothing here in Siena to occupy my spare time. The city is like a ghost town. It appears even the criminals have gone into hiding. I'll let you know if I find anything else." Antonio wasn't surprised by her reference to Leonardo. He and Chia had met only weeks before, during the search for Raphael, but their relationship had blossomed instantly.

After hanging up they spent a few minutes discussing their observations from the meeting. Gabriella's ire rose up when Antonio mentioned Rocco, and the comment he had made. "I want to start our surveillance tonight," she said. "Are you with me?" she asked Antonio.

"Of course."

"Giulia wants to help, too," Gabriella added.

Antonio looked at Giulia, who nodded. "I don't think …"

"We've already been through this, Antonio," Gabriella said.

"Okay, okay. I guess we'll get more sleep that way. God knows I could use it. By the way, one more thing I wanted to tell you. Did you notice that Marianna Bellini was missing from the meeting today? I inquired at her table. Nobody had an explanation."

"Hmmm, odd," Gabriella said. "I have her number." She dialed it and let it ring until it went to voice mail. She left a message.

*****

They arrived home about 4:30. Chiara addressed the family. "I don't know about the rest of you, but I don't feel like cooking tonight. Let's go out for pizza. Our favorite place is Giacomo's. Our treat. He uses some of my cheeses on his menu."

"I'll call to make sure they'll be open," Sylvio said. He did, then reported, "We're in luck. It's his last night. He's had a surprising number of winemakers making reservations, but said he can accommodate us if we come for an early dinner at 7:00."

"Early works for me," Chiara said. "I'm exhausted."

"After dinner, the three of us are going straight to Carpinteria to begin our surveillance," Gabriella said. She turned to Antonio and Giulia. "Charge your phones before we leave. And if you need anything, bring it with us. We should bring pillows and blankets for those who are resting. And we need our guns." She turned to Sylvio. "Do you have an extra shotgun or hunting rifle we can bring? I want to be prepared for the worst."

"I hope that's all you want them for," Umberto said. "Promise me you'll stay off their property."

Gabriella assured him, then turned to Sylvio again. "And do you have binoculars?"

"Of course." He disappeared and came back five minutes later with a 12-gauge shotgun, a Winchester hunting rifle, two boxes of shells, and binoculars.

Chiara spoke up. "I have something else you may need. Hold on." She left the room and came back with a digital SLR camera. "My Nikon D810," she said. "I switched the lens to a four hundred zoom. I use it for birding. For shooting at night, I suggest setting the ISO as high as it will go."

"*Perfetto! Grazie,*" Gabriella said. "Looks like we're all set."

"Almost," Angelica added. "You'll need coffee to get you through the night. Mom has a couple of thermoses. I'll brew coffee just before we leave for Giacomo's. And I'll see what I can put together for the late-night munchies."

They packed everything in Gabriella's Audi. They hid the handguns under the seats and the shotgun and rifle under the hatch in the rear.

Chapter Thirty-five
Saturday Evening

Giacomo had opened an hour early, to accommodate their family and a few others. Antonio thought about how vastly different the cultures were. He thought of his own restaurant located in the small town of Woodinville, Washington. If he opened at 8:00, he would do little if any business.

No wonder Sylvio and Chiara love this place, Antonio thought when they entered. Giacomo welcomed them with hugs and kisses upon the cheeks of the women, and led them to a table in the inner courtyard, beneath a pale-yellow canopy. The tables were widely spaced. Giacomo told them he had removed some because of the pandemic. There were huge pots with olive and lemon trees. The lemon trees were loaded with fruit. The space felt magical to Antonio.

The family was uncharacteristically quiet during dinner. They had begun the day with little sleep, then the *consorzio* meeting had sapped what energy they had left. Their limited conversation centered around what they learned that day, which wasn't much. But they felt it had given them a pulse for the mood of the growers and winemakers. Gabriella was still fuming over the cavalier comment by Rocco. Sylvio said that as they were leaving, two of the growers told him they no longer planned to sell grapes to *"that family."*

Sylvio, Chiara, Umberto and Angelica shared a bottle of Rosso di Montepulciano with their pizzas. Antonio, Gabriella, and Giulia drank only mineral water. Antonio ordered a pizza with porcini mushrooms, sausage, mozzarella and a Marzolino cheese made by Chiara. He savored it in silence. It may have been the best pizzas he'd ever eaten. He saved some for a late-night snack.

Gabriella was anxious to leave before they even finished. They excused themselves and three of them took their leftovers and stepped outside into the cool night air. They headed down the dimly lit cobblestone street toward their car. They had only walked for a minute when Antonio spotted the familiar glow of a cigarette in the shadows. The man was wearing a cap, but Antonio was sure it was the same man he'd seen the night before. He thought about confronting him, then had second thoughts. *Probably just a local,* he thought, *whose wife won't let him smoke in the house.* But his gut suspected otherwise. He turned back to look again before they turned a corner. The man had turned his back and was on his phone.

The three of them climbed into the Audi with Gabriella behind the wheel. It had been an hour since the sun had set and the moon had not yet risen. Darkness enclosed the country roads like the wings of a raven. They had driven a couple of kilometers from the city when Gabriella raised an alarm, "There is a car behind us with no headlights on. Maybe he is drunk. Seems early for that though. I think he is following us. I think I saw the car earlier … on the road not far from Sylvio and Chiara's." Antonio turned to look. The large, dark sedan was about twenty meters behind them. It appeared to be a classic Mercedes, possibly decades old. He couldn't make out a license plate.

What occurred next came without warning. The Mercedes accelerated rapidly and shot past them, nearly sideswiping them. Antonio tried to make out the driver but the interior of the car was dark. Even the instrument panel lights were off. Antonio instinctively grabbed the dash as the car swerved in front of them, inches from Gabriella's front end. *"Che diavolo!* What the hell!" Gabriella shouted.

Antonio stared after the car, evaporating into the night. It disappeared over a rise. He breathed a sigh of relief, but it was short-lived. When they came over the rise the Mercedes loomed right in front of them, facing them head on. Seconds later the car turned on their high beams and launched toward them. The driver was playing a game of chicken. It felt like a scene from one of his dreams.

Antonio's could feel his heart pounding in his chest. *"Merda!"* he swore as he braced himself with one hand and grabbed for his gun case with the other. He opened it, pulled out the gun, and flipped off the safety. "Get down Giulia!" he yelled. The car was closing fast, his headlights blinding them. He looked at Gabriella, wondering how she would handle this. The veins in her neck stood out. *Will she panic and veer dangerously or hold her course, hoping the other car swerves?* he wondered. She did neither. With nerves like steel, she waited to just the right moment then tore onto the dirt shoulder in a controlled skid as dirt and rocks went flying. The other driver stayed his course. *Would he have swerved to the other lane if she hadn't?*

"Guns!" Gabriella barked. He pulled out the other gun cases and handed each of them their own. The girls pulled out their guns and readied them. They waited, but the dark sedan never returned.

"Dio mio," Giulia said, followed by language Antonio had never heard from her lips. "Who the hell was that?"

"I wish I knew," Gabriella said. Antonio could see the pulse pounding in her temple. "Maybe someone working for the Tarantino's. More intimidation tactics I suspect."

"We might be blown," Antonio said. "Will our surveillance accomplish anything if they're onto us."

"We don't know that for sure."

"I think it is time that we call the local Carabinieri," he said.

Gabriella shook her head. "No. I'd have to explain why I am operating on their turf without their knowledge. Word would get back to Marcello."

"Damn it, Gabriella! How long are we going to play this game? Operating under the radar without authorization? It's dangerous not having backup to call on."

She stared at him hard. "Remember, Antonio. I never asked you for your help. You can bail anytime you want."

He locked eyes with her, once again considering if he should walk away. He knew he couldn't. "And leave you to fight this battle alone? I hope you know me better than that."

She turned and stared out the front window, then slammed her hand on the steering wheel. Tears rolled down her cheek. She released her foot off the brake and pulled onto the road. Another kilometer and they saw the turn for the winery ahead. She doused her headlights and pulled behind a copse of trees across the road from the entrance. She hid the car as best she could, while still allowing them to see the house and most of the winery buildings. "I doubt you can see much from back there, Giulia. We will move you to the front when it is your turn."

"I'm fine," she said, leaning forward. "Tell me what we're looking for."

"Anything unusual or suspicious," Gabriella said. "The building on the left with some lights on is the main house." Giulia leaned forward to see. "The two just beyond are guest houses. I believe the sons live in those." Only one window was illuminated. "The long, low building on the right—built into the hillside—is the winery. We think the one behind it is the truck and tractor garage. When it's your watch, wake us if you see any vehicles coming or going, or any other movement."

"Got it. Who has first watch?"

"I propose we all watch for now," Antonio said. "I don't know about you guys, but my adrenaline's pumping too hard to sleep any time soon." They agreed.

"Alright," Gabriella said. "We'll start our rotation at eleven. I'll take the first watch, then you, Antonio, then Giulia. Two-hour shifts. At 5:00 AM we head home."

"Turn off the automatic dome lights," Antonio said. "I'm going to open the car door to retrieve the rifle and shotgun. I want to be prepared after that incident."

He pulled the guns from beneath the rear hatch and placed them within easy reach behind the rear seat. Then he pulled out the binoculars.

*****

The night proved uneventful. Antonio's hunch was that this was a waste of time. If these guys were guilty of anything, and if the Tarantinos drove that car—or someone who worked with or for them—then they weren't going to show their hand now. But he knew it was time to keep his opinion to himself.

He reclined his seat at eleven and finally dozed off sometime near midnight. He slept a fitful hour until Gabriella woke him. He brought his seat up straight, drank a cup of lukewarm coffee, and did all the things he knew to do to drag himself fully awake. He got out and relieved himself. The chill breeze felt like it was coming off the mountains. He shivered, then pulled off his coat and sweater. *The colder the better,* he thought. He stretched, then got back in the car. Still, it wasn't long before he was struggling to keep his eyes open. He decided to utilize a technique he'd been taught in his detective days. He applied deep acupressure starting from his head and working down. First was the top of his skull. Then the spot behind his temples. Next, he used his thumbs to apply pressure on either side of the spine near the base of the skull. Moving to his hands, he squeezed the pad between the thumb and forefinger, then the outside of the leg bone, a few inches below his knees. All of these points had names, Asian mostly, but he couldn't remember them. All he cared was that they worked.

The cold made him famished. He pulled out his box and ate his leftover pizza slices. It was just as good cold as it had been at dinner. He was fully awake now. Soon, that alertness became a hyper-sensitivity. He became aware of every sound … every bird that fluttered in the trees, every cricket's trill, every breath from the girls' lungs. Occasionally, the dogs at the winery barked at something in the night. He was conscious of the slightest movements … each branch that swayed in the wind, and every bat that darted in front of a star. He drank a second cup of coffee. Every few minutes he scanned the grounds with the binoculars. At around 2:00 AM most of the lights in the main house went out. Someone was a night owl. He watched closely with the binoculars. A few minutes later the front door opened and someone came out. It appeared to be Donato, the younger son. He walked to the nearest house and entered. A few minutes later it went dark.

Being as wound up as he was, he made use of the time to examine every detail of the case, and consider alternative theories. And he thought about Gabriella—her emotional state—and his own role in all of this. *What do you want, Antonio?* he asked himself. *Three people are dead and someone's trying to intimidate us.* He realized he wanted justice as desperately as Gabriella did. He hoped it wasn't revenge he craved. But more than that, he wanted to protect her. He knew it was his job to keep her from doing something stupid—something she'd later regret. And there was one other thing ... he wanted her back, the woman he'd known before all this began.

He doubted that he'd be able to sleep in this condition, so he didn't wake Giulia when it was her turn. Then about 3:45, his mind and body began to shut down. He woke her and they switched places. He put his sweater back on, pulled a blanket over himself, and laid his head down on a pillow in the back seat. He closed his eyes, and fell fast asleep in seconds.

*****

He heard the engine start and sat up in the back seat. The clock on the dash said 4:50 AM. "Good morning," Gabriella whispered sleepily. "Let's get out of here before it's light." The slightest grey light was beginning to show in the eastern sky. *What a waste of time this was,* Antonio thought, as she pulled onto the road. He laid back down, closed his eyes, and became dead to the world again.

Chapter Thirty-six

Sunday morning

Gabriella had to shake Antonio awake when they arrived at the house. He sat up begrudgingly. The first thing he saw was Chiara coming out of the barn with a pail of milk in each hand. The laughter was gone now that Serena was. She carried them into her cheese making room, where she had a commercial refrigerator. Gabriella stepped out of the car and removed the rifle and shotgun from the back and carried them into the house. She looked like a soldier. He reminded himself that the Carabinieri actually are a military police force who serve both at home and abroad.

Antonio woke Giulia. She leaned on his shoulder as they shuffled into the house. Not another soul was stirring. He smelled the delicious aroma of fresh coffee. He was tempted, but decided against it.

Chiara came in, took one look at them and frowned. "*Buongiorno*," she said softly, assuming they were as dead on their feet as they appeared. "Anyone want something to eat before you crawl into bed?" They all shook their heads. "Okay, I'll have some pastries and fruit when you wake up. And fresh coffee. Angelica and Umberto will be attending church with us this morning. We normally go to the nine o'clock service, but we can go to the eleven if any of you would like to join us. They're moving the service outdoors today. It may be the last one for a long time. I'd be surprised if it's well-attended. Many of my friends are afraid to go."

Antonio hadn't even realized it was Sunday.

"That would be lovely," Gabriella said. She looked at Antonio and Giulia. They both nodded.

"Okay, we'll leave at 10:40."

As Antonio passed by the pastries, he changed his mind. It was the aroma that got him. They were warm, and flaky, with a light filling of cream cheese and berry jam. He picked one up and ate it in three bites, then wandered off to bed. He set an alarm on his phone for 10:00 and went to sleep in his clothes. It took about two seconds.

*****

Antonio was in the middle of a dream when he was awakened. He could only remember bits and pieces, but that was disturbing enough. In one scene, the Mercedes was bearing down on the three of them with headlights glaring like evil eyes. It morphed into a big delivery truck. That's when it dawned on him that the truck that ran Andrea and Bria off the road was the same kind of truck that killed Randi and Christina in Nice. Odd that it took a dream to make the connection. In this dream, instead of being in Gabriella's Audi, they stood exposed in the middle of the road, frozen in place. Gabriella grabbed his shoulder and began to shake it, crying out, "Antonio, move. We need to get out of the road!"

He peeled his eyes open and realized the shaking was real. But it wasn't Gabriella. It was Sylvio.

"Antonio, wake up. Something terrible's happened!" In his stupor, the dream still had a grip on his mind. He sat up abruptly, expecting to be told that Gabriella and Giulia had been run down by the truck.

"Huh, what?" he asked. Gradually, his mind found its way back to reality.

"The widow Bellini … she was found dead in her home," Sylvio said breathlessly. "It looks like she was murdered! I received a call from Vito Crivello, the president of the *consorzio*. He was worried so he went to check on her. He'd been unable to reach her."

Antonio was suddenly wide awake. "Have you awakened Gabriella yet?"

"Not yet."

"I'll do it," Antonio said. He stood up, looked down and realized he was fully dressed except for his shoes. He slipped them on and stumbled up the stone stairs to Gabriella's room. He knocked gently and entered. She heard the door squeak and opened her eyes. "What time is it, *amore mio?*"

Now she decides to be nice to me, he thought. He pulled out his phone. "Just after eight."

She moaned and rolled over. "Give me another hour."

"Gabriella, there's been another murder … Marianna Bellini."

"Huh?" she sat up even faster than he had. The blanket fell away and he saw she was wearing a sheer nightgown. It made him think how much he looked forward to their wedding day. She saw him smile and pulled the blanket up. "What happened?"

"I don't know any details. Sylvio got a call from Vito Crivello. He couldn't get ahold of her so went to check on her."

"Have the Polizia Municipale been contacted?"

"I don't know. You now know as much as I do."

"Get out of here. I need to get dressed."

Antonio left the room. He went and poured a cup of coffee. Chiara hadn't made the fresh batch yet. The old stuff would have to do. He grabbed another pastry and headed toward his room. He ate too quickly and washed it down with stale coffee. He went in the bathroom, looked in the mirror, and cringed. He ran his head under cold water, and splashed some on his unshaven face. He dried his hair, ran a brush through it, brushed his teeth, and changed into some clean clothes. Suddenly a wave of sadness washed over him like a tsunami. He plopped down on the bed and put his head in his hands. He had really liked this woman, and had felt sorry for her, living in that big estate house all alone.

He returned to the kitchen for more coffee and found Gabriella leaning on the counter, drinking a cup of coffee and eating an apple. She hadn't bothered to put make-up on but didn't need it. She looked surprisingly fresh.

"Are you coming with me?" she asked. All business again.

He didn't even ask what she meant. "Ready when you are."

Chiara walked into the room. "I heard what happened," she said, a grave look on her face. She looked older than Antonio remembered.

"Is Sylvio around?" Gabriella asked, "I want to ask ..."

"Right here," he said, as he limped into the room looking somber.

"Can you tell me anything more about what happened?"

"Vito found her on the floor of the kitchen, lying in a pool of blood. Her two dogs were standing guard next to her." Antonio remembered the two small white Bolognese dogs. "A knife was on the floor next to her body. He didn't want to move her, but felt for a pulse. Her body was cold and stiff."

"She's probably been dead for more than a day," Antonio said. He looked at Gabriella. "Do you think she took her own life? She had a certain sadness about her … like her life had become meaningless."

"Possible, but I don't think so." She turned to Sylvio, "Any idea if Vito called the Polizia Municipale?"

"He told me he called the Carabinieri."

She groaned and a shadow crossed her face. That was not what she wanted to hear. "Do you know anything about who runs the local Carabinieri?"

"A captain, I believe. Name of Zampari," Sylvio answered.

She shook her head. "I do not know him."

"You still want to go?" Antonio asked.

"Yes."

"Should we wake Giulia?"

"No. Let her sleep. She can go to church with the family." She turned to Chiara. "Will you make sure she gets up?"

"Of course." She stepped up and nestled Gabriella's hands in her own. "We'll be praying … praying for Marianna's son, and for your safety. I'm getting worried for you," she looked at Antonio, "both of you. Please be careful. Serena needs you."

Gabriella locked eyes with her and nodded. "We will." Then she picked up her car keys and tossed them to Antonio. "*Andiamo.* You're driving. I've got a couple of calls to make."

Chapter Thirty-seven

Sunday Morning

The morning sun shone through the tall Italian Cyprus trees lining the long drive, sloping gently upward toward the pale orange-coral colored Villa Sant'Angelo. The formal gardens and pond were flourishing with life. Birds fluttered about, each singing their assigned song. A pair of bunnies nibbled on her flowers, and the fish continued their path among the lily pads in water kept fresh by the water pouring from the mouth of the lion. It felt so idyllic that it seemed impossible that they would find Marianna's dead body here.

Several vehicles already occupied the circular drive in front of the villa. There were two black Carabinieri sedans, and a paramedic vehicle—white with orange and blue stripes down the side. *Ambulanza* was printed across the front. There was also a Porsche Cayenne SUV. Antonio trailed Gabriella up the broad steps to enter the grand foyer. She donned a pair of latex gloves and handed him a pair. They followed the voices to where they found two Carabinieri in the kitchen, along with two *paramedico*, a man and a woman wearing orange jump suits. Vito Crivello stood to the side, his face frozen in sorrow as he rocked back and forth. The stench of death permeated the house. Antonio saw bloody paw prints heading off toward the outdoor patio where they had taken lunch three days prior. He assumed the dogs had been shooed away or scared off by all the strangers in the house.

Gabriella showed her badge. "I am Colonel Ferrara. You must be Captain Zampari." He was a relatively short man with mottled dark skin. By his looks and dialect, Antonio guessed him to be from Calabria or Apulia.

"Yes. May I ask why you're here?" he sputtered. "I didn't call for backup. How did you find out? I haven't even reported this yet. Where are you from?" His voice betrayed more and more annoyance—bordering on anger with each question. Everyone in the room turned to watch the conversation, including a young Carabinieri corporal who stood behind the captain with a slightly amused look on his face.

"Slow down, Captain. One question at a time, *per favore*. I am the head of the investigative unit in Siena. We are investigating some possible wine fraud and a series of homicides which have taken place surrounding that investigation."

"Siena? Montepulciano is not in your territory. Why was I not informed? And wine fraud? That's not a Carabinieri task." He was becoming increasingly bombastic.

Antonio watched a growing irritation come over Gabriella's face. "Breathe, Captain. Do you always ask so many questions at once? You are right about one thing: wine fraud investigations are not normally our responsibility. It is the purview of the Wine Commission. But their man who came to investigate was murdered on his return trip, along with his wife who accompanied him. There was a wine chemist who was analyzing the samples who was also murdered, and his lab set on fire." She stopped and looked at Marianna's stiff body, lying in a pool of congealed blood. She was dressed in a satiny pale fuchsia suit.

It looked expensive. Her silver hair was perfectly styled. "And now we have a fourth victim."

"This woman wasn't murdered," Captain Zampari blustered, "She committed suicide."

"This woman has a name, Captain … Marianna Bellini. Please use it. You are certain this was a suicide?"

"Absolutely. We found a suicide note. And this chef's knife near her hand," he pointed at the bloody knife. "There was a single stab wound to the heart."

"May I see the note?" Antonio asked. The corporal handed it to him. It was typed, *E diventato tutto troppo. Mi dispiace.* Meaning "It all became too much. I'm sorry." He handed it to Gabriella.

The *paramedicos* had rolled in a stretcher. They lifted the board off in preparation for moving the body. "Do not move her!" Gabriella said firmly.

Captain Zampari's face turned red. "You can't start barking orders here. This is my jurisdiction!"

"May I remind you, Captain Zampari … that I outrank you. This is my crime scene now, which means I have some questions. Have you called in a forensic team?"

"The nearest forensic unit is in Arezzo, a small, two-person department. There's no reason to bring them in for a suicide."

Gabriella turned to Antonio. "Please contact Major Marina Gallo for me. See if she is available to come to the scene this morning." She turned back to the captain. "Marina is the chief forensic person for all of Tuscany. She is stationed in Firenze."

Antonio turned to walk outside to make the call, thankful for the excuse to escape the smell. As he was leaving the room, he heard the captain objecting once again.

Gabriella had apparently had enough. "That will be *all,* Captain Zampari. If we need further assistance, I will call on you. You are dismissed."

Outside, Antonio dialed Marina Gallo's number. She answered on the second ring. "*Pronto*, Antonio. How can I be of assistance?"

Antonio explained. "No problem," she said. "With the non-existent traffic I should be there in just over an hour. I'll be bringing a new member of my team. Don't touch anything until we get there!"

"Of course. *Grazie,* Marina. *Grazie mille!*"

"*Prego.*"

He was ending the call when Captain Zampari stomped past him, muttering curses. His corporal followed, still looking amused. Antonio suspected he enjoyed seeing the captain being put in his place. He was probably a pain in the *derriere* to work for. They got in their respective cars. The captain roared off. The corporal nodded to Antonio and smiled, then pulled away casually.

Antonio turned and found Vito Crivello standing nearby. "She didn't kill herself," he said. "I *know* her. She would never have done such a thing!" The way he said, "I know her," sounded intimate, as if their relationship had been just that. "You saw how she was dressed," he added. "She was dressed to attend the *consorzio* meeting. She was looking forward to it."

The same thought had occurred to Antonio when he saw her. "Do you know if anyone has contacted her son?" he asked.

"Not that I'm aware of."

"Do you have his contact information?" As they were talking, the *paramedicos* walked past rolling their empty stretcher. They climbed in their unit and drove slowly away.

"I do. Would you like me to contact him? I've known him since he was a boy."

"*No. No, grazie.*" *We'll want to see how he reacts,* Antonio thought.

Vito pulled out his phone and shared the number.

"One more question," Antonio said. "Did you touch anything in the house?"

"No. Of course not. I was very careful. I know about such things ... from watching the movies."

"Good, thank you." Antonio didn't think he believed him. There had been a brief flicker downward in his eyes. "Gabriella will have additional questions for you," Antonio added. "Best if you wait out here. The more we avoid the crime scene, the better."

When Antonio returned, Gabriella was the only living person in the room. "Marina will be here in about an hour with a new member of her team," he said. "I asked Vito if he touched anything. He says no. I'm not sure I believe him. He doesn't think this was suicide. He said, *I knew her,* in a way that made me think it was more than as an acquaintance." She looked up at him and nodded sadly. Antonio continued, "I told him to wait outside ... that you would have more questions. I think you should let him sweat for a while."

Antonio went to the opposite side of Marianna's body and knelt down for a closer look. She was face down in the pool of blood. Her eyes remained open. There was a look of terror in them. Once again, he was overwhelmed with sadness, mixed with anger. So many senseless deaths. It's one thing to hear about a death, quite another to see the body of someone you know, lying in a pool of their own blood.

He tried to push those feelings aside so he could think clearly. Emotions have their place. They can provide motivation and purpose. But they can cloud one's judgment—blinding you to the obvious. One thing he knew for certain. He was going to see this through.

He studied her body and the scene, and began to formulate questions. How did they know the stab wound was to the heart unless they had moved her? There was no blood on her side or back indicating she had been rolled over. Did they make an assumption? Or had they lifted her just enough to see? It would have had to be done very carefully. If this was murder, why her? What could possibly be the motive or connection? Did she know something she hadn't told them?

"Do you think she killed herself?" he asked.

"No. I think that she was preparing to leave for the *consorzio* meeting yesterday morning when someone killed her."

"What makes you think that?"

"A few things. She is dressed to go out to an event. She put on her make-up but no lipstick yet. I think she was waiting until she finished that cup of coffee on the counter. And why would she bother to make coffee and only drink a few sips?"

Antonio stood and looked at it. It was less than a quarter gone. *This woman's a damn good detective*, he thought.

"There are those suicides that are spur of the moment decisions," he said. "Sometimes a person has thought about it for a long time, then makes a rash decision and does it before they lose the courage." *Courage isn't the right word*, he thought, but didn't correct himself.

"I know that's true," she said. "But then the suicide note makes no sense. If she made a last moment decision it would have been handwritten ... or there would not have been a note at all. Besides, this fits a pattern. I just don't know what it is yet." She stood. "I'm going to go and talk with *Signor* Crivello."

"After that, we should call her son," Antonio said. "Vito offered... says he's known him since he was a boy. But I told him no."

"Good call," she said, and headed toward the front entrance. Antonio suddenly became aware of a whimpering behind him. He turned and saw the two little balls of fur looking lost and forlorn. The red on their paws looked like Christmas gloves. They tilted their heads and whimpered again, in unison. It occurred to him that they had not eaten for at least a day. He stood and began to search for some food, being careful not to disturb anything that could be of interest. On the counter he noticed a knife block. The spot where the chef's knife should have been stood empty. The handles on the other knives matched the one on the floor. They used her own knife. He wondered if it was premeditated.

He opened a pantry door and found canned and dry dog food on the shelf. He settled on dry for now. He saw two clean dog bowls, each with double concave openings. He put water in one side, barely touching the faucet handle with the back of his hand. He put food in the other side, and put them where they could get to them. He felt sorry for them as they hungrily attacked the bowls, and wondered about their future.

He had a sudden urge to escape the room ... leaving the ugliness and the stench behind. But the detective in him wouldn't allow that to happen. He planted himself in the middle of the room and let his eyes scan every corner, looking for the tiniest clue.

Chapter Thirty-eight

Sunday, mid-morning

Gabriella returned after about ten minutes. "I sent Vito home. Your instincts were right about two things," she said. "Vito and Marianna had been having an on-again, off-again affair, ever since her husband passed. He is married … wants to stay that way, so pleaded with me to be discreet. Let's keep it between the two of us for now. My first concern is that makes him a suspect. A lover's quarrel. It is possible, but I can't see it. He claims to have an alibi, that he was home all morning with his wife until he left for the meeting. Of course, we cannot verify that without raising her suspicions. But I saw no signs of stress in him at the meeting yesterday, at least not until the meeting itself brought it on. Besides, I think he genuinely cared about her."

"You said I was right about a couple of things?"

"Yes. He lied to you about not touching anything. He removed a few items from the bedroom and bathroom. A toothbrush, hairbrush, a few items of clothing."

Antonio nodded. Part of him wanted to judge the man, but he'd made his own mistakes. It almost cost him his marriage.

"I should warn you now," she added. "If you ever do that to me, I will know the moment I see you. You are a lousy liar, you know." She stared at him seriously for a moment, then laughed.

"Don't worry, *amore*. I trust you. I would not be marrying you otherwise." She leaned over and gave him a short, but warm kiss. "Now we need to call Marianna's son. I hate these calls. What was his name again?"

"Jacopo." Antonio pulled out his phone and gave her the number. He tried to remember what he knew about him. *Oh, yeah. The playboy son who has no interest in the winery ... fancies himself a movie producer.* It saddened him that the family heritage of the winery may have come to an end.

"Can we go outside to make the call?" he asked.

"Of course." They walked outside but the odor followed them. By now the aroma of death and decay had permeated their clothing and skin. Gabriella dialed and put the phone on speaker. After several rings, she was about to hang up when a sleepy voice answered, sounding annoyed, "*Pronto*. Who is this?"

"My name is Colonel Gabriella Ferrara with the Carabinieri."

They heard a scoff, "Yeah, right, and I'm Al Pacino. Who is this really? Is that you Ilaria? Don't mess with me! It's too early." Antonio looked at his phone. It was nearly 11:00 AM in Tuscany.

Gabriella ignored him and forged ahead, "I am sorry to wake you, Jacopo Bellini. But I am afraid I have some bad news for you. Your mother, Marianna. I am sorry to tell you she is dead."

There was a pregnant pause. "What? *Merda!* No, it can't be! I just spoke with her yesterday morning." He paused for several beats. "She was getting ready to go to the meeting of the *consorzio*. Wait! Are you the woman detective who came to see her a few days ago with the American?"

"Yes. That was us. My associate, Antonio Cortese, is on this call with me now. We are here at the villa."

"What happened? Did she have a heart attack? You know she had a pacemaker."

"I was not aware of that. But no, *Signor* Bellini. She was stabbed. It appears to have happened shortly before she left for the meeting. Probably right after you talked to her. I need to ask you. Was your mother ever suicidal? There was a note found."

There was silence again. "No," he finally said. "I don't believe so. She was a very positive person. But lately she was sad … lonely. First, the loss of my father, and then her winemaker and estate manager retiring. Some of her friends have died, too. *Merda!* I should have been there."

The words sounded right. But there was something in the voice that didn't sound convincing to Antonio.

"And what was her frame of mind when you spoke?

More silence followed. "I'm afraid we had a fight. She hasn't been happy with my choices. She doesn't … didn't understand why I don't want to run the winery. And why I would want to have my own people making the wine if I never intended to run the estate. I got angry. *Dio mio!* I hope I did not push her over the edge."

"We are not convinced this is self-inflicted, *Signor* Bellini. We have a forensic team coming to assist with our investigation."

"But you said …"

"Yes. There was a note. But it was typed. We have reasons to be suspicious that this may have been foul play."

"What kind of reasons?"

"I'm afraid I am not at liberty to say. But I need to ask you some questions. What time did you speak with your mother yesterday?"

"About 10:30. She called me."

"Did she call from a landline, or cell phone?"

"Her cell. She no longer has a landline." Antonio looked around the room. He had seen no sign of a cell phone.

"And where were you when she called you?"

"Portofino. I arrived Thursday to meet with some other producers ... trying to sell them on a project ... a co-production."

"And you have been there since?"

"Yes, why are you asking?"

"Just doing my job, *signor*. Thank you for your patience. I have a couple more questions. Why *did* you want to put your own people in place here at the winery?"

"I wanted to make sure we had the most qualified individuals. Someone who would apply modern winemaking techniques. Villa Sant'Angelo has the best vineyards in the entire viticulture region, but if I may be frank, our previous winemaker was old school in his approach. I felt it would have a negative impact on the value of the winery."

"Which you are planning to sell, I presume?"

"Yes. It would provide the funds I need for my productions."

"When we visited your mother a few days ago, she said that she had given the new winemaker and manager a few days off. Were you aware of that? We've seen so sign of them here."

"They have been here in Portofino. They left this morning. They should be arriving there this evening."

"They were there with you? You said you were meeting other producers."

"Yes. We're friends."

Hmmm. Convenient alibi for all of them, Antonio thought, before those thoughts were interrupted when Gabriella's phone made a noise, notifying her of an incoming call. The screen announced Marcello Bianchi. *Uh, oh. Trouble!* Antonio thought. Marcello was her boss, the General, from whom she'd been hiding her activities.

Gabriella pushed the button to ignore it and asked for the names of the estate manager and winemaker. She wrote them down.

"*Signor* Bellini," she said. "Do you know anyone who would want to harm your mother? Anyone who would have motive?"

Another pause. Antonio wondered if he was just thinking, or making up a lie. "No one that I can think of."

"One last question now then. Do you know anyone who drives a black, older model Mercedes sedan, possibly a 300SEL?

An even longer pause, during which Gabriella's voice mail notification sounded. "No. No one in Italy."

"Somewhere else?"

"In Cannes. But trust me, there's no connection."

"Will you be returning to Montepulciano soon, *Signor* Bellini?"

"Is it a problem if I do not return until tomorrow evening?" he asked. "I have meetings scheduled for today and tomorrow."

"It's your decision, *Signor* Bellini. But I'll probably have more questions. So please be attendant to your phone."

*****

Antonio had thoughts to share, but before he could say anything Gabriella hit the button to return Marcello's call. Instead of putting it on speaker, she turned and walked away. Exhaustion suddenly overtook him and he sat down on the broad entrance steps. He could hear the water pouring into the pond from the lion's mouth and the birds singing, as if nothing out of the ordinary had happened here. It was such a beautiful, peaceful place, now forever sullied in his mind.

A moment later the two tiny Bolognese dogs showed up. One sat down on his left, the other on his right. They cocked their heads and looked at him inquiringly. He scratched one, then the other, and wondered what they were thinking. They both lay down on their bellies, red paws extended forward. He was concerned about how their wandering was affecting the crime scene. It was too late now to do anything about it. They'd been on their own with Marianna's dead body for almost twenty-four hours.

Gabriella returned a few minutes later. She took a seat near Antonio and scratched the dog sitting between them. Antonio wished he knew their names. She didn't speak a word for a couple of minutes. Antonio just waited. She finally opened her mouth, "I got my butt chewed out."

"I expected as much." He wanted to add *I tried to warn you*, but bit his tongue.

She looked him in the eyes. "You don't need to say it."

"I wasn't planning to."

She bumped him with her shoulder. "Thanks. Though you had every right to."

"What did he say?"

"He got a call from Captain Zampari, which caught him off guard, of course. But he acted like he knew about me being here. He told him he had assigned me to the case. And that it was a sensitive situation, so was kept under wraps."

"So, he covered your rear end."

"Yes … and no. He's like that, you know. Always supporting his people in front of others."

"But?"

"But he read me the riot act. I think that's what you Americans call it?"

Antonio nodded and smiled. Different cultures.

"Did he rein you in?"

"No. Thank God!" She breathed a sigh of relief. "After I explained everything, he just told me to be careful. Of course, he was angry that I hadn't told him what I was up to."

"As he should have been."

"I told him that I knew he would not have allowed me to be involved if I had asked. He said I was right. But if I ever pull a stunt like this again, I should plan on retiring before he fires me."

"That's it? You're free to work the case? I'm surprised."

"One caveat. He's sending Chia to assist us. He's sending someone to cover her in Siena for a few days. He said we have forty-eight hours, then he's pulling the plug. Also, if there are any arrests which need to be made, Chia has to be the one to make them. For obvious reasons."

"For obvious reasons," he repeated. "Did you tell him she and Marina have already been helping us?"

"Of course not. But he knows you're here."

"What did he say about that?"

"He was surprised. But glad that I had someone watching my backside."

"Oh, I love watching your backside. It might be your best part."

She elbowed him hard. "If I wasn't going to marry you, I would probably fire you."

"No time for that. We have less than forty-eight hours."

Chapter Thirty-nine

Sunday, mid-day

Antonio checked the time. Almost noon. Marina would arrive soon. Gabriella received a text from Chia saying she should arrive around two o'clock.

"Thoughts on the phone call with Jacopo?" Antonio asked.

"He definitely has motive. Selling the winery would give him some much-needed capital. I have a feeling he burns through cash like crazy." She paused. "He is a selfish man … putting his business dealings ahead of coming home to attend to his mother's death."

"Her death makes me sad. I really liked her. I'm so angry, I want to hurt someone. I wanted to hurt him when he said that."

"Me too."

Antonio shoved his anger back into its cage and padlocked the door. "Do you think he did it? Came down, either alone or with his friends?"

She shook her head. "No. But I feel like there is some kind of connection to him."

"I have the same sense. By the way, how did you know what model Mercedes that was?"

"I looked up the classic models on the internet before I went to sleep this morning. I also asked Captain Zampari and Vito if they knew anything about the car. They both said no, but I think Zampari was lying."

"That's big, if he is." He thought for a moment. "Maybe he's just angry, so he doesn't want to share information."

"Possible."

"Or he could be involved."

"Also, possible."

"Are you aware that someone may have been following us when we went to Montepulciano last night?" Antonio asked. "And possibly the night before? Whoever this is has resources we don't know about."

She nodded. "I saw him, too. Had my suspicions. But he did not tail us the whole time, so I thought maybe I was just being paranoid."

"Me too," Antonio said. "But maybe he was just reporting our comings and goings to whoever broke into the house, and whoever tried to run us off the road."

She nodded as she stared off into space, deep in thought.

"So, what do we know for certain?" Antonio asked.

"We know that Andrea's investigation touched a chord. So, someone murdered him and Bria, and then the wine chemist."

"Motive?"

"Cover up something they knew, or that the killers at least thought they knew."

"Something bigger than wine fraud," Antonio said.

"Almost certainly."

"And now we have another murder, with no obvious connection, but feels like it is somehow."

"Has to be."

"Possibly not," Antonio said.

"It is."

"Motive?"

Gabriella thought for a moment before answering, "Maybe they want to gain control of the estate."

"And they couldn't do that until she was out of the way."

Gabriella nodded.

"A theory then … Jacopo had an arrangement to sell the estate to someone after the death of his mother. So, they killed her to expedite the process. With or without his knowledge. My guess is without. And they tried to make it look like suicide. Otherwise, he would back out of the deal."

"All plausible. But who are the *they* we are speaking of?" Gabriella asked.

"I know you have your favorite suspects."

"Yes," she said. "If Alida is connected to the *Sacro Corona Unita,* either directly, or through her stepfather, then that provides the means—the resources—to accomplish this. It could also explain the cover-up if there is mob related activity that they are trying to hide."

"It could also be one reason we've yet to find a truck that matches the description of the one which ran Andrea and Bria off the road," Antonio said. "Maybe it came from down south."

"Maybe the Mercedes, too."

He nodded his assent. "We also know they've been going out of their way to grow their production. Any other suspects that make sense?"

"For wine fraud maybe. Or the murder of Marianna … maybe. But not for all of it. Not *if* it is connected."

"Which it is."

She nodded.

"I couldn't find a cell phone," Antonio said.

"Me neither. But we did not do a thorough search. We should wait for Marina."

On cue, the two dogs suddenly sat up. Moments later they saw Marina Gallo coming up the drive in her Carabinieri SUV, an Alfa Romeo Stelvio. She parked behind Gabriella's car and climbed out. A young woman got out on the other side. "*Buongiorno!*" Marina said cheerfully. Antonio wondered how she could be so upbeat, knowing she had a decaying body to examine. "Let me introduce my new associate, fresh out of the academy. This is Ginevra Barbieri."

Ginevra walked up confidently and shook Gabriella's hand, then Antonio's. It was a firm handshake. "Call me Gini," she said. "The last person who called me Barbie ended up with a broken arm," she said with a laugh.

Antonio half believed her. Still, he could see why someone might give her such a nickname. God had blessed her with long blonde hair, blue eyes, and a tall, slender body. Her accent sounded northern, possibly from Trentino-Alto Adige, which borders Austria. About the only asset that diminished her Barbie look was her stately southern European nose.

Marina retrieved two sets of light blue Tyvek coveralls and handed one to Ginevra. As they were pulling them on, she said,

"I got the strangest call from General Bianchi on our way here. He said that he knew you had called me to come to the scene here, and that I should be available to help you as much as possible for the next forty-eight hours. Did you speak with him?"

"Yes," Gabriella replied. "He found out I was working the case here. We crossed paths with a Carabinieri captain here. A man named Zampari. He was not happy with me taking over his crime scene so he called Bianchi."

"Of course, he did. I've met the man. He defines the word pompous. Anyway, just wanted you to know Marcello was on a fishing expedition. He beat around the bush, trying to find out if I'd been helping you all along. Thankfully, he didn't ask directly. I'd hate to lie to him or create problems for you." She sat down on the rear opening of the SUV and pulled covers over her shoes, and grabbed gloves and respirator masks for her and Ginevra. Antonio wished they'd had masks like that. Experience told him that it could take days before the aroma of death left your nostrils.

"Thankfully, he didn't pull me off the case," Gabriella said. "But he has given us forty-eight hours before he pulls the plug. He is sending Chia to be of assistance, and to be the front person if any arrests are made. I'm glad actually. I would never forgive myself if justice did not get served because I overstepped the boundaries."

"We better get started then," Marina said. She pulled a camera from her car. "Show me the body, but keep your theories to yourself for now. I want to look at this with a fresh set of eyes."

"Just follow the bloody paw prints," Antonio said. "These guys were the only ones with the body until she was found this morning."

"No wonder they look so sad. Poor little guys," Ginevra said, bending down to pet them. She had a tender way with them. Antonio suspected she'd grown up with dogs.

Gabriella spoke. "While you are attending to the body and surrounding area, do you mind if we search the other rooms? We're looking for her cell phone."

"That's fine," Marina said. "You know the rules. Grab shoe covers for your feet and fresh gloves if you need them, and there are paper masks if you want them."

*****

They gave up their search after about a half hour. Every room, every drawer, every nook and cranny had been gone through painstakingly. They had even checked the outside patio where they had taken lunch with Marianna. They found no phone, nor little else of interest. Gabriella had found a tube of lipstick sitting out on the bathroom counter. It was a color which she said would be a perfect pairing with Marianna's pale fuchsia outfit.

They reconvened on the front steps. A cool breeze had risen. They breathed in the deliciously fresh air. "I've been thinking," Antonio said. "If the truck which forced your brother off the bridge came from the south, then the guys driving it may have had southern accents. We should call Lodovico, the guy who owns the pizzeria in Buonconvento to ask him. What was his last name?"

"Muratori."

"You still have his card?"

"In the glove box." She pointed toward the car. Antonio retrieved it.

"You make the call," Gabriella said. "I am exhausted." She crossed her hands on her knees and leaned her head on them.

Antonio dialed. When the phone answered, he started to speak, then realized he was listening to a recorded message, announcing that the pizzeria was closed until further notice. It finished with, "If you would like to speak with me, Lodovico Muratori, leave a message and I'll call you back." Antonio did so. "Signor Muratori, this is Antonio Cortese, the detective working with Colonel Ferrara. We spoke to you a few days ago about the murder incident. A question has come up. We think it's possible that the men who drove that truck came from the south, possibly Apulia. Can you please call us and let us know if they had any noticeable accent? It would be much appreciated."

They sat silently for a time, lost in their own thoughts. Then Marina and Ginevra emerged from the house and pulled off their respirator masks. The dogs followed. Ginevra was carrying a bowl of soapy water. She knelt down and began to wash their paws. "If only you little guys could talk," she said. "It would save us so much trouble."

Marina planted her feet a few steps below Antonio and Gabriella at eye level. "Not a suicide. Among other things, Signora Bellini's fingerprints were on the knife, but not in the right places if she'd been holding the knife herself. And they would have been smeared by the force needed to penetrate her sternum. Someone held the knife handle to her fingers. You can see their own smudges, but they were obviously wearing gloves, so as not to leave any fingerprints of their own, nor anywhere else we could find."

"Any other signs of foul play on her body?"

"Some slight bruising on her left arm. I'm sure they grabbed her there during the attack. But I think it was so sudden that there was no sign of her fighting back."

"Do you think she knew her attacker?" Gabriella asked.

"Maybe," she paused a few beats and looked down at her notepad, "We also found her computer. We dusted the keys and the printer. We should have found her fingerprints but there were none. The keys had been wiped clean by whoever typed the note. Then there was the note itself," she added. "No fingerprints on it either. It was obviously handled with gloves."

"And why would she type it?" Ginevra said. "She was all dressed up for something which tells me she was planning to go out. So, it was not pre-meditated. If this was a spur of the moment decision, you don't go and fire up your computer to type a note."

Antonio looked at Marina. "You've added a bright mind to your team. We had the same thoughts. You probably also noticed that she had not put on her lipstick, and that she had coffee on the counter which was barely touched."

"Yes. All this makes me certain it was murder," Marina said. "They were careful in some respects ... no fingerprints, no shoe prints, no obvious cleanup, no forced entry. But they were not professionals with enough experience to fool you and us."

"They fooled Captain Zampari," Gabriella said. "If we had not arrived when we did, much of this evidence would have been gone or compromised."

"They were probably counting on that. I'll place a call to the medical examiner to pick up the body. I want him to double-check our findings. But if I were you, I would proceed with your investigation assuming this is a murder."

As she was speaking, Antonio heard the sound of an engine. He looked up and saw another vehicle coming up the drive. Major Chibuogo Umeh, fondly known to them as Chia, arrived in her Carabinieri vehicle, a small Fiat Bravo.

Chapter Forty

Sunday, early afternoon

B*uongiorno!"* Chia greeted them. *Come va?"*

"I have been better," Gabriella answered.

"Heard you had another murder. You think it's related?"

"Not sure yet. Seems too coincidental though. We interviewed her a few days ago. We have a theory that we think is plausible." She explained their thoughts, and what they knew about the murder.

Chia considered this. "Could be. Or maybe she just knew something that worried them. Or they thought she did."

"Possible," Antonio said.

Chia turned to Marina Gallo, "May I see the body? I don't want to mess up your crime scene."

"Of course. We've finished our examination. But first I'd like you to meet the newest member of my team." She introduced Ginevra.

"Come with me," Gabriella told Chia.

While Marina placed her call to the medical examiner, Ginevra began pulling off her coveralls, and repacking the SUV. Antonio walked to the manmade pond and took a seat on a concrete bench near its edge. He wanted to get away from the stench and clear his head. The gentle splash of the waterfall was soothing, but added to his melancholy. The sun fought its way through the trees and glinted like a patchwork quilt on the water. He watched the fish swim lazily among the lily pads. Every time they passed through a sunny patch the sun reflected off their scales.

Something else shiny caught his eye. At first, he thought it was a fish. But it didn't move. Was it dead? He leaned over for a closer look, slowly coming to a realization of what he was seeing. He peeled off his shoes and socks and jumped into the pond, feet first. Brackish silt kicked up when his feet hit the bottom, clouding the waist-deep water. He stood shivering and let it settle, then reached down and picked something up.

He climbed out, picked up his shoes, and traipsed barefoot toward the house, dripping water. Gabriella and Chia were just coming out of the front entry. They saw him and Gabriella began to laugh. "Did you fall in? Or did you decide to go swimming to wash away the stench?"

Antonio held up the cell phone and everyone stared with astonishment. *"Bravo!"* Marina said. "Way to throw yourself into your work."

Gabriella spoke up. "Chia also found something interesting. Probably not as significant as that, but it might tell us something."

Chia held up a clear plastic bag. It contained small bits of soil. "Found this just inside the door. Looks like it came from the sole of a boot. I doubt it came from Marianna's shoes. I heard about those who were here when you arrived. Did anyone notice what kind of shoes they were wearing?"

Antonio spoke, "The Carabinieri and *paramedico* were wearing shoe covers." He thought for a moment, "Vito Crivello was wearing dress shoes. I noticed they were shiny but had dirt splatters. But they definitely had flat leather soles."

"It may have gotten tracked in by your perpetrator then," Chia said. She turned to Marina. "Can you have the soil analyzed?"

"Yes. But it won't tell us much without a comparable sample." She turned to Ginevra. "Take a variety of soil samples here for comparison. I'm going to send you back to Firenze. Take my car. I'm staying. I'll ride with Chia." She glanced at Chia for approval. She nodded. "Take this soil sample and Marianna's phone. The soil sample you should take to Captain Caramino in the crime lab. Try to dry out the phone and see if you can get anything from it." She handed Ginevra her keys, which elicited a smile.

"May I see the phone, *per favore?*" Ginevra asked, holding out her hand.

Antonio handed it off. She removed the case and pulled out the sim card. Then she opened the back and pulled out the battery, something most newer phones rarely allow anymore. "So, these can start drying out," she said. "I'm going to see if I can find clean, dry cloths and a container to sit these in for the trip back."

"I've heard that immersing it in uncooked rice can help," Antonio said.

"It can," Ginevra answered. "But rice is often dusty, which can create problems. We have stuff at the lab that's better. I'll immerse it as soon as I get back. Hopefully, I can get something from it by morning."

Gabriella looked at Antonio. "Why don't you wash up in her bathroom and dry off as best you can. And borrow some towels to put on my car seat."

Antonio headed that way, passing by the body as quickly as he could. He'd seen enough of it. He was just washing up when his cell phone rang. It was the owner of the pizzeria in Buonconvento.

"*Pronto, Signor* Muratori. *Mille grazie* for returning my call."

"*Prego, prego.* I'm glad you called. I never thought of it until I heard your message. But yes, those men had southern accents. And their features were typical southern."

"*Grazie, grazie!* That's very helpful. One more piece of the puzzle falling into place."

"Glad I could help. But you better find the other pieces quickly, *Signor* Antonio. I suspect we'll all be in quarantine any day now."

Antonio thanked him again and hung up. As he dried off, he pondered the truth of Jacopo's final statement. That was probably why Marcello gave them forty-eight hours. He wrapped a dry towel around his waist. They were thick and luxurious. He felt guilty for soiling them but knew it would not matter to Marianna Bellini. He rejoined the others, and told them about his phone call.

"Everything is pointing in one direction," Gabriella said.

"Yes. It is," Antonio said. "But don't forget, assumptions can be dangerous, causing us to overlook other things. We still need to consider every possibility."

Gabriella appeared distracted, as if she hadn't even heard him. She turned to Chia. "I assume you brought your laptop?"

Chia confirmed it. "Good, you are skilled at research. I am wondering if you can check financial information on a couple of people."

"Technically, I should have a warrant for that."

"Not possible. Time is running short. If you find anything, we will have to find a way."

"Who?" Chia asked.

"The local Carabinieri captain. Name of Zampari." Antonio looked at her with surprise, but then thought it made sense.

"One of our own. You're sure we should do that?"

"Positive. And I want you to check Jacopo Bellini, Marianna's son. And find out what you can about the estate manager and winemaker he hired." She looked at her note pad and provided their names. "Oh, one more thing. See if you can find a black Mercedes 300SEL registered in this area. I looked it up. They were first released in 1968. I think this one may be that old, or early seventies."

Chia nodded, "I'm going to need Wi-Fi."

"We'll head back to Chiara and Sylvio's. They have decent Wi-Fi."

"And the two of us need to figure out a place to stay tonight," Chia said, gesturing toward Marina.

"No need. You will be doing surveillance with us tonight. In the morning we will find you a bed to catch a little more sleep."

"That's exciting!" Marina said. "I've always wanted to try my hand at surveillance."

We'll see if she still feels that way in the morning, Antonio thought.

"Did you bring a gun?" Gabriella asked.

"I did." She went to her Alfa Romeo Stelvio and pulled it out of the glove box. She checked the magazine and grabbed an extra.

They heard engine noises and looked up to see the *Ambulanza* returning, followed by a tiny red Fiat 500. It was the *paramedicos* and medical examiner. They pulled close to the stairway. The *paramedicos* pulled out their rolling stretcher without acknowledging any of them. Antonio figured they were annoyed at having to make the return trip.

The medical examiner, a small, man of about forty with a thin, stylish moustache came and greeted Marina with a kiss on both cheeks. They obviously knew each other. She introduced him as *Dottore* Vittano. They turned and followed the *paramedicos* up the stairs.

Gabriella looked at Chia. "Are you okay to wait for them? I would like to get back and shower."

"Of course, just give me the name of the winery. I'll find it on Google maps."

"Fattoria Montieri," Antonio said. "You'll love it."

As soon as they were back in the car, Antonio rolled down the windows for fresh air before speaking. "I should text Chiara to make sure it's okay to have two more for dinner."

"Offer to pick up something. And tell her we will help cook tonight." Antonio smiled, realizing they had done almost no cooking together. She had usually been injured.

"Not sure if anything will even be open. They should know." He texted Chiara and received a prompt reply. *No problem. At the coop now. They received a shipment. Stocking up.*

Great. Gabriella and I will help you cook tonight.

She sent a thumbs up. *You'll be helping Angelica and Umberto. They said they are barring us from the kitchen again tonight. I'm getting spoiled.*

Chapter Forty-one

Sunday afternoon-evening

Giulia stood glaring in the doorway. "Thanks for inviting me!"

"Trust me, Giulia," Antonio said. "You didn't want to be there."

"Can you at least tell me about it?"

Gabriella turned to Antonio. "You tell her. I'm heading for the shower."

"Let's talk outside," Antonio told Giulia.

"Please. You smell really bad."

"That's why you should be glad you missed it."

"That bad, huh?"

Antonio nodded. "Heartbreaking."

"She was murdered?"

"They tried to make it look like suicide. The evidence says otherwise."

"All this violence," she murmured softly. "Firenze … here." She sighed and stared out at the vineyards as if they would give her the healing she was looking for. She turned back to Antonio as if seeing him for the first time. "You're wet."

"Took a little swim." He told her the highlights. "I'll fill in the details later. The family will want to hear."

They sat quietly for a few minutes, lost in their thoughts. Giulia broke the silence without looking at him "Are you still going home after this?"

He nodded and took a few seconds to reply, "For now."

"God, I'm going to miss you."

"I'll miss you, too. You know you're like a second daughter to me." He looked at her. A tear ran down her cheek.

"I suppose you have to go?"

"I'll be back."

"Who knows when."

Gabriella showed up in the doorway and looked at Giulia with concern. Her hair was swaddled in a towel, and she was wearing a shiny robe. She looked fresh and inviting. "You will want to wait a while," she said to Antonio. "I used all of the hot water."

"Gee, thanks!"

"You are so welcome."

He was trying to come up with a sarcastic reply when they heard the sound of Chia's car coming up the drive.

"You didn't tell me Chia was coming," Giulia said, perking up. "Leonardo will be jealous."

"Is he still in quarantine?"

"Yes. Not sick though. But they told him two weeks to be safe. He's going crazy."

Gabriella changed the subject. "We're doing surveillance again tonight, Giulia, if you want to join us."

"Absolutely. Same routine?"

"Similar. But two vehicles. We will take up positions north and south. I want to be as inconspicuous as possible."

Giulia looked at Chia's Carabinieri vehicle coming to a stop in front of them. "They won't be very inconspicuous in that."

"I'm going to ask Chiara if we can borrow her car," Gabriella said. "We'll leave right after dinner."

*****

Antonio checked the time and excused himself. He decided to call Shane while the water heater was recovering. He'd been dreading it. He walked away from the house. A cool breeze hit him, sending a shiver through his damp body. He saw clouds coming in from the south.

He was much relieved by the tone of the conversation. It seemed that Shane was adjusting to the additional stress and responsibilities.

"I've laid off most of the servers and some of the kitchen staff," he said. "You told me you wanted to give them severance money to help bridge the gap until their unemployment kicks in. I hadn't heard from you so I made an executive decision and gave them two weeks for now. Hope you're okay with that because it's already done."

"That's fine," Antonio said. "Sorry I didn't call sooner."

"I imagine it's crazy. How is your investigation going?"

Antonio filled him in. Shane hung on every word, then changed the subject back to the restaurant. "I think we should close down on Mondays and Tuesdays for now. It's costing us more to open the doors than we're bringing in."

"Okay, do it."

"You sure?"

"Yeah. I trust your decision," Antonio said.

"That went easier than I thought. Let's talk about doubling my salary while we're at it."

"Now you're pushing it."

"Just making sure you were actually listening, since you were being so agreeable and all," Shane laughed. "Any idea when you're coming back?"

"It has to be soon. Whether we solve these murders or not. Are you going to give me your usual warning now?"

"Absolutely! I'm surprised you've managed to stay out of the hospital this long. And I sure don't want it to be the morgue. Be careful, *Zio* Antonio!"

*****

It felt life-giving to be in the kitchen with Gabriella and the family. The specter of death had been looming over him all day. Angelica and Umberto were planning to leave tomorrow, and wanted to cook one last meal tonight. Chiara and Sylvio dressed up for the occasion and hung out in the kitchen with Chia and Marina, watching the busy preparations and drinking Malvasia. Chiara had been allowed one contribution, one of her cheeses— formaggio Raveggiolo—made from the milk of her sheep. It was rich and creamy, with a fresh, almost sweet flavor.

Angelica appointed herself head chef. "Okay, Antonio and Gabriella, you're in charge of the soup, minestra di farro. Everything you need is there," she pointed to the end of the island. "The borlotti beans have been soaking since this morning."

"Aye, aye, Chef Angelica!" Antonio said.

"Enough trouble from you, *cugino!*" She pointed a chef's knife his way and laughed like a teenage girl, then went back to giving orders. "Giulia, you get to help me with the involtini. Umberto is making Cacio e Pepe pasta with some of mama's pecorino, and a side of sautéed Swiss chard."

Antonio loved Cacio e Pepe pasta, a simple Roman dish of spaghetti with pecorino cheese, butter, and ample black pepper.

Gabriella went to work dicing onions, carrots, and celery, while he went out to Chiara's garden and returned with a sprig of rosemary, Italian parsley, and sage. The sage plant was just beginning to recover from its winter hibernation. He minced the sage and parsley, and set the rosemary sprig aside. Gabriella was now dicing the pancetta, so he grated the aged pecorino cheese, also made from sheep's milk.

A loud pounding made him look up. Giulia taking out her aggressions on the veal cutlets, as she pounded them very thin. She would roll them up with fillings for the involtini.

Gabriella pulled down a stockpot from the rack above the range and placed it on the burner over a medium flame. She added olive oil. When it began to shimmer, she threw in the pancetta, onions, carrots and celery. She sautéed them for a few minutes, creating what the Italians calla sofrito, then nodded to Antonio and he added the diced herbs to the pot. She stirred those for a minute, then added a few glugs of white wine to deglaze the pan. It occurred to him that he and Gabriella cooked really well together with unspoken communication.

When the wine had cooked down, Antonio added a jar of whole peeled plum tomatoes from Chiara's pantry, breaking them up with his hands over the pot. Some of the juices squirted Gabriella. She threatened him with the wooden spoon in her hand.

He lifted his hands. "The women in this kitchen are dangerous," he laughed. It felt good.

"Time for the vegetable stock," Gabriella instructed. "Try to keep it in the pot." Antonio poured it carefully, then added the beans, which he had drained. He threw in the rosemary stem. She reduced the heat and put a lid on the pot. It was time for them to enjoy a little wine and cheese with the others.

"Half glasses, Sylvio, *per favore*," Gabriella said. "We're working again tonight."

"I was afraid of that," Chiara said. "Can you tell us about today now?"

She and Antonio took turns explaining what they had found, as well as their theories. They left out the part about their suspicions of Captain Zampari, and the research Chia had begun that afternoon.

Umberto, who had been listening intently while stirring the pasta, spoke up. "I know it must be frustrating. Your theories make sense, but still not enough that a magistrate will issue you a warrant. I hope you find something tonight."

"I hope so, too," Gabriella said. "My instincts are telling me we will."

"Keep me posted," Umberto said. "We're planning to leave late-morning tomorrow."

Antonio checked the beans. They were just tender. He used a hand blender to puree them until some were fully pureed, while others remained whole. Most Italian cooks continue to puree until everything is smooth. He preferred his way, which gave the soup more texture. He added salt and pepper, then the farro, and let it simmer. When the farro appeared to be al dente, he tasted it, and declared it a masterpiece. They passed the pecorino around at the table to sprinkle on top.

*****

Antonio knew that he would miss these family meals when he made it home. He thought about all the meals he'd taken alone since losing Randi and Christina. The thought of doing it again made his melancholy mood return. *Maybe I should sell the restaurant to Shane,* he thought, *and stay here.* But he knew it wasn't the right time. Not yet.

Their minestra di farro received rave reviews, as did Umberto's Cacio e Pepe. But the highlight of the meal was the vitello involtini—veal roll-ups—stuffed with prosciutto, spinach, mushrooms, and sage leaves. It would be etched in his memory for a very long time.

Chapter Forty-two

Sunday, late evening

C hiara agreed to let them borrow her car, a black Volvo XC90 SUV. It had over two hundred thousand miles on it, and the smell of cheese permeated the inside. Otherwise, it was in spotless condition. Chia drove, with Marina as her passenger. They found a good surveillance spot and took up position in an olive grove, about a hundred meters north of the entrance to Tenuta di Carpinteria. Gabriella, Antonio and Giulia found a spot in a wooded glen to the south. It was well concealed but slightly elevated, giving them an excellent line of sight. It was almost 10:00 PM.

They decided to change up their rotation. They would start at 11:00 again. Antonio would go first, from 11:00 to 1:00, then the girls would take ninety-minute shifts. Gabriella would take the mid-shift, followed by Giulia. They would knock off at 4:00 AM. Gabriella texted Chia their plan and asked for their schedule, so they would know who to communicate with if needed. Chia would be taking their first shift.

Antonio poured a cup of coffee, hoping the caffeine would dissipate by the time he was ready to sleep. He took a sip and looked at Gabriella. "Tell me about these instincts of yours that make you think we're going to find something tonight?"

"Just a feeling. I have learned to trust them, though I cannot always explain why."

He considered that. He had experienced similar things. But his were only right about half the time. He hoped hers were better. "I saw you and Chia go off to talk after dinner. Did she learn anything this afternoon?"

"Yes. Zampari has a lot of money."

"How much?"

"More than four-hundred thousand Euros in various accounts. There may be others she has yet to find."

"That's a lot for a Carabinieri Captain. He didn't appear to be beyond his late thirties. Could be an inheritance. Any large deposits recently?"

"She did not get that far yet. She has someone working on it."

"What? Who? Are you sure that's a good idea?" Antonio asked.

"Our Europol friend, Marco Calore? Apparently, he feels he owes her for all her help in Firenze."

Antonio understood. Chia's research skills had been a key factor in finding Raphael and exposing a plot against the prime minister of Italy.

Giulia leaned forward at the mention of Marco's name. Antonio had suspected for a while that she had a crush on the handsome Spaniard, twenty years her senior.

"You think Zampari's on the take?" Antonio asked.

"It would not surprise me."

Antonio nodded. "Marco is a valuable asset to have on our side. Have they discovered anything unusual about Jacopo Bellini?"

"Only that he is cash poor and living beyond his means."

"We suspected as much. Does that change your thinking about him as a suspect for his mother's murder?"

"Not really," Gabriella answered.

"Because of your instincts?" Giulia piped up from the rear seat.

Gabriella turned toward her. "Yes. Because of my instincts."

They stopped and watched a pair of headlights pass by. The vehicle did not look familiar, and passed by the turn into the winery. "What about Jacopo's associates?" Antonio asked. "The guys he put in place at the winery?"

"Still unknown."

Gabriella's text notification sounded. It was Chia. She read it aloud. "Marco says Zampari has been depositing $25,000 euros a month for the last year."

"I'd say that confirms your suspicions," Antonio said. "No wonder he got upset when you took over his crime scene. He was probably covering for someone."

"Or maybe he did it himself," Giulia said. They both turned and looked at her.

"Very possible," they both answered, almost simultaneously. Giulia smiled victoriously and plopped back on her seat.

*****

The first hour dragged on like Seattle freeway traffic on a Friday evening. Antonio was getting antsy. He had his doubts about Gabriella's instincts. The clock rolled past midnight and he needed to relieve himself. He made sure the dome light was switched off and quietly opened the door. He could tell by their breathing that the girls were asleep.

He emptied his bladder behind a tree and walked back to the car. The night was getting cold, but he decided to remain outside to stay alert. He leaned against the car and looked up. The cumulus clouds, moving southwest to northeast, covered about a third of the sky. The remaining sky was as clear as crystal. It seemed like he could see a million stars. In some places it was hard to tell where the stars left off and the scattered lights on the distant hills began. The clouds to the east were backlit by the rising moon.

A sky like tonight's never failed to put life in perspective. He felt small—a grain of sand in a universe with no end. *Did you really create all of this God?* he wondered. He had never given credence to the theory of evolution. The universe was too vast, too complex. And here he was on this miraculous planet— earth—with conditions perfectly balanced to sustain life. Then there was the astonishing complexity of the human mind and body. He thought it was more farfetched that it all came about by a series of accidents, than by design.

Are you out there, God? He whispered. He heard no reply. He thought about all the evil he'd seen in recent weeks. He couldn't get the image of Marianna's body out of his mind. *Why, God? Why do you allow such evil to exist?* It was a question man had wrestled with since the beginning of time. You could read it in the Psalms. He believed that somehow the answer lay with the free will which God had granted to man.

Once again, he became keenly aware of the night sounds. Crickets—known as *la cicala*—sang their tune, accompanied by the gentle sound of the leaves rustling in the breeze. Somewhere in the distance he heard the hoot of an owl. It was more than the sounds that filled his senses. His nose picked up the aromas of the night, the scent of early spring blossoms on the trees, and the musty aroma of the earth.

His mind began to wander. He found himself thinking of his family back home. He missed his son, Jonathan, and wife, Leah. He wondered how their brewery was doing with the pandemic. He especially missed their twins, five-month-old Randall and Christina, named for their grandmother and aunt whom they would never know. He thought about his mother, recovering from Covid-19; and his brother-in-law Matthew, recovering from an operation to remove a cancerous brain tumor.

The feeling of being torn in two returned. It would be easier if he knew he could come and go as he pleased, but travel restrictions were getting tighter by the day. *If you're there, God, it sure would be nice if you would tell me what I should do.*

Seemingly from nowhere, a thought came into his mind … *I have called you to help bring justice in this world … to make right those things which are wrong.*

He was stunned. He wondered if he had just heard the voice of God? It felt like it. He wrote it off to an overactive imagination. But he couldn't shake the feeling.

As his mind wrestled with these thoughts, the distant whine of an engine rose above the other night sounds. It didn't sound like a car—more like a diesel truck. *Like the kind of truck that drove Andrea and Bria off the bridge,* he thought. The whine grew louder, until it became a deep vibrato. It was coming from the south. He moved next to a tree to get a better view that direction. After what seemed like forever, the truck appeared over a rise. It looked just like the truck in the CCTV photo Chia had sent them. He tried to see if there was any visible damage on the passenger side. He was on the wrong side of the road to tell.

He stepped behind the tree as the truck drew closer, then passed by. It turned into the entrance to the winery. He opened the car door and roused Gabriella. She awoke in a momentary stupor. "A truck pulled into the winery," he said. She sat up quickly and climbed from the car.

Antonio retrieved the binoculars. Gabriella pulled out Chiara's camera with the long lens. Giulia came to and clambered out of the back seat. "What's going on?" she whispered sleepily. Antonio explained without taking his eyes from the binoculars. His ears picked up the deep, aggressive barking of the Cane Corso dogs as the truck rolled past the house and stopped in front of the building that they believed to be the truck barn. A floodlight came on, probably set off by a motion sensor. Four people emerged from the main house: Alida, Rocco, Donato, and a man he didn't recognize. Antonio heard the camera clicking away. Then he heard the text notification on his phone. He handed the binoculars to Giulia.

It was from Chia. *You seeing this?*

Yes.

Not a great view from here. Should we move?

Antonio checked with Gabriella. She confirmed his opinion. *No,* he typed. *Lay low. We have a good view.*

He took the binoculars back and raised them to his brow. Two men climbed down from the truck and were shaking hands with the others. All except Alida, who walked over to a keypad next to the large metal door on the truck garage. She punched some buttons and the door rolled upward. Antonio could see a second truck in the garage; it appeared to be the same model. The two men climbed back into their truck and pulled into the garage. They opened the back and began to unload some wooden crates, which they stacked against the wall. There were about a dozen of them. They appeared larger than wine crates.

Gabriella held up her camera and zoomed in on one of the photos. "It's them," she said breathlessly.

"You sure?"

"Positive." She showed Antonio the image, then pulled out her phone and showed him the photo Chia had sent her a few days ago. The images were pixelated and blurred to varying degrees, but he was pretty sure it was the same guys.

"Might be the same truck, too," he said. "If it is, it appears to have been repaired. I couldn't tell for sure. But it has license plates now."

"Did you see those wood crates they were unloading?" she asked.

"Yes. They don't look like wine crates. And I've never seen drugs stored in wooden crates. If I were a gambling man, my bet would be on weapons."

"My thoughts exactly."

She pulled out her phone. "I'm calling Umberto."

Antonio was about to remind her it was the middle of the night, but she was already holding the phone to her ear. She must have had his number on speed dial. He listened as she spoke. "Umberto. Gabriella. There is a truck that arrived here. It is being driven by the same men who ran Andrea and Bria off the bridge. I have photos to prove it. We think it might be the same truck, too. It's definitely the same model. I need a warrant."

She listened for several beats, nodding. "Yes, I'll send them to you," she said. "*Bene, bene, grazie.*" She hung up. "He is going to call his friend, the magistrate in Arezzo. He needs these pictures. How do I get him the ones from the Nikon?"

"Doesn't Giulia have her laptop? We could download them."

"That's right. But I doubt the email would work out here."

He nodded. "You'll need to take a shot of the picture with your cell phone then. Hand me the camera." He pulled up the image and zoomed in. She snapped a picture. It wasn't perfect, but it would have to do for now. She texted the pictures to Umberto.

"Now we wait," she said with a shiver. "I'm calling Chia." She got in the car, while he lifted the binoculars to his eyes again. He leaned against the car, scanning the garage. After unloading the crates, they closed the garage and everyone entered the villa. Long minutes rolled by. There was no movement.

He suddenly felt a pounding vibration and turned to the car. Gabriella was slamming her fists against the steering wheel. Her whole body was shaking with sobs.

Chapter Forty-three

Sunday, late evening

Antonio climbed into the passenger seat and put his hand on Gabriella's shoulder. "What's wrong?*"*

It took her a minute. "The magistrate refuses to give us the warrant!"

"Wait, I thought you were talking to Chia?"

"I was. Then Umberto called. The magistrate says the quality of the pictures are not good enough to prove that these are the same men."

"Show me those pics again." He studied them carefully, trying to see without bias. He told her what she didn't want to hear, "He's right, Gabriella. And you probably know the quality suffers every time you text them … you to Umberto … Umberto to the magistrate. And it's possible we're just seeing what we want to see … what we believe to be true."

She looked at him like he was from Mars. "You are wrong! I know it is them!"

"What were you planning with Chia?"

"To go in and make the arrest."

"All of us, or the two of you?"

She shook her head. "You know I can't take you or Giulia. And Marina doesn't have the right experience."

"So, you were going in there two against six? What the hell were you thinking?"

"Don't try to tell me …" She buried her hands in her face. After a minute she sat up straight. "Those men killed my brother and Bria! And they have killed at least two others that we know of. If they kill somebody else, that is on me. They have to be stopped!" She pulled out her Beretta.

"You're right, Gabriella. But not like this! Not in this frame of mind, you'll get yourself killed! Chia, too."

"It is our job, Antonio."

"Not without a warrant, it isn't! Even if you make it out alive, you'll compromise the case. Any half-way decent lawyer would have these guys back on the street before breakfast."

She stared out the window. A look of defeat crossed her face. "That is what Umberto said."

"And Chia? She was willing to go in there, just the two of you?"

She shook her head slowly. "She did not think we should go in without backup. And only then if we were able to get the warrant."

Gabriella's phone rang. She put it on speaker. It was Chia. "The truck is coming up the drive."

"We are on them!" Gabriella said. "Stay on surveillance."

"But what will …" Gabriella had already hung up. They watched the truck come down the drive with no headlights. It turned south on the road, then turned their lights on. Gabriella rolled down the window and told Giulia to get in. She looked at them with concern. The truck rolled past and Gabriella pulled onto the road about fifty meters behind.

"*Merda,* what are we doing, Gabriella?" Antonio asked. "You're blowing our cover! What do you hope to accomplish? We can't stop them."

"Stop trying to control my every move!"

Antonio was ready to explode but knew he had to stay in control. He was angry at Gabriella. Angry at the magistrate. Mostly he was angry at the men who had killed several people, and were now likely driving the truck in front of them— probably headed back to the safety of Apulia.

Angry or not, he had to do the right thing. He had to keep Gabriella from doing something she would regret. He was trying to decide his best course of action when the truck pulled onto the shoulder. Gabriella did the same, keeping her distance. She checked her gun. Antonio checked his. He heard a click from behind him and knew Giulia was doing the same. They sat in tense silence, staring at the red taillights of the truck. Antonio stole a glance at Gabriella. Tears ran down her cheeks. He kept his mouth shut. But inside, he was deeply worried about the future of their relationship, a relationship built on a foundation of crisis. *God, I sure could use your help about now,* he thought.

Moments ticked by. A few minutes felt like hours. Then without a word, Gabriella put the Audi in drive, pulled a U-turn, and headed back toward Chia's location. Antonio turned his head and watched the truck pull back on the road and continue their journey south. He wondered what would have happened if they had approached them, or driven past. It might have become a war zone. He breathed a sigh of relief.

Chapter Forty-four

Monday morning

Antonio heard gunshots in the distance. Or did he? His mind hovered somewhere between a dream and reality. He tried to make sense of the dream. He remembered a long tunnel which got darker and darker, until there was no light at all. He couldn't see anything. But somehow, he knew Gabriella was at the other end of it reaching out to him. Then he remembered her whisper, "Antonio, help. Save me." It left him with a sense of dread.

He looked at the clock. It was just past seven. He had slept maybe four hours. The sun shone gently on the sheer white curtains. All he could hear now were birds singing, and the sound of a tractor far off. Then he heard them again … faraway gunshots.

He pushed back the curtains and opened the old wood-framed window. He leaned on the sill, breathing in the fresh Tuscan air. On either side, pale green shutters were pushed wide, their paint fading. He saw Chiara coming from the barn, humming some tune he didn't recognize. Her wavy hair, streaked grey and black, was pulled up in the back. She was not an elegant woman, but had her own beauty. Tall, slender with sinewy muscles, she strode with her chin high. The word *noble* crossed his mind.

He pulled on a pair of jeans and a t-shirt and went barefoot up the cool ceramic steps to meet her, drawn by the aroma of fresh coffee. She walked in the French doors and looked at him, shaking her head. "It's going to take more than coffee to make you human again."

"*Grazie!* Love you too, *zia*." He kissed her on the forehead. "Did I hear gunshots or was I dreaming?"

"Hunters. Common around here."

"Are we the only ones up?"

"You missed Gabriella. She was up at the crack of dawn. Said something about going to take soil samples. She seemed anxious. Is she okay, Antonio?"

"God, I hope so." He had left his phone in his room. He rushed down the stairs, pulled it off the charger and dialed her number. It went straight to voice mail. "Damn it!" he said. *Where are you?* He sent her a text. He sat on the edge of the bed, waiting. After a few minutes he tried calling again. This time he left an urgent voice message.

Nature called him into the bathroom. He looked in the mirror and understood what Chiara was talking about. He looked like someone he would avoid on the street—with bloodshot eyes and his hair every which way. He washed his face, wet his hair and combed it, put in eye drops, and threw on a clean shirt. Looking less like an ogre, he headed back upstairs, still barefoot, looking for the cup of coffee he'd left behind.

"Marginally better," Chiara said, running her fingers through his hair. "Dump out that cold coffee and pour a fresh cup." He obeyed, and took a seat at the kitchen table. "Were you able to get hold of her?"

"No. I'm worried, Chiara."

She sat down and gripped his hands in hers. "I've been praying. God will watch over her. He listens to me you know. A lot better than your uncle Sylvio does." She laughed. "Let me make you some breakfast."

Before he could answer, his phone rang. He grabbed it, expecting Gabriella. It was General Marcello Bianchi.

"*Pronto*, Antonio. I've been trying to reach Gabriella. She tried to call me but it only rang once. She didn't leave a message."

"I'm worried, Marcello. She left while I was sleeping … told my aunt she was going to take soil samples. I assume at Tenuta di Carpinteria. We've wanted samples from there but haven't been able to get a warrant." He explained about the soil found at the home of Marianna Bellini, and their suspicions.

"She went alone?"

"Yes. She must have slept little, if at all." Antonio explained the high points about their stake-out, what they had seen, and their failed attempt to get a warrant.

"I'm guessing she did not react well to that?"

"Not at all." Antonio didn't want to say more, afraid he'd already told Marcello more than he should. But Marcello and Gabriella had been investigative partner in Siena for years. He probably knew her better than Antonio did.

"Yeah, I can imagine. She's always been bull-headed."

"You should have warned me," Antonio said. He heard a laugh on the other end. "Marcello, I need to go. I need to find her. She probably sneaked onto their property for soil samples. I can bring Chia with me."

"No. We need more backup. Something might have happened. Either way, we need that warrant, unless we find evidence they've abducted or harmed her."

"We haven't given up on the warrant. Last night Chia called Marco. He feels obligated to her after Firenze. She says they have more advanced software for cleaning up photos. She sent him the original file of the photos Gabriella took. That in itself will improve it. She also asked him to look at the CCTV footage again for a better shot of the guys driving the truck. He and his people are working on it."

"Another of my people going behind my back. We'll deal with that later."

"There's one other possibility, too. Ginevra Barbieri is trying to dry out the phone I found in the pond at Marianna's villa so we can access it. There was no phone in the house so we're pretty sure it's hers. It might give us a clue. There has to be a reason her killer would try to get rid of it. Sheer dumb luck that I found it."

"Ask Chia to follow up on that. I'll head your way in a few minutes, after I see if I can round up any officers on short notice. It's a challenge right now. One of the people in our station got Covid-19 so we had to quarantine everyone who'd been in contact with him. I'll call Captain Zampari also … see if he or his people can join us."

"I wouldn't do that," Antonio said. Marcello went silent on the other end.

"*Merda*! Don't tell me." He paused a few beats. "My gut's been telling me not to trust him. What can you tell me?"

Antonio filled him in.

"You think the people under him are compromised?"

"No idea. But I met a young corporal who was at the villa with him yesterday. Name patch said Garza. He seems trustworthy, if my instincts are any good."

"I'll see if I can reach him without raising any red flags. Listen, no one, I repeat, no one, goes on that property until I get there! Where's a good spot to rendezvous?"

Antonio thought for a moment. "The church of Madonna di San Biago below the town. It's only a few kilometers from the winery. Do you know it?"

"Is the Pope Catholic? I'll let you know when I'm thirty minutes out."

*****

Antonio found Chia and Marina asleep in Gabriella's room. Gabriella had told them she would share Giulia's room. He woke them and told them what was going on. He debated if he should wake Giulia, and decided on a yes. She would rightly be angry if he left her in the dark. He told her about Gabriella, and asked if she had come to bed last night.

"Yeah. For a little while. She was so restless she was keeping me awake. I finally dozed off. A while later I woke up and she wasn't here. I'm so sorry, *Zio* Tonio. I should have checked on her."

"Not your fault," he said. But the look of guilt on her face didn't go away.

"Let me try to call her," she said, grabbing her phone. "She might just be avoiding you after last night."

"I was only trying …"

"You don't need to explain it to me, *zio*. You said what you had to say. I was proud of you, actually." She dialed. It went straight to voice mail. She left a message, then followed up with a text.

Within fifteen minutes, everyone had congregated in the kitchen, including Sylvio, Umberto, and Angelica. Chiara was busy at the stove. Antonio could smell a wonderful aroma that reminded him of his childhood.

Angelica walked up and hooked her arm in his. "We're going to stay until you find Gabriella," she said. He tried to convince her it wasn't necessary but she wouldn't hear it. "Maybe we can be of some assistance," Umberto added.

Chiara walked over to the table carrying a platter loaded with pancakes. "Necci," she said. "I remember how much you liked these when you were a kid, Antonio." Memories flooded back … *Nonna* Valentina mixing the chestnut flour with water, and making these crispy pancakes in her flat cast-iron pan known as a *testi*. "I inherited her pan," Chiara added. "I layered these with my homemade ricotta, sweetened with honey from my neighbor."

"You shouldn't have troubled yourself, *zia*," Antonio said, though there was no way he was turning them down. "We haven't time."

"Nonsense! You're not leaving this house on an empty stomach. Besides, the general said he would give you thirty-minutes notice of his arrival. You haven't heard from him yet and the church of the Madonna is ten minutes away. Those of you who need to go can eat first. There are more coming. *Mangiamo!*"

Antonio slid a few of the pancakes onto his plate. No one bothered to sit down. They ate standing around the kitchen island while Umberto made more coffee. Antonio wished he had time to relish each amazing bite, but he wolfed them down, thinking of things which needed to be done. He pulled Sylvio aside. "Can we borrow your rifle and shotgun again? Our pistols were in Gabriella's car."

"Come with me," Sylvio said. He led him to his den where he kept a gun safe. He opened it and pulled out a rifle and shotgun, and boxes of shells. There were two additional hunting rifles and another shotgun. "And here," he said, handing Antonio a handgun. "My pistol from when I served in the Royal Italian Army."

"I didn't know …"

"It was in the sixties. You were only a *bambino*." He took the pistol back, pulled it apart, and peered down the barrel. "Beretta M1934. Nine-millimeter. That's the year they first made them but they remained in production for decades. I keep it like new." He reassembled it, except for the magazine, and handed it to Antonio. It was a compact, semi-automatic, with a relatively short barrel. Sylvio was already loading the magazine. He handed it to him along with the rest of the carton of shells.

Chapter Forty-five

Monday morning

Chia was hanging up her phone when they emerged. She looked at the guns and shook her head. "Self-defense only. Understood?" She wasn't kidding. Antonio was beyond caring.

"That was Ginevra," she said. "I called to see where we're at. She says Marianna's phone is dry enough that they should be able to access it, but it's password protected. She found a computer tech willing to come out of quarantine to work on it. She thinks she'll have something later this morning."

"Good. Really good," Antonio said. His sense of dread eased a little. He knew every step in the right direction was crucial. Suddenly, a thought came to mind, "Chia, can't they put a trace on Gabriella's phone?"

"We already tried. No signal. Either it's off, the battery's dead, or it's out of range." She looked at him intently. "There's one more thing, Antonio … Ginevra says Gabriella called her before six o'clock this morning … inquiring if the soil samples taken from Villa Sant'Angelo matched what we found in the house. They didn't. That explains why Gabriella was so set on getting samples from Carpinteria. She's desperately looking for a way to get that search warrant. But she's not thinking clearly. Those would be inadmissible anyway without the warrant first."

He nodded as he stared off into space. "But why no phone signal?" he murmured, knowing that no one in the room knew the answer any better than he did. *Maybe she just turned it off,* he thought, *so I couldn't bother her. She must have known I'd try to stop her.* But the longer they went without hearing from her, the more worried he became. He was afraid she'd gone looking for more than soil samples and got herself in trouble. He refused to even consider the worst-case scenario, but it hung over him like a dark cloud somewhere in the back of his mind.

*****

Antonio convinced Giulia to stay behind. He didn't need anyone else to worry about. She wasn't happy about it. He rode with Chia and Marina, in Chia's Carabinieri Fiat Bravo. If they needed to go onto the winery property, it would be an official visit this time. As Chia negotiated the winding road, Antonio tried Gabriella again. Same results. His fear was now beginning to cloud his judgment. *Please, God. Please keep her safe.*

As if to bolster his faith, La Chiesa di Madonna di San Biago came into view. The Renaissance masterpiece, built of travertine, stood tall and majestic in the morning sun. It was located at the bottom of a drive—lined with cypress trees—coming down from Montepulciano. Antonio knew a little about its history. It had been designed and built by another Antonio—Antonio da Sangallo the Elder—in the sixteenth century. The story of its origin was linked to a purported miracle. Two women and a shepherd—passing in front of a fresco of Saint Francis and the Madonna—the Christ child on her lap—claimed they saw the Virgin's eyes move. He didn't know what to think of the story, but was desperate for a miracle of his own.

Chia glanced at him with concern. She was about to say something when her phone rang. It was linked to the car via Bluetooth. She hit the answer button on the steering wheel.

Marco Calore's voice came over the speakers. *"Pronto,* Chia. I have an update for you. We're making progress. I have a member of my team working on the photo Gabriella shot last night. Having the original file made a big difference. And I spent the night crawling through surveillance footage and found something. The truck left the highway onto a small country road after the bridge incident. I thought I lost them, but got lucky. They showed up a while later on a highway heading south. Just so happens there was a new high-resolution CCTV on the road. I got a better shot of your two guys. It's definitely the same two guys that showed up at the winery last night. I'm going to email these photos so that we don't lose resolution. Where should I send them?"

"We're on the road. I'd like you to send them to Umberto, Antonio's cousin …"

"I know who he is," Marco said. "Send me his email."

"I'll have Antonio text it to you." She thought for a moment, then added, "Can you also text those pictures to Antonio for us to look at?" He agreed and was gone.

Antonio phoned Umberto to get his email address and told him to expect Marco's email shortly. Umberto promised to forward that to the magistrate immediately and follow up. He forwarded the email address to Marco, and took a deep breath. Moments later he received a text reply with a photo, then another, then a third.

The first was a much-improved image of the photo Gabriella shot last night. The second was a close-up taken from the CCTV footage that Marco found. There was no sun glare on the windshield, and it showed their faces clearly. The third was a broader view showing the whole truck with damage to the passenger side clearly visible. It appeared the hubcap on the front tire was missing. *If I were a magistrate,* Antonio thought, *these would be good enough for me.*

He looked up from his phone and saw they had arrived at the church. There was no sign of Marcello or his people yet. Antonio showed the photos to Chia and Marina, then got out to stretch his legs.

He was surprised to see the doors of the church open. He wandered over and out of the sunlight into the dimly lit interior. It took a minute for his eyes to adjust. The only soul to be seen was an old janitor swirling a mop across the floor.

The baroque interior inspired awe. The floorplan was laid out like a Greek cross, with a central dome, flanked by two bell towers, situated in the arms of the cross. Above the ornate altar a stained-glass window depicted the Madonna surrounded by angels and saints. Within one of the arches to the side was a fresco—painted by Angelo Righi—of Jesus hanging on the cross. Antonio became transfixed upon his broken and bloodied body, absorbing all that it meant. He remembered something Father Bruno told him recently. "Comfort doesn't mean that the pain goes away." He was now facing new pain … new fears. He whispered another prayer and felt a certain peace and comfort come over him.

He felt a hand on his shoulder. "General Bianchi is here," Chia whispered. He turned without a word and followed her into the bright sunlight, squinting to see the Carabinieri vehicle, an armored Jeep Cherokee. He knew the man standing next to the general. Carlo Ricci had been Chia's partner when Antonio first met him in Firenze. He considered how little he knew about the man, even though they had been in and out of each other's lives for more than a week.

"This is everyone we've got for now," General Marcello Bianchi said. He was wearing his general's uniform, something Antonio had only seen a couple of times. Carlo Ricci looked handsome in his lieutenant's uniform. "I managed to get the number for that young Corporal Garza. I called him directly and asked if we could talk privately. He told me no. Later, he was able to get away and called me back. He's traveling with Captain Zampari today. He was glad I called … said he had some things he needed to tell me, but only in person. That's as far as we got. I didn't want to raise any red flags by trying to pull him away. We'll deal with Zampari later."

Antonio showed him the photos that Marcello had sent, and explained their renewed efforts to get a warrant. "Chia has additional photos taken by Gabriella last night on her phone." Chia pulled out her phone. There were pictures of the truck, Alida opening the garage, and wooden crates being unloaded and stacked. The general asked her to forward them to him.

"I hope to God that warrant comes through soon," Marcello said gravely. "I can call the magistrate myself …"

Chia's phone rang, interrupting him. She looked at it, answered, and put it on speaker. "*Pronto* Ginevra. I've got General Bianchi and the others listening in. What have you got?"

"We were able to pull a phone and text log from Marianna Bellini's phone. There were three calls in and out on the morning of her death. The first was a call from her friend, Vito Crivello, president of the *consorzio*. The second was an outgoing call to her son. Shortly afterward, she received a call and a text from a burner phone. There was no name associated with it in her contacts list. The call was about an hour prior to her estimated time of death … the text, about 45 minutes later, said '*Just arriving*'."

"Any way you can track the burner phone?" Marcello asked.

"Your computer tech is sharp. In the best of times, it would be a long shot. But with so many of the shops closing down, I highly doubt it."

"*Grazie*, Sergeant Barbieri," Marcello said. "Good to have you on the team. Now, a question. Are you available to head back this way and join us?"

"Absolutely, sir. I can be there in an hour."

"And who is the computer tech assisting you?"

"Amara Bertoli, sir. Like I said, she's a sharp one."

"See if she can join you."

Ginevra disappeared for a moment, then returned. "She'd be delighted, sir."

"Have her bring her laptop and whatever else she needs for downloading cell phones."

"Got it." She hung up.

Antonio looked at Marcello. "We're not waiting that long, are we General?" He usually called him Marcello but decided on the formality in front of his troops.

"Depends on that warrant. We could go and ask questions, but we wouldn't be able to search the property without it, unless they gave their permission. From what you've told me, that'll never happen. Do you know which magistrate Umberto is dealing with? I can call to find out the status. I've …"

They were interrupted again, this time by Antonio's phone. He put it on speaker. Umberto got right to the point, "*Pronto,* Antonio. You've got your warrant. Or more accurately, he wants to send it directly to General Bianchi. He says he knows him. Has he arrived yet?"

"I'm standing right here," Marcello said. "What is the magistrate's name?"

"Donati, Matteo Donati. You guys know each other?"

"You can say that. Glad we had you on our side. He and I have had our run-ins."

Umberto laughed. "I'm not surprised. Glad to be of assistance. The warrant should show up on your phone within minutes. By the way, Chiara had the television on. The newsman announced that the quarantine lockdown has been extended throughout all the northern regions. They expect it may go nationwide any day now. Godspeed to you. Find our girl."

"Let's move," General Bianchi said. "Antonio, you're with me and Ricci."

"I have some weapons in Chia's vehicle, sir. I know I'm not authorized …"

"Leave them. You're right. You can't carry. But if you need to defend yourself, I have all the weapons you'll need. While I'm driving, text Ginevra Barbieri and tell her to meet us at the Tenuta."

Chapter Forty-six

Monday, late morning

L ess than two weeks ago, Antonio had been Marcello's driver in Firenze after the General was injured in a knife attack by a Nigerian henchman. Now, Marcello drove the armored Jeep Cherokee like a man possessed, with Chia's little Fiat trying to keep up.

They pulled into the long driveway of Tenuta di Carpinteria and sped past the immaculate rows of budding vines. They pulled into the circular drive, which brought them toward the grand front entrance. Marcello came to a skidding stop, inches behind Alida's red Ferrari. Antonio trailed the General and his troops as they marched up the stairs to the door and rang the bell. It took a few minutes before anyone answered. Finally, Alida opened the door, dressed in a short, low-cut black dress. She didn't speak a word … nor make an effort to invite them in … just stared at them like they were unwanted visitors from another planet. That didn't stop General Bianchi. He presented the warrant and entered, followed by his team.

"We've come to search your premises, *Signora* Tarantino."

"Fontana," she corrected, with a stony glare.

"My apologies. Now, if you'll excuse us, we have a search to conduct. If any buildings are locked, we'll need access. I need you to gather your family and anyone else on the premises.

Nobody touches or moves anything until we've completed our search. And no calls. We'll need to gather your cell phones for phone searches." He held out his hand. She handed her phone over with a look that could kill a lesser man.

"My son, Rocco, isn't here," Alida said. "He's gone to make one more delivery while we're still able."

Merda, Antonio thought, his heart sinking. *He probably has Gabriella.*

"And where exactly is this delivery to take place?" General Bianchi asked.

Antonio watched her eyes flicker, then decide to tell a lie. "A wine shop in Montevarchi." Antonio knew that Montevarchi was about a half hour north. He figured she would choose a place in that direction to misdirect them. If they were transporting Gabriella somewhere—alive or dead—it would probably be south—likely all the way to Apulia. He saw a look of disbelief on Chia's face. She pulled out her cell phone and fired off a text.

"We will need his cell number then," Chia said. Alida rattled it off. Chia typed it into her phone and fired off another text.

"What is the purpose of your search, General ..." Alida looked at his name patch ... "Bianchi?" She spit it out like a dirty word.

"I know you've been questioned about the truck and drivers who killed the wine inspector, Andrea Marinelli, and his wife, by running them off the road. We know that the men who drove that truck visited your winery late last night."

"You are mistaken, General, we ..."

"Don't bother finishing your lie, *signora*. We have photographs. Would you care to see them?"

"I'm sorry. If any such activity occurred, it was without my knowledge."

"Oh, you knew about it. It was you who opened the truck garage for them. That's where we would like to begin our search. You can give us access. Then Lieutenant Ricci," he waved his hand toward him, "will accompany you to gather the remainder of your family and workers. He'll bring everyone here and keep an eye on you." Ricci nodded.

They walked together to the truck garage and Alida entered the combination on the keypad. Antonio expected her to be nervous. She wasn't. As soon as it opened, he saw why. The wooden crates were gone. The garage was large enough to hold three trucks. Only one remained.

"Where are the crates that were unloaded here last night, *signora*?"

She decided not to deny their existence. "Those were wine crates, General Bianchi … staged for today's delivery."

The General pulled out his phone and retrieved the pictures. "Those do not appear to be wine crates to me, *signora*. And why would they come off another truck?"

"I'm through answering your questions, General, without my counsel present. You haven't believed a word I've told you."

"Maybe because you haven't spoken a word of truth." He stared hard at her. "Are the other buildings unlocked, or will you have to let us in?"

"I'll need to let you in."

"You can unlock them while you are gathering your people. But first I need you to unlock the padlock on the back of that truck."

"I'm afraid I don't have the key. Transportation is Rocco's job. As I ..."

"No problem," Marcello interrupted. He turned to Antonio, "There's a pry bar in the rear compartment of the Cherokee. Please retrieve it for me." He handed him the keys. "Meanwhile, Lieutenant Ricci, please accompany *Signora* Fontana as she unlocks the other buildings and rounds up the others. Take them to the house and collect all of their cell phones. Keep everyone in one room but far enough apart that they can't whisper to one another. I don't want them conspiring about what additional lies to tell us." He made eye contact with Alida Fontana as he spoke those final words.

Antonio watched Ricci and the *signora* walk toward the wine production building as he headed toward the Jeep Cherokee. A few minutes later he returned, and pried off the clasp which held the padlock on the back of the truck. He rolled the door up. It was empty except for some straps used to secure loads.

Marcello began to give orders, "Chia, you and Marina search every nook and cranny of this building. Anyplace that a person could be hidden. Forget about the little stuff for now. Our priority is to find Gabriella, if she's here. Antonio, you and I will check out the wine production building. If we don't find her, we'll divide up the remaining buildings. We'll do the main house last. If they're hiding Gabriella, that's likely the last place it would be. Stay alert, everyone! These people are deceptive and dangerous."

"General," Antonio said. "My gut tells me Rocco has Gabriella. They're probably headed ..."

"South." Marcello finished his sentence. "I thought of that. Chia ..."

"Already done, sir," she interrupted. "I texted Marco Calore. He and his Europol people are checking the CCTV feeds heading away from here and attempting to track his cell phone. I told them to look south first." She looked at Antonio and smiled knowingly, then added, "They are also using the GPS from Gabriella's vehicle to look for her car."

"Good job," Marcello said. "Let us know as soon as you hear anything."

*****

They searched every building on the grounds and found nothing. No sign of Gabriella. No evidence of anything unusual. They returned to the main house just as Ginevra Barbieri and Amara Bertoli were arriving in Marina's Alfa Romeo Stelvio SUV.

They entered the main house together. General Bianchi instructed Amara Bertoli to begin downloading the cell phone data. She took them outside to work out of the back of the Alfa. He then asked Chia, Carlo Ricci, Marina, and Ginevra to search the house, while he and Antonio stayed with the others. There were five people present: Alida, her son Donato, the unknown man they had seen last night, and two others. They all had the look of southern Italians. Antonio looked carefully at the two he had not seen previously. They were not the men who drove the truck last night. They appeared to be farmhands.

General Bianchi asked Alida to introduce the others. He then said he'd be taking each one aside to speak with them, while Antonio watched the others.

"They won't talk to you without an attorney present," Alida said. Antonio was sure her message was heard loud and clear by all present.

"That will be for each of them to decide for themselves, *signora*," the General answered.

He started with Alida's son, Donato. One by one they left the room, and one by one they returned after several minutes. Antonio watched Marcello's face. If he was getting nowhere, he didn't betray it. *He must be one hell of a poker player*, Antonio thought. Through it all, Alida appeared calm.

The others returned while the General was outside with the last person. He was the man Antonio had seen last night. It turned out his name was Ettore Alghero. Alida had introduced him as their winemaker. He may have been, but Antonio suspected it wasn't his only role.

Chia's phone rang. She stepped outside to take it. When she returned, she looked worried. The General returned a couple of minutes later.

"Now that you've found nothing, are you through with us, General?" Alida asked sharply.

"Chia, please check on the status of Inspector Bertoli's phone search," he said.

She went out and returned a few minutes later with the cell phones. "She was just finishing up, sir." She handed him a bag with the phones. He handed it to Alida Fontana. "*Buona giornata, signora.* We'll be in touch."

They exited the house, closed the grand doors, and gathered beyond the hearing of Alida and the others. Chia looked at the General. "Marco called, sir. They found Gabriella's vehicle. According to the tracker, it's just south of here, probably parked in the same copse of trees you guys hid in last night," she said, looking at Antonio. "Still no luck tracking her cell, nor Rocco Tarantino's. He probably powered it off. But we were right, the truck started north, but then took SP326 east and caught the A1 south. He left about an hour before we arrived. He was able to identify the driver as Rocco, but no sign of anyone else. He's watching all of the cameras. They are sporadic, but so far, they've tracked him beyond the turnoff to Orvieto."

"He's got a huge head start," Marcello said, as he grabbed his phone. "I'm calling in a chopper."

Chapter Forty-seven

Monday, mid-day

Antonio realized they had driven right past Gabriella's vehicle on their way to the house. She had hidden it further back in the trees than when they were surveilling the house last night. It felt like days ago. Marcello pulled his Jeep onto the shoulder. The others pulled up behind him. They all got out to inspect it and found it unlocked. There was nothing unusual, no sign of foul play. Antonio checked under the seat and found the lockboxes with the handguns. All three were accounted for. From all signs, if Gabriella had been abducted, it took place away from the vehicle.

Marcello received a text. They had located a pilot. A helicopter would be in the air within thirty minutes. He turned to Antonio. "Is there a place for a chopper to land at your uncle's winery? I'm going to have them pick up Captain Umeh and Lieutenant Ricci."

Antonio thought for a moment. "Not really, but there's plenty of open space at San Biago. I imagine the parking lot would still be empty."

"Of course. Of course. I should have thought of that." He called to make the arrangements, then turned to Chia and Ricci. "I'm putting the two of you on that chopper. It should arrive at San Biago in about forty minutes. So, you can help us search here for a while. There will be one additional officer onboard with the pilot. I'm forwarding you a copy of the search warrant. Your goal is to intercept the truck and inspect it. If you find anything, take Rocco Tarantino into custody."

"General, may I accompany them?" Antonio asked.

"Out of the question! I understand your frustration, Antonio. But it's too dangerous. If they find Gabriella, you'll be the first to know."

Antonio hung his head. He knew he would make the same decision. *Come on, Antonio. Pull it together*. He lifted his head and went to work.

Marcello placed a call to Marco Calore for an update on the truck's progress, then called his flight dispatcher. Meanwhile, Amara Bertoli continued analyzing the data she had downloaded from the phones of Alida and the others. While they were busy, Antonio, Chia, Ricci, Marina, and Ginevra began to search the area. Antonio was glad to have two forensic experts with them. It took only moments to find footprints, appearing to belong to Gabriella, which led from the car toward the road. It made sense that she would have crossed over to the vineyards. They crossed the road and found more of her prints. The soil was softer, making them easier to follow. About a hundred feet from the road, they found a spot where it appeared she had dug up some soil.

Ginevra bent down and used her hand to scoop some into a plastic bag. "She would have wanted multiple samples," she said, "from various parts of the vineyard. The soil changes."

The footprints continued deeper into the vineyard. They found a second spot dug up, then her steps turned toward the house. Antonio looked up. The upper floors of the house were visible over the top of the vines. *If it was light, they could have spotted her*. They found two more places where the soil had been dug up. Ginevra collected samples at each. They were still following Gabriella's trail when Marina Gallo spoke up. "Look," she pointed, "another set of footprints. They appear to be a man's boots." She bent down and touched one of the imprints. "They're fresh. They came from the direction of the house, then turn and intermingle with Gabriella's heading back that direction." They followed them until they reached a paved area. They had no idea which way they went from there.

Chia turned to Lieutenant Ricci. "We need to get going to meet that chopper." They all walked back to where Marcello was talking on his phone. He hung up and Chia gave him a quick update.

"News for you," the General said. "The truck is still on the A1 heading south. He's north of the E35 turnoff toward Roma. Marco will be watching to see which way they go there. I'm betting he'll stay on the A1. The chopper just lifted off. You better get moving." She and Ricci climbed into her Fiat and sped off toward the south.

General Bianchi gathered the others. "I hope they are watching from the house so they'll see us driving away. As soon as it's dark, we'll return for surveillance. Not likely there will be any comings or goings after our search, but you never know. These people have been unbelievably brazen." He turned to Antonio. "It would be helpful if we had Wi-Fi access. Do you think it's possible for us to set up a command post at your aunt and uncle's house?"

"I'm sure it will be. Let me call them to make sure." He dialed and spoke to Sylvio. "We're good."

*****

It was early afternoon when they drove past the faded wood sign announcing Fattoria Montieri, through the wrought iron gate, and up the long drive. The sun was warm but it appeared the weather was about to turn. The tall cumulus clouds gathering to the northwest looked menacing.

Sylvio invited them in for lunch. Marcello tried to decline, but Sylvio was not to be denied. They entered the house and found the rest of the family in the kitchen. Antonio's nostrils picked up the aromas of hot oil and melting cheese.

Everyone stopped what they were doing, anxious to find out about Gabriella. Amara and Ginevra interrupted, asking if there was a place they could work. Sylvio showed them to his den. When he returned, Antonio filled them in, answering dozens of questions in the process.

With anxiety written all over their faces, the family went back to their preparations. Angelica was prepping asparagus. Giulia was cutting up chunks of day-old bread, while Chiara was cutting up raw meat. Antonio saw Umberto furiously whisking something in a double boiler on the range. He leaned over his shoulder, and saw that it was egg yolks into melting cheese and cream. When it was smooth, he added butter and whisked some more.

Chiara spoke up. "We didn't have much time to prepare," she said. "So, we're having *fonduta,* a simple affair. There's hot oil, lamb, asparagus, and bread. You can cook the lamb and anything else you want in the oil. The cheese dip is made from Fontina Val d'Aosta. Antonio's favorite."

Antonio smiled, despite himself. Food had been the last thing on his mind until the aromas hit him and his stomach began to growl. They gathered around the large rustic table. The fondue was divided among four pots, two of oil, two of cheese. Giulia sat down next to Antonio. She gave him a worried look. "You okay?"

"No."

Before she could ask more, Marcello took charge, talking between bites. "As you know, Amara's been working on the phone and text logs from their phones. There were calls to and from Alida Fontana to two different burner phones which we've yet to identify. Neither were the same burner that contacted Marianna. There was a text from one of them about a half hour before we arrived. It simply asked, *Is it done yet?* To which she replied, *Yes.*"

"What's that supposed to mean?" Antonio asked, not even wanting to consider the possible implications.

"Wish we knew," Marcello said. "We could ask her but I'm certain all we'd get is more lies, or she'd play the attorney card again. I'd say one of those phones has to be Rocco." He turned to Ginevra Barbieri. "Fill them in on what you told me a few minutes ago."

She smiled proudly. "I brought a portable soil test kit with me. The soil samples we took from the vineyard this morning appear to be a match to the soil we found at Marianna Bellini's villa. Each sample was slightly different, but one in particular is extremely close. I'd say about ninety-nine percent accurate."

"That would be enough to uphold it in court," Umberto said. Antonio was seeing more and more what an asset he had been to them the last few days.

Marina added her two cents, "Everything points toward this Fontana-Tarantino family. But we still don't know who did what. We need more." Umberto nodded in agreement.

Marcello's text notification sounded. He looked at it. "From Chia," he said. "They've spotted the truck. They're looking for a good place to make the intercept." Marcello fired off a return text, *Proceed cautiously. Soil samples from winery matched the soil from Marianna's villa.*

He went quiet for a few beats, *"Merda,* I hope they can apprehend him without a gun battle. From everything you guys have told me, Rocco sounds like a loose cannon."

"He is," Antonio said. "Definitely is." The room went quiet. There were worry lines on every face.

Aunt Chiara did what she always did in times of crisis. She said a prayer out loud. Everyone nodded and said amen. Even Marcello, a man who said he had no faith.

After a few quiet moments, Umberto spoke. "I know you've had your concerns about Captain Zampari. Have you considered that he's the one using the other burner phone?"

"Crossed my mind," Marcello said. Antonio nodded agreement.

"Why don't you text his corporal, Mario Garza?" Antonio said. "See if he knows if Zampari has a second phone?"

Marcello didn't respond right away. His mind was elsewhere. "Good idea," he finally answered, then fired off a text message.

The return text was prompt. *Yes.*

Marcello texted back, *Any idea what he uses it for?*

Moments later, *No.*

Marcello texted again, *Where are you guys?*

Station.

Marcello considered his options. "Time to confront Zampari," he said. "I'm going outside to make this call." Antonio followed. Marcello didn't send him away, as he half-expected him to. Instead, he dialed his number and put it on speaker. There was no answer. It rang four times and went to voice mail. Marcello turned to Antonio. "Get those burner numbers from Amara." Antonio did so, considering what Marcello had in mind. "Which one first?" Marcello asked.

"The first one," Antonio said. "That's the one that texted Alida's phone." Marcello nodded and dialed. It rang and rang until they finally hung up. Obviously, it had no voice mail set up.

They looked at one another. "You thinking what I'm thinking?" Antonio asked.

"I believe so. I'm going to try the other number, too."

At that moment, Marcello's phone rang. Antonio's figured it was Zampari calling back. Marcello answered. His face turned serious as he put it on speaker. Chia's breathless voice came on. "Rocco's dead. When we approached the truck, he opened fire with an Uzi. Ricci took two rounds in the chest. Thankfully, he was wearing a flak vest which they had on the chopper for us. He's still hurt pretty bad. I think he has bruised or broken ribs. At least he's alive, thank God."

Antonio stared hard at the phone, waiting for the other shoe to drop. He finally asked the question he was afraid to hear the answer to. "What about Gabriella?"

Chapter Forty-eight

Monday afternoon

No sign of her," Chia answered. "I tried to get an answer from Rocco. He tried to whisper something, but it was unintelligible. I think I understood one thing though. He said, 'I didn't kill Marianna.'"

"Damn, we're back to square one in our search for Gabriella," Marcello said. "We searched every inch of their property. Either we missed something or she was moved somewhere else."

Antonio watched Marcello's face become pensive. Then he asked, "What was on the truck?"

"Weapons mostly, as you suspected. Twelve wooden crates of small arms of all types. My guess is they were acting as a distribution point of weapons coming up from Apulia. When things got dicey, they decided to send them back south for now. There was one other thing, too. Four barrels of wine. We'll have to test it, but my guess would be it's a southern varietal being sent back. It's a much less serious infraction but they may have been cutting their Sangiovese after all."

"What's your plan?" Marcello asked.

"We're not far southeast of Roma. I suggest we call the local Carabinieri and have them take care of Tarantino's body and the truck. Then the chopper could drop me back at the church to be there to help you. Ricci doesn't want to get treated in Roma. He'd prefer to get treated back home in Firenze."

"Good call. I'll call General Peluso. I believe he's in Roma now." General Peluso was General Marcello Bianchi's superior. "You guys obviously need to stay with the truck until you're relieved. Shouldn't take long. Are you sure Ricci is up for the bumpy chopper ride?"

"He says he is. It will be painful. The chopper pilot gave him some pain meds."

"Alright, let me know when you're ready to lift off. I'll text you as soon as I've talked to General Peluso."

"Got it, General. *Grazie*."

Marcello immediately dialed General Peluso. As it was ringing, his phone notified him of another call coming in. It was Corporal Mario Garza. Marcello pointed to it and asked Antonio, "Can you call him while I'm handling this?"

Antonio nodded. He looked up the number and dialed as he walked away from the house. The sky caught his attention. The clouds had moved closer. They looked threatening and a cool breeze had begun to rise. "*Pronto*, Corporal Garza. The General is on an important call. He asked me to call you."

Garza got right to the point, "Did the General try to call Captain Zampari?"

"Yes. There was no answer."

"And did you try to call his other phone?"

"We called a number that we suspected might be his burner."

"I think you got it right. He ignored two calls, then bid me *Buonasera*. Said he'd see me tomorrow, then left in a rush."

"And you're suspicious?" Antonio asked.

"Yes. I have been for a while. Nothing solid. It'll take some explaining. I'd prefer to be telling the General."

"Understood. Listen, are you available to join us? Colonel Ferrara has disappeared. We believe she's been kidnapped or worse, possibly by the Fontana-Tarantino family. The General can explain more, and you can tell him all about your suspicions of Captain Zampari. We could use an extra hand."

"Certainly. Where are you?"

"We've set up a temporary command post at Fattoria Montieri. The winery belongs to my aunt and uncle."

"I know it. Fantastic wine. I'll be there in fifteen."

"Excellent. May I suggest you bring your Beretta PMX? More than one, if you have them." The PMX was a sub-machine gun. "There's a chance you may need it."

"Absolutely. We have three at the station. I'll bring them all. *A presto, Signor* Cortese."

Antonio walked back to where the General was finishing his call. He hung up and spoke. "Things are coming together. Peluso is heading over to the truck site himself with a team. Says he can be there in less than thirty minutes. Hold on a moment." He sent off a text to Chia. "Now, tell me what Corporal Garza had to say."

Antonio explained.

"And he's on his way here?"

"Yes. He should be here in less than fifteen minutes. Fully armed."

"Good. As soon as he gets here, he and I need to talk. Then we gather everyone for a strategy meeting."

*****

Antonio stepped over the threshold into the steaming shower to clear his head. It didn't help. He was only half-done toweling off when he heard his phone ring. He was surprised to see the picture of his son, Jonathan, on the screen. He looked at the time and did a quick calculation. It was about six in the morning in Seattle. Jonathan and Leah owned a brewery in the Ballard area of Seattle and worked a lot of nights.

"*Ciao*, Jonathan. Is everything okay? It's early in Seattle."

"You forget we have twins that are less than six months old, Dad. Our sleep schedule isn't what it used to be."

"Right. But the question stands, are you okay?"

"Yeah. Everything considered."

"Everything being?"

"Well, our business is down about seventy percent. Most of the beer we're selling is growlers. I've had to lay off most of my service staff and two of my brewers. We're down to a skeleton crew. We've shortened our hours, though, so I get home earlier. What really worries me is that the governor may be shutting down all in-house service in restaurants and breweries."

"I've heard. Will you guys be okay? Financially, I mean?"

"Depends how long this goes on. Breweries are a profitable business. More so than restaurants, you know. We've got a nest egg that'll last a while. I'm just thankful we're healthy. The hospitals are filling up. Hospital workers are overwhelmed. People are dying. This is serious stuff. Is everyone okay there? I hear it has hit Italy hard."

"Yeah. It has. Everything here is shutting down, too. Probably even faster."

"Are you okay, Dad? You sound …"

"Gabriella has disappeared."

"Shit! What happened?"

Antonio gave a brief summary of a complicated story.

"And here I'm worried about my business and finances."

"You should be. I'm glad to hear that you've got some money to last a while. The little ones are fine?"

"Yeah. They're good, Dad. Listen, call me as soon as you know something. I don't care if it's the middle of the night. I'll keep everyone else in the family posted. We'll be praying."

"Thanks, Son. I gotta go. We're getting together with General Bianchi to plan our next steps. And yes, I'll call you as soon as we find her."

Chapter Forty-nine

Monday evening

A torrential rain was pummeling the Jeep Cherokee. It had begun with a few huge drops. Now, it felt like the apocalypse. Marcello's Carabinieri vehicle shook violently when a clap of thunder exploded above. It must have been right on top of them. A blinding flash of lightning lit up the black sky, hitting one of the trees in the small grove they were parked in. A large branch crashed to the ground, just missing Gabriella's abandoned Audi.

"This is useless," Antonio said, lowering his binoculars. "I can't see twenty meters." He was reluctantly following Marcello's plan: more surveillance when he wanted to storm the villa, sirens blaring, and tear the place apart.

"This storm's supposed to blow past pretty quickly," Marcello said.

Amara was in the back seat, staring out the window with eyes wide, holding her hands tight so no one would see them shaking. Antonio wasn't sure if it was the storm, or what might lie ahead that frightened the computer tech. The thunder and lightning struck again, eliciting a string of Italian curses. Some of them were new to Antonio, probably because of her Sicilian heritage.

Antonio was sitting behind the wheel. Marcello had asked him to drive so he could make some calls. *This guy's breaking every rule in the book*, Antonio thought. He'd been following a different set of rules—rules of his own making—since Gabriella had disappeared. *At least he won't be able to blame Gabriella for doing the same.*

As with the previous night, teams were watching from both north and south of the long driveway heading to the winery compound. The forensic team of Marina Gallo and Ginevra Barbieri, with Corporal Mario Garza, were keeping watch from Marina's Alfa Romeo Stelvio. They had expected Chia to touch down soon at the church, but Antonio wondered if that would happen in this weather.

"She's alive," Marcello said out of nowhere. "For what purposes, I don't know. But I know it in my gut." Antonio wanted to have such certainty. It was eluding him.

Marcello was looking at his phone when Antonio caught sight of headlights piercing the rain from the north. They passed the other surveillance position. Amara must have seen them too because she leaned forward, just as it doused its headlights. Marcello looked up from his phone as it was turning into the driveway. Antonio lifted the binoculars but could no longer make it out through the rain, though it was beginning to lighten somewhat. A bolt of lightning flashed at that moment and he caught a brief glimpse of its silhouette. It appeared to have stopped part-way up the drive. Something was up, and he had no idea of what it was.

The radio crackled. "You guys see that?" Marina Gallo asked.

Marcello lifted the hand-held radio and gave an affirmation. "Could that be Zampari?" he asked. There was silence for several seconds.

"Mario doesn't think so," she said. "It was not a Carabinieri vehicle, nor Zampari's personal car. Looks like it stopped half-way up the drive."

The rain came to a stop as quickly as it had begun. More thunder rumbled, but less violently. The storm cell seemed to be moving to the southeast. Antonio ran the windshield wipers for a few swipes, and could now make out the car a little better. It was an SUV, and looked familiar. *Where have I seen that car?* His mind was foggy with exhaustion and worry. The lightning flashed again. He caught a brief glimpse of a man moving away from the car toward the house.

"Whoever that is, is now moving toward the house, General. He's crouched down. He doesn't want to be seen."

Marcello lifted his radio again and depressed the talk button. "We have a situation here," he explained. "Time to move. Make sure you're wearing your flak jackets. We're going to follow him in. I want the three of you to circle behind the house through the vineyard. It's probably muddy as hell, but I think I saw a gravel track back there. Time to go silent. Radios off. Phones on vibrate. Let's go to text communications. Call only if you have to."

Marcello made eye contact with Antonio and handed him a Beretta 92FS, standard Carabinieri issue. "This is against my better judgment, but we have a bunch of rookies and forensic people. Self-defense only! Am I clear?"

Antonio nodded. He made sure there was a round in the chamber, and checked the magazine. He double-checked that the safety was on, and tucked it in his rear belt as they exited the vehicle. The air was bracing; cold and damp after the squall had passed.

Antonio followed Marcello across the road. In the distance he saw the silhouette of the other team doing the same. They moved along the road's shoulder until they came to the long, winding drive. It didn't take long to reach the car. Antonio now recognized the Porsche Cayenne SUV. He tapped Marcello on the shoulder, "Vito Crivello's car, the president of the *consorzio.*"

"What the hell is he doing here?" Marcello asked, not really expecting an answer.

As if to answer his question, they heard gun shots from the direction of the house. One, two, three, Antonio counted. He saw flashes of light in a window. *Merda! Somebody just died,* he thought.

"Move, now!" General Bianchi barked. He moved quickly, but cautiously, staying low. Amara Bertoli followed. Antonio fell in behind. Someone needed to watch her back. At the end of the drive, they found what cover they could behind the budding vines. Here the drive split. To the right it went past the winery building and the two houses which the sons occupied. *Only one now*—Antonio thought sadly—though he had no love for the dead son, Rocco. Beyond that was the truck garage and a small parking area near the swimming pool and guest houses. To the left, about twenty meters away, lay the circular drive leading to the grand entry door of the villa. Alida's Ferrari was parked in its usual spot.

They watched for a moment, seeing no one, including the dogs. *Where the hell are they?* Antonio wondered. Marcello waved them forward. He crossed the drive and took up a position out of view of the front door. Amara and Antonio followed.

Marcello moved to the edge until he could see the front door. Seeing no one, he continued on. With gun raised he moved like the soldier he was. He stopped to one side of the grand entrance door and waved Amara to take a position behind him. He directed Antonio to the opposite side of the door. Marcello pulled out his phone and sent a text, presumably to notify the others. Then he pointed, and whispered to Antonio, "You ready?"

Chapter Fifty

Monday evening

The door was unlocked. The only light in the entry foyer spilled out from the formal living room in front of them. They heard voices—mostly one voice—that of Vito Crivello. "I didn't want to kill anyone," he said breathlessly. "He shouldn't have come at me."

They heard sobs and angry accusations from Alida. "You bastard! Of course he came at you. You come into our home—brandishing your gun—making baseless accusations. We didn't kill Marianna!"

So that's what this is about, Antonio thought. His phone vibrated in his pocket. Possibly Marina Gallo. This was no time to check.

"Enough!" Vito said, his voice strained.

General Bianchi crept forward, gun raised. Antonio followed, waving Amara to get behind him. Vito had his back to them, unaware of their presence. There were three other people in the room, one of whom appeared to be dead. Donato's body was lying in a pool of blood. Vito had his gun leveled somewhere between the other two. One was Alida, the other, Ettore Alghero, her winemaker. Ettore's eyes flickered in their direction. Vito began to turn.

General Bianchi spoke firmly, "Lower your gun, Vito."

Vito turned his head some more, enough to see Marcello in his uniform. "No, General," he answered. "One of these people killed Marianna Bellini. I intend to find out who."

"That's our job, Vito. Let us do it!" Antonio felt a presence behind him. He turned and saw Marina Gallo, Ginevra Barbieri, and Mario Garza spread out to their rear, each carrying a Beretta PMX. He wondered if Marina and Ginevra had ever handled one.

"Vito, I'm telling you again, lower the gun! Justice is our job, not yours! We need to see if Donato's alive."

"He's dead. I shot him through the heart."

"You still need to stand down ... unless you want to end up like him."

"I don't care. My life is of no use now. The woman I loved—truly loved—is dead. And I'll go to jail for the rest of my life ... what's left of it."

"Not if you acted in self-defense," Marcello said. "You don't have to go to prison. Besides, which one of those two do you shoot? Do you want to kill someone who's innocent? If I see your finger even twitch on that trigger, you're dead."

Vito turned the gun toward Alida. "She's responsible, whether she pulled the trigger or not. She wanted Marianna's vineyard. She knew her son would never sell it until Marianna was gone."

"Vito, listen! You don't want your life to end this way." Marcello's voice was calm, reassuring. He had done this before. "I'm going to step toward you now. I'm lowering my weapon and asking you to do the same." He holstered his weapon and stepped forward slowly. Vito began to lower his, then had a sudden change of heart. The weapon started to come back up toward Alida Fontana. The General leapt forward with the speed of a man half his age. He knocked Vito's arm toward the floor, grasping for the weapon, which discharged. The sound was deafening as it echoed off the hard surfaces of the room. The bullet dug a large chunk out of the tile floor, and ricocheted into a chair next to Alida, barely missing her. Marcello knocked the weapon to the floor. Before anyone else could get it, Alida had it in her hand.

"Perfect timing," they heard from behind them. Alarm bells went off in Antonio's head. He turned and his heart dropped. Captain Zampari was standing just inside the doorway, holding Gabriella from behind, a gun to her head. Her mouth was gagged. Two others stepped up behind him, brandishing sub-machine guns. These were not the farm hands from this afternoon. Antonio recognized them as the men that drove the truck. Alida raised her weapon as well, the Glock she had just plucked from the floor.

"Now I want all of you to lower your weapons and place them on the floor," Zampari ordered. "Then, move to the middle of the room." Antonio looked at General Marcello, who nodded. He and all the others did as they were ordered.

"Ettore, retrieve their weapons and take their cell phones," Zampari said. "Then find some rope. Tie their hands behind them. We're going to take a road trip."

Zampari moved to Alida's side. "I'm sorry I didn't arrive in time to save Donato, *cara mia*. This man will pay for it." He raised his gun toward Vito Crivello. "But in case you're wondering, Vito. By sheer luck you killed the right man. He's the one that killed your lover. But it was on my orders. My first faked suicide. I learned some things for next time."

"Don't kill him here!" Alida said. "His death needs to look like an accident."

"*Brillante, amore mio!* This worked better than I imagined. All of the Carabinieri in one place. We'll take him south with them. Your father can help us decide how to dispose of them." He looked at Mario. "I'm sorry to see you here, Corporal Garza. I liked you. You had a bright career ahead of you. But that will teach you to stick your nose into matters which don't concern you."

Mario stared at him defiantly. "Justice will find you, Zampari. I won't dignify you by calling you *Capitano*. But let me ask you. How do you expect to explain all of us dead?"

"In case you hadn't noticed, Corporal, the entire country is in chaos. In a couple of days, the whole of Italy will be shut down. Besides, we're very good at covering our tracks. We may have to take out a few others as well to make sure there is no one left to make trouble for us." He looked at Antonio with arrogance. "Such as the *Americano's famiglia.*"

Merda! Antonio thought, fear rising in his gut. It left him as quickly as it came, replaced by an unexplainable confidence. *This isn't over,* he thought. *None of us are dying tonight.*

Zampari continued to blow smoke. "My loyalty was never to the Carabinieri. My uncle and godfather, Lorenzo Tarantino, is the one who took care of me. He even got me into the Carabinieri. He knew some day it would be useful. But my Carabinieri days are behind me now. Time to return to my Apulian roots."

Antonio was beginning to understand. Zampari had been taken care of by the same man who was Alida's stepfather. The man she had grown up thinking of as her real father. It appeared that Lorenzo Tarantino was the head of a crime family.

Ettore finished tying them up. It occurred to Antonio that it was the first time in his life. They herded him and the Carabinieri out the front door. They rounded the ell of the house and the classic black Mercedes 300SEL came into view. *Of course,* Antonio thought. *It belongs to Zampari! It's probably registered in Apulia. That's why we couldn't find a local owner.*

They led them toward the truck garage. Alida punched in the code and the electric motor pulled the door upward. One of the men with Zampari opened the rear sliding door on the lone truck—the same truck they had inspected earlier today. "Everybody in," Zampari said. He removed Gabriella's gag and shoved her toward the truck.

She turned, and all of her regrets poured forth. "I'm sorry." Her eyes scanned from Antonio to Marcello, then the others. "If I had not been so stupid, you would not be in this position."

"No regrets," Marcello said. "If we die tonight, let's die with our heads held high."

We're not going to die, Antonio thought again, wondering where this confidence was coming from.

Chapter Fifty-one

Monday night

Antonio turned to the guard with the beard. "Hey, I'm desperate here. Any chance I could relieve myself before the long trip? I don't think you want piss all over the back of your truck. And I'd rather not meet this Lorenzo Tarantino with soiled pants."

The guard looked at Zampari. He nodded. "Over there," he pointed. "Let him water the vines." The vineyard was about thirty meters away. Antonio walked that way with the guard following him. He knew he should stop at the first vine but kept walking until the guard ordered him to stop. He was about ten meters in.

Antonio turned to the guard. "Either you're going to have to unzip my pants, or untie my hands." The man chose the latter. Antonio unzipped and relieved himself. He hadn't lied about being desperate. When he was done, he stayed in that position until the guard got impatient. "Zip it. Let's go." Antonio paused a few more seconds, until the guard walked up and jabbed him in the back with his gun. It was the precise moment for which he'd been waiting. He spun as quickly as his fifty-five-year-old body could move. His right hand pushed the Beretta submachine away in case it went off, then his hand got a grip on the gun, twisted it, and yanked hard. It was a move he'd learned in training. The guy let out a startled sound. Antonio stepped back and leveled the gun at him and put a left finger to his lips.

Zampari called out, "Everything okay over there, Salvo?"

"He was just getting impatient with me," Antonio called out, hoping to buy a few seconds. His mind raced through the split-second calculations. He decided that trying to take on Zampari, Alida, Ettore, and the other guard would likely lead to his own death and possibly some of the others. He kept the submachine gun pointed at the guard as he walked slowly backwards. When Zampari called out again, he pivoted and ran as fast as he could. The mud grabbed at his feet. He nearly slipped and fell. Moments later he heard cursing and footsteps behind him. He turned and let go a burst of shots, then ducked left under the wire which held the vine tendrils, into the next row. A salvo of bullets ripped through the vines to his right. He stumbled headlong toward the road, then ducked under the wires and moved several rows over. He paused to return fire, then moved the opposite direction, hoping they would think he was still moving left. An explosion of bullets to his left told him his ruse had worked. He could hear distant yelling and curses from Zampari.

To his own amazement, he reached the road. He crouched and listened, trying to determine where the guards were. He assumed the one who'd accompanied him had been re-armed by now. He heard the sucking sound of footsteps in the mud behind and to his left. Voices yelling instructions told him he was right.

He was about to cross the road when he heard the sound of Alida's Ferrari Tributo screaming down the drive. He moved back to the cover of the vines and lay flat in the mud. She turned south on the road and screamed past him at high speed. He lifted his head but saw nothing but taillights. As the high-pitched sound of her car faded, he listened for the sound of the guards. They'd gone silent. He swiveled his head, searching. Then his ears picked up the slosh of a man's boots trudging through a puddle. It was close by on his left. He saw the silhouette of the bearded man, barely visible against the dark sky.

What to do, Antonio? You can shoot this guy. Then you're down to one-on-one but it will alert the others. Or ...

He decided on a second option. He hated to kill a man unless he had to. *He might die anyway for letting me get the drop on him. Not my problem.*

The guy passed him on his left and stared across the road. Antonio rose silently, ready to spring. Then he whispered just loud enough to be heard, "Lower your weapon or die here." The man stopped in his tracks. Antonio was hoping that the guards had spread out. He spoke quietly, "Engage the safety. With the barrel pointed away from me, reach back and hand me your gun." The man did as he was told. "Now, as quietly as possible, walk straight backward down this row. If you run, or alert your partner, I'll put a bullet in your chest."

The man began to move, slowly in the mud. All of a sudden, Antonio became aware of barking. Where had the dogs been all this time? *They must have been locked up somewhere.* When the man was about forty meters away, Antonio heard his partner's voice call out quietly, "Salvo, where are you? I haven't found anything."

As soon as he heard the voice, the bearded Salvo dove to his right under the wire. He yelled out, "He's by the road!"

Just then, Antonio heard a growl and the first dog appeared, running straight toward him. He shot a quick burst just as the dog was beginning to lunge. The dog went down and stared at him with glassy eyes. The other dog appeared. Antonio lifted his gun, ready to shoot, but suddenly the second dog stopped by its partner. It sat down, laid its head on its front paws and whimpered. It had chosen to mourn instead of continuing the chase. Antonio's heart cracked in two.

Chapter Fifty-two

Monday night

Antonio tore his eyes away from the dogs and sprinted toward the road. He looked left, then crouched, holding a submachine gun in each hand. He was across the road in moments, headed toward a grove of stone pines, when he heard an explosion of shots. Something stung his ear like a wasp. He put his hand to his ear and felt a trickle of blood. *God, that was close!* But he kept moving and made it behind a tree. He poked his head around and saw a muzzle flash. Bullets struck the tree. He crouched and returned fire. He moved, staying low, and returned fire again. He heard a scream followed by Italian curses. It sounded like the scream of a wounded man, not of death. He didn't stay to find out. He circled away from the road and found a gravel path which took him toward Marcello's Cherokee. There were no more shots. He reached the Jeep in about two minutes, and fumbled for the keys in his pocket. He climbed into its armored interior, closed his eyes, and breathed a sigh of relief.

*****

It only took mere moments until Antonio's eyes sprang open as he realized he was safe but the others were not. He put the key in the ignition—murmuring thanks that he was the one who had them—and started the car. He threw the Jeep in reverse, grateful for the all-wheel drive in the mud. He backed as far out of sight as possible. He no longer needed to see the winery—only the road. He kept the engine running.

He found a first aid kit and bandaged his ear, which was minor. He then turned his mind toward trying to figure out how to rescue the others. No plan would come together. His mind was racing but his thinking was muddled. He wondered why Alida Fontana-Tarantino had raced off on her own. Was she trying to escape the situation, or simply getting a head start? He had no idea. He only knew it would serve no purpose to chase her. He'd never catch her in a million years.

The wait seemed to drag on forever. Finally, he heard the grinding of gears and the whine of the truck engine approaching. The bearded man named Salvo—the man he'd disarmed—was driving, but there were two men in the front. He assumed it was the other guard. Apparently, his wound was not that serious.

Behind the truck came Zampari's classic Mercedes. *It really is a fine-looking vehicle,* Antonio had to admit. Someone sat in the passenger seat. He thought it was Ettore, the man they called a winemaker, but now appeared to be a family enforcer.

When the Mercedes was about two hundred meters up the road, Antonio pulled out behind it, leaving his headlights off. Maybe they would see him, maybe not. He only wanted to keep them in view, though he was pretty certain where they were headed.

The truck and Mercedes maintained a steady speed. If they had spotted him, they showed no signs of it. But after a while he decided there was no way they hadn't seen him. The Mercedes was a powerful car, but there was no way the truck would ever be able to outrun him. That left them one option. Sooner or later, they'd have to deal with him. *Be smart, Antonio. They'll be looking for a spot to set an ambush.* They knew these roads better than he did, especially once they got south of Montepulciano.

They had gone about three kilometers when there was a bend in the road that caused him to lose sight of them. He accelerated rapidly around the curve and over a rise, wanting to bring them back into view. Emerging from the curve, his first thought was that they had set their trap. The truck and Mercedes were stopped in the middle of the road. He hit the brakes hard, sending the Jeep into a skid. He expected a hail of bullets any moment. He wondered if they knew his vehicle was armored. It was an irrelevant question. No shots came.

Antonio's understanding of the situation shifted in milliseconds as his mind took in the scene. His skid had brought him sideways, within inches of Zampari's Mercedes, blocking his escape. There was no way he would have escaped anyway. Six people surrounded the truck and Mercedes. Chia, Carlo Ricci, Sylvio, Giulia, Umberto and a Carabinieri officer he didn't recognize. They were armed to the teeth. Beyond the class six truck, the road was blocked by Sylvio's pickup truck and Chia's Fiat. Behind them, the Carabinieri chopper sat menacingly, its flood lamps illuminating the scene. Its rotors were slowly turning. He let out a sigh of relief.

Antonio piled out, bringing the Beretta submachine gun with him —as if there wasn't already enough firepower. "There are hostages in the back of the truck," he yelled. Umberto was the first to react. He turned the heavy steel handle and slid the door upwards. He shook his head when he saw how many people were tied up. General Marcello Bianchi looked out at the assembled rescuers. "About time you guys got here!"

Gabriella spied Antonio. For a brief moment her head dropped to her chest. Then she lifted it and flashed a relieved smile at him. She slid to the edge on her bottom, threw her legs over the side and let herself down. She walked unsteadily toward him. He stepped behind her, untied her hands, and turned her around.

She buried her head against him, then pulled away and began to beat on his chest. "Damn you, Antonio. Damn you. I thought you were dead!"

He grabbed her hands and pulled her close. Her body quivered. After long, healing moments he stepped back and lifted her chin until their eyes met. "I'm okay. But now you're covered in mud," he said with a grin. He noticed an ugly red scrape on her forehead. "Are you okay?" She nodded as he looked up to see the others climbing down. "Is anyone hurt?"

"We got jostled around a lot when the truck had to slam on its brakes. I don't think anyone is seriously hurt."

Everything seemed to be happening at once. Sylvio, Giulia, and Carlo Ricci were holding the two men in the truck cab at gunpoint as they directed them to step down. Antonio reached into the Cherokee and handed Gabriella the other submachine gun, a SIG MPX. She dug deep and found her strength again and joined her old partner, Marcello, as they directed Zampari and Ettore to step from the Mercedes. Corporal Garza patted Zampari down, making sure he had no hidden weapons. "Told you justice would be served," he said, with little satisfaction in his voice.

"There isn't enough justice in the world, Zampari, to make up for all you've done," Marcello said. "Tell me now, where are the guns and phones you took from us at the villa?"

Zampari nodded toward the trunk. "Keys are still in the ignition," he said smugly. "No key fob on this classic," he gave his Mercedes a sorrowful look, probably knowing he'd never see it again.

Marcello retrieved the keys and opened the trunk. The guns and phones were in a black leather duffle. He pulled them out one-by-one and distributed them. He handed Marina Gallo and Corporal Garza their weapons, and asked them to guard Zampari, while he planned for their extraction. He called aside Antonio, Chia, Gabriella, Carlo Ricci and the Carabinieri lieutenant who had been on the chopper. His name patch said Carbone. The pilot remained in his seat aboard the helicopter.

"I didn't expect to see you here, Ricci," Marcello said. "You okay? Last I heard, you were on your way to the hospital in Firenze."

"Hurts like hell, sir. I'll live. We smelled trouble when we couldn't reach any of you. We called Giulia to see if she'd heard from you. As you can see," he smiled, "she brought along some help. The chopper dropped us at the church. They were just getting airborne again when they spotted the truck and Mercedes with your Cherokee following, and directed us where to set up a blockade."

Antonio suddenly remembered his phone vibrating while they were being held. He pulled it out and saw he had missed several texts and attempted calls from Chia, and a couple from Giulia.

The General turned to Lieutenant Carbone, "How many can you fit on the chopper?"

"It's an older Bell 206, sir. Six max, including the pilot."

"Alright, here's the plan. We have …"

The scene was shattered by a gunshot and a harrowing scream. Everyone ducked as they turned and saw Zampari on his knees, holding his stomach. Blood oozed between his fingers. His face was pale. His eyes were wide with shock and disbelief.

Gabriella was the first to reach him. She calmly laid him to the ground and applied pressure to his wound with crossed hands. Chia sprinted to her Fiat and returned with a first aid kit. She pulled out gauze and handed it to Gabriella, who applied it to the wound. Corporal Garza stood over him, looking dazed, his gun limp at his side. "I… I didn't mean to shoot him!" he stuttered. "He lunged at me … grabbed for my gun."

General Bianchi began to bark orders, "Listen up! We need to airlift him to the hospital. We'll send the wounded guard with him. Major Umeh, Lieutenant Ricci … I want the two of you and Lieutenant Carbone to accompany them on the chopper. Chia, we'll need your keys. Go! We'll handle the rest from here."

"There is a portable stretcher on board, sir," Lieutenant Carbone said. He rushed to the chopper, ducking under the lazily rotating blades. Moments later he had the stretcher on the ground next to Zampari. He and Corporal Garza nodded to Gabriella; they lifted him onto it, while she maintained pressure on his wound. They lifted the two ends of the stretcher

Chia stepped forward. "I've got him, Gabriella." She switched places with Gabriella and walked alongside the stretcher, somehow managing to keep her hands on Zampari's abdomen as they slid the stretcher across the floor between the two pairs of facing passenger seats. She climbed aboard awkwardly. Carlo Ricci followed with his weapon leveled at the injured guard. From the looks of his shredded pants and bandage, Antonio's shot had caught him in the calf. They took seats opposite one another, while Chia remained on her knees next to Zampari, who appeared to be unconscious. Lieutenant Carbone climbed into the front next to the pilot and pulled on a headset. The rotors increased speed, and a minute later the black chopper lifted off and slowly disappeared into the night sky. Antonio hoped Zampari would make it, if only so he could face a court of law.

Chapter Fifty-three

Monday night

T he thump-thump-thump of the helicopter faded, and the scene became utterly quiet. Ettore the winemaker, and Salvo the truck driver, sat on the ground, guarded by the civilian band of Sylvio, Giulia, and Umberto. The Carabinieri trio of Marina Gallo, Ginevra Barbieri, and Amara Bertoli sat on the rear tailgate of the truck, looking happy to be alive. *Consorzio* President Vito Crivello had been moved to the rear of the Mercedes, his hands still tied. Marcello informed him—almost apologetically—that he had to arrest him for the murder of Donato Tarantino. Vito put up no resistance. Gabriella climbed in next to him and began to ask him questions.

Corporal Mario Garza stood leaning against the black Mercedes, staring at the ground as if he might find some solace there. Antonio was sure it was the first time he'd shot a man. It appeared he was running it over-and-over in his mind, trying to figure out how it could have been avoided. There was a lot to admire in the young Carabinieri, including a sound conscience. He had done what he had to do, but that didn't make it any easier.

Marcello returned after wandering off to make a phone call. He stood quietly rubbing his chin, as if it helped his brain work better. Finally, he swung into action again. "We need to get these vehicles off the road," he said. Under normal circumstances, blocking a road like this would have stopped post-dinner traffic, drawing curses from infuriated Italian drivers. But tonight, not another vehicle was about. It felt like one of those movies where all of humanity had been abducted by aliens.

Once the cars were all on the shoulder, Marcello gathered the odd mix of Carabinieri and civilians and handed out instructions. He turned to Sylvio, Umberto, and Giulia. "Things may have turned out far differently if you hadn't been here to help. *Grazie. Grazie. Mille grazie!"* Antonio watched their reaction. Sylvio stuck his chest out with pride, while Umberto lifted his chin and nodded. Giulia stood holding her rifle like a commando. *What happened to the little girl who used to make us teddy bear pancakes?* Antonio wondered, looking at her with a mix of pride and angst.

General Bianchi continued to organize what needed to happen. "We have almost as many vehicles scattered as we have people. These five vehicles," he waved his hand, "plus Gabriella's and Marina's vehicles back on the road near the winery. Is anyone experienced at driving one of these trucks?" He pointed at the class six.

"I am," Ginevra said. They all turned to her in surprise. She was the last person Antonio expected to answer affirmatively. "My uncle had a produce business. I used to drive his truck to the farmer's markets."

"Good," Marcello said. "You get to drive this all the way to the Carabinieri station at Palazzo Pitti in Firenze. We'll lock these other prisoners in the back. I'll be following behind you in case they try to bust out of that box somehow. Vito Crivello will ride with me. Marina, tomorrow morning I want you and Barbieri to do a complete forensic analysis on the truck and Mercedes. Amara, you drive Chia's vehicle and drop Marina at hers. Then the two of you can caravan with us." He paused and thought for a moment, "Antonio, I'm entrusting you with the Cherokee. Take Gabriella to retrieve her vehicle. No need for the two of you to come to Firenze tonight. As for me, I'm going to be selfish and drive this classic Mercedes. Garza, you're with me. We have some debriefing to do. I'll bring you back tomorrow when I come to pick up the Cherokee."

"What about Alida, sir?" Antonio asked. "She's on the run. And what about the dead body of Donato?"

"I called the medical examiner. He's on his way to the winery with an ambulance to handle Donato's body. I also called General Peluso. He's got the highways being watched. With so little traffic, it shouldn't be hard to spot a red Ferrari in the middle of the night. If she gets past us, we'll find her later. She's probably heading home to her stepfather in Apulia."

Antonio looked at the time. It was after midnight. Exhaustion suddenly washed over him like a rogue wave. He felt like he was going under.

"Antonio. Hey, Antonio," Marcello spoke, pulling his mind back to the surface, "I'll be back mid-day tomorrow to pick up the Jeep. I'll need to debrief you and Gabriella so we can file our arrest reports."

"It's going to be complicated," Antonio replied.

Marcello nodded. "Sure as hell is. Always seems to be that way when you get involved." Antonio wasn't sure how to take that but Marcello smiled and he sensed that he had come to earn the man's respect.

Marcello turned to Sylvio, Umberto, and Giulia. "You're free to go. We'll take over with the prisoners. *Grazie* again!" He turned and nodded to Marina, and the trio of ladies climbed down from the rear of the truck and herded Ettore and Salvo inside.

Antonio walked over to the Mercedes and leaned in. "You ready to go?" he asked Gabriella.

"In a moment," she said. She turned back to Vito.

Antonio climbed in the Jeep. A minute later he watched Gabriella exit the Mercedes and walk over to the men in the back of the truck. She spoke something to them. He wished he could read lips. She turned away, her face full of emotion. She slid into the passenger seat. "Let's go," Gabriella said tersely, as if she'd been the one waiting.

Antonio waved to the others as he pulled onto the pavement heading back toward the winery. "What was that about?" he asked.

"Not now," she said, as she turned her head toward the passenger window. He decided not to press. He wondered what she'd said to Salvo, the man who'd driven the truck when they ran Andrea and Bria off the road. *The guy's probably safer in prison, than if Gabriella were alone with him,* Antonio thought. *And certainly better off than if he arrived in Apulia after I disarmed him twice and escaped.*

They drove in silence. Gabriella's mood swings continued to be so dramatic, he didn't know what to think. Ten minutes ago, everything seemed fine between them. Now, he wondered if it over really would be. They reached the copse of trees where her car was located. She got out and leaned her head back toward him. "Thank you, Antonio, for giving me space to breathe. You look exhausted. I'll follow to make sure you get home safely." She smiled weakly and closed the car door. He waited for her to get in her car and start the engine, then pulled onto the road and turned south toward Montepulciano. She pulled in behind him.

~~~~ **TUESDAY, MARCH 10** ~~~~

Chapter Fifty-four

Tuesday, after midnight

They had not traveled far when they saw the oncoming headlights of the small caravan. Antonio rolled down his window and waved. He kept it down so the chilly night air could keep him alert. A few minutes later they passed the spot where the rescue had occurred, now just another spot in the road. An hour ago, everything had seemed hopeless. To his hazy mind it felt like one of his dreams.

The half-moon had risen and illuminated the landscape as they passed several hectares of tilled fields, lying fallow on both sides of the road. They weren't far now from the church of Madonna di San Biago. Antonio rounded a bend in the road which came to a Y. He took the left fork, then suddenly slammed on his brakes and pulled quickly onto the shoulder to make sure Gabriella didn't rear-end him. He couldn't believe what his eyes were seeing. Alida's red Ferrari Tributo was about ten meters off the road, its front end wrapped around the grey trunk of an aged olive tree. He assumed she'd come around the bend at high speed and didn't handle the Y in the road. Gabriella pulled onto the shoulder just beyond him. He was first out of his car, but she beat him to the Ferrari. Its door stood open and the interior was lit by the dome light, but there was no sign of Alida Fontana-Tarantino. Only footprints from high heels in the muddy soil.

Antonio looked inside, surprised to see the airbag had not deployed. He looked at the front end of the car, and saw the collision was not as bad as it first appeared. He pulled out his phone and turned on the flashlight to give himself a better view. It looked like she had tried to back the Ferrari away from the tree but her tires had spun themselves deep into the mud. *A problem with high-powered rear-wheel drive vehicles,* he thought, not really surprised.

"We have to find her!" Gabriella said. "I am not letting her get away again. Not after all she has done." She was carrying the SIG MPX submachine gun he'd given her at the rescue scene. He was worried about her state of mind.

"I hope you aren't planning to use that," he said, with a wave of his hand.

"You really think …?" she let her words hang in the air. "Only if I have to defend myself."

"Okay. You're right. She's probably armed. I'll grab my gun, too. It shouldn't be hard to track her with this mud."

Antonio returned to the Jeep. He placed the handgun in his belt beneath his jacket and grabbed the Beretta submachine gun from the passenger seat. He opened the glovebox and found a Maglite flashlight. He and Gabriella started next to the Ferrari and followed the muddy prints, which headed back toward the road, and crossed over. They found them again on the other side and tracked them toward a wooded area which rose up the hill toward the walls of Montepulciano.

They crossed the muddy field, watching, listening. Antonio spoke quietly, "If she's reached the town, we'll never find her."

Gabriella didn't reply. She moved silently, like a tracker of big game. Coming to the edge of the woods they came upon a gravel trail. In one direction it skirted the edge of the woods. In the other, it led into them. Antonio bent down, shining the flashlight on the path. It appeared the muddy footprints crossed over the path. He lifted the flashlight a little and saw a pair of muddy high heels.

Gabriella whispered, "She took her shoes off so she would not leave a trail for us to follow. There is enough stone in this path that she could avoid the muddy parts. I suggest we split up. You've got the Maglite. Follow the path through the woods. I'll follow it this way. The moon should give me enough light."

"Okay," he agreed, reluctantly. He didn't like the idea of splitting up, but knew it provided their best chance of finding her. "But pay attention to your phone. If either of us spots her we should notify the other before engaging."

She nodded. He hoped she was agreeing, and not just placating him.

He turned uphill into the woods, moving as quickly as the ground would allow. The woods became dense in a hurry. Luckily, they appeared to only be about a hundred meters wide. He was almost to the other side when the sound of two gunshots shattered the night. It was not Gabriella's submachine gun.

"Merda!" he said, as his heart sank. When no screams came, he pulled himself back from the abyss and quickly assessed his situation. The shots had come from somewhere to his right. *Am I better off returning the way I came, or leaving the path and crossing through the deep woods?* He considered a third option, which was to continue upward toward the base of the town and look for a way around the perimeter of the woods. He took off running. A dozen long strides and he emerged from

the woods. He turned right, putting the stone wall of the city to his left, a stone's throw away. The thicket of woods was to his right. But now he was back on muddy ground. It forced him to slow, which was more prudent anyway. If he ran headlong, Alida might spot him before he knew she was there.

He doused his Maglite that made him an easy target. He stopped to let his eyes adjust and listen. He didn't hear a thing. He released the safety on his Beretta M12, and held it at ready. He moved forward, fully alert now, senses keen from the adrenaline, hoping he wasn't walking into Alida's view. But that's exactly what he did.

Chapter Fifty-five

Tuesday, after midnight

S top right there." He heard a low, husky voice, barely loud enough to be heard. It came from the shadows to his left. "Lower your weapon." He did. "Now, walk backward this way." He followed her commands, praying with every step. "I'll take that Beretta," she said. "Reach back and set it on the ground, facing away from me." As he set it down, he turned his head just enough to see she was pressed tightly against a boulder in the shadows near the base of the wall. "Now take three steps forward and turn around," she said. "I've never shot a man in the back." Antonio turned slowly, looking for an opportunity to disarm her. Unlike the guard earlier, she had established the perfect distance – close enough for an easy shot, too far for him to make a move.

All he could do now was try to buy time. *Where are you, Gabriella?* He knew most perpetrators liked to talk about the things they'd done and their reasons behind them. Some people thought it was their pride that made them do so. He had always thought it was their way of justifying their evil choices. No one wants to think of themselves as truly evil. Usually, they've made themselves out to be a victim.

"Why do you want to shoot me?" he asked, keeping his voice low. He knew if he spoke too loudly, he'd be inviting her to shoot him now. "I've done nothing to you. I don't even have evidence that you've done anything wrong. I see now that Zampari was the mastermind behind all of this."

She doesn't know he's been shot. Or that Gabriella is no longer held captive, he thought. *So, what did she shoot at?*

"Ha! You think that buffoon was pulling my strings? He thought so, too. But I was calling the shots. Men are so, so easily manipulated, you know. I could get him to do anything I wanted and make him think it was his idea. And whatever I wasn't able to accomplish directly, I accomplished through my father."

Antonio realized he'd been wrong. For Alida, it was purely pride and a desire for power that drove her.

"No more talking. See, I've given away my little secret, so now I have to kill you. On your knees."

As Antonio slowly knelt, he continued to buy precious moments. "Do you know that I was able to free the others? As soon as you shoot me, they'll be all over you!"

"Nice try," she said, her voice still barely loud enough for him to hear. "But I was watching. I know it's just you and Gabriella. A minute ago, she was a couple of hundred meters that way," she nodded her head left, "where I fired my first shots to get your attention. She may come running into my trap any moment now, or certainly as soon as she hears your dying screams. She's lost her head, you know. Her emotions have taken over her ability to reason. And after she's gone, the labyrinth," she nodded toward the wall, "will swallow me up."

Antonio had heard that within the caves and secret passageways under Montepulciano, some of them provided escape routes to hidden places in the outer wall. He wondered if she'd found such an entry point. If so, they would almost certainly never find her, even though the gunshots would bring the local authorities. He was surprised they hadn't showed up already, but then again not. Nothing was the same as it had been just weeks before.

"*Arrivederci, Signor* Cortese. It's a shame to see such a noble and handsome man die on his knees." She slowly raised the gun.

"Drop your weapon!" He heard Gabriella's voice ring out, though he couldn't see her. She stepped from the shadows. "Drop it now or you're a dead woman."

Alida just smiled sadly. "Go ahead. Kill me. Let's see who can pull the trigger first. There's already been an abundance of death. What's one or two more? You've taken both of my sons away … along with everything else that means anything. What do I have left to live for? I'd rather die than rot in some hellhole prison!"

"I'm not playing games, Alida! You brought those things on yourself!" Antonio watched her inch forward. "But you were right about one thing. I have lost my head. Killing you right now would be perfect revenge, but I'd rather see you suffer in prison for the rest of your life. You had my brother killed … his lovely wife, and so many others. You told them to kill me, too. And now you want to kill the man I am going to marry. I'm counting to three and that weapon better be on the ground!"

Alida didn't even wait for the count of one. Her gun came up quickly, toward her own temple. Gabriella reacted in a flash, flying toward her arm to pull it away. The gun went off and Alida let out a blood-curdling scream. Blood ran down her face and she fell to her knees. Antonio expected her to fall over dead, but she didn't. She stayed there, staring into space with a look of shock. Then she lost consciousness and tumbled forward.

Gabriella and Antonio were on their knees beside her in moments. "I think it is a deep flesh wound. But it might have cracked her skull," Gabriella said. She tore off her own long-sleeve blouse, leaving herself with nothing but a bra to protect her against the chilly night air. She pressed the blouse firmly against the wound and Alida moaned. For the second time tonight, Gabriella was trying to save the life of someone she thought deserved to die. "Call 113!" she shouted.

113 is the Italian equivalent of 911 in the States. He dialed. It rang and rang. He was about to hang up, when someone finally answered. He spoke in his best Italian. *"Emergenza! Una donna e stata fucilataq.* A woman has been shot! *Ci serve un'ambulanza."*

"Mi dispiace, signor. I'm sorry. Due to the shutdown, services are limited. The nearest available ambulance is forty minutes away. Can you transport the victim?"

"Looks like we'll have to!" He hung up, exasperated. "We're on our own!" he yelled, louder than he needed to.

"Get the Cherokee! You should be able to get fairly close with the all-wheel drive. Go!"

Before he went, he tore off his muddy jacket and placed it around Gabriella's shoulders. He turned and ran, slipping and sliding. It was more down than up, which proved treacherous. He almost went down a couple of times, all the while looking for the best path to bring the Jeep back to where they were. He reached the Cherokee, got in, started the engine, and put it in all-wheel drive. He crossed the road and headed back up the incline. It was a bumpy ride, but a few minutes later he reached a spot about forty meters from them, as close as the terrain would allow. He jumped out, opened the door to the rear seat, and laid the middle seats down.

When he reached them, Alida was still unconscious. "I need to keep pressure on the wound, Antonio. Can you carry her?"

"As long as I don't fall in the mud." He knelt, fought off a leg cramp, and placed his right arm under her knees and his left arm under her shoulders. "Ready?" he asked. She nodded and he lifted her. They picked their way carefully down the hill. Antonio, unable to see his own feet, tested every step before putting the weight of two bodies on it. They managed to make it to the Jeep without falling. Gabriella climbed in first, scrunching down awkwardly. Antonio slid Alida in as gently as he could. She still appeared to be unconscious, but managed to emit another moan.

He climbed in the driver's seat. As the crow flies, they were probably less than a kilometer from the Ospedale di Montepulciano. But the city wall lay between them and the hospital. He'd have to go around. He backed down the hill until he found a spot to turn around.

"Hurry, Antonio! Her pulse is weak."

"Okay. But it's going to be bumpy." He accelerated and the ride got rough. Fortunately, it didn't take long to reach the smooth surface of the road. He turned north on the Via del Canneti.

"The siren," Gabriella said.

"There's nobody on the road."

"But what if someone is coming around a corner? And once in the city it will alert any pedestrians who might be out."

"If you insist." He turned it on. It had been almost twenty years—since his patrolman days in Newport Beach—that he'd driven with a siren blaring. This siren sounded far different than the ones on the American patrol cars.

Antonio's phone rang. He had no choice but to ignore it. In less than two minutes, he reached SP17 and turned south to enter the city. Minutes later he pulled up in front of the hospital. He jumped out and burst through the doors looking for someone to help.

"Signor, signor. Fermare! Stop!*"* a frenzied nurse yelled. "You have no mask!" Despite being dressed like a space woman, he could see the exhaustion on her face. She was in no mood for back talk.

He quickly explained the emergency in his broken Italian. She shooed him out the door, saying the emergency staff would be right behind him. A minute later two orderlies showed up, rolling a stretcher. They were dressed like the nurse. They rolled Alida inside while the nurse barred re-entry to Gabriella and Antonio. "We'll take care of her," she said. "No way you're coming in here. Not if you want to live. *Andare!* Go! Find the Carabinieri station and file a report."

Gabriella pulled out her badge and showed the nurse, who simply nodded and retreated back inside. Gabriella stared after her in a daze, then rushed to the door, yanked it open and yelled after the nurse, "This woman needs to be restrained. She is a danger to herself and others."

*****

Antonio and Gabriella stood on the well-worn cobblestone street in front of the hospital. The golden light of the old streetlamps pushed back against the blue-black shadows of the night. The only sign of life was a stray cat that darted across the empty street. They were muddy, bloody messes as they stared at one another with a sense of relief, jumbled together with disbelief. Gabriella's tears suddenly broke loose and she leaned into his chest. He put his arms around her, trying to act strong. Reality was, he didn't feel strong at all on the inside.

After a minute, Gabriella looked up at him. "You have no idea how badly I wanted to kill her. Part of me wishes I had."

"But you didn't. You probably saved her life." He paused a moment. "You saved mine, too."

"You never would have been in danger if it was not for me. I was reckless. Alida was right, you know … about my emotions getting the better of me. You tried to warn me."

She was right, but he wasn't about to tell her that. He understood. "You're being too hard on yourself. We're all susceptible when it comes to the people we love. I know how much you loved your brother. I saw it the day he and Bria visited you in the hospital in Siena … the way your eyes lit up." He watched her face as she recalled the memory of that day.

"I thought justice would make me feel better. Damn it! I know better. I let it consume me." She leaned into him again. They stayed that way for several minutes, trying to find the people they'd lost. Finally, she stepped back and wiped her tears with her sleeve. Her face was a mess.

Antonio's phone rang. He pulled it from his pocket and saw it was Sylvio. He had attempted several calls.

"Dio mio, Antonio! What's going on? You guys should have been here a long time ago. When you didn't answer, we were beginning to worry. Has somethi …?"

"We're fine, Sylvio. We crossed paths with Alida. She's in the hospital. Long story. We'll be back soon and explain to anyone who feels like staying up to hear it."

Chapter Fifty-six

Tuesday, mid-morning to mid-afternoon

Antonio peeled his eyes open, not knowing for a moment where he was. If his bladder hadn't woken him, he might have slept 'til noon. It took a few moments before he decided yesterday's events were real, and not one of his dreams. He felt grateful to be alive. Even more so that Gabriella was.

It had been after three in the morning when they'd finally gone to bed. When he and Gabriella returned, she'd left the room to call Marcello. That left Antonio to answer the questions that bombarded him, fast and furious. Even Chiara and Angelica were still up, padding about in nightgowns and slippers. He almost didn't recognize Angelica without her make-up. They raided the pantry and refrigerator to find some much-needed sustenance. Of course, Vino Nobile was offered. Antonio had a tall glass to settle his nerves.

There were questions arising that only Gabriella could answer. She finally finished her conversation with Marcello and rejoined them. He was surprised by her willingness to talk about the day's experiences. She explained how Rocco had gone out to hunt pheasant at dawn and stumbled upon her in the vineyard. It gave him great pleasure to bring her at gunpoint to the villa. Alida was almost giddy—like a spoiled little rich girl who had gotten her way. She had wanted to shoot Gabriella right on the spot ... but her sons convinced her otherwise. "Best not to have her blood on your hands, Mother," Donato had argued. "Let your father, Lorenzo, take care of the dirty business." Apparently, her stepfather had enough connections in Apulia to smooth over most crimes he committed, especially when it didn't involve the locals.

"Where were they hiding you?" Antonio asked. "We searched everywhere, once we finally got the search warrant."

"Inside one of the empty *botti*. In the far corner of the wine cellar." *Botti* are huge oak wine casks which hold 800 liters of wine. "They said that if anyone came looking for me ... if I made a noise, they would shoot the searchers on the spot. I could hardly hear a thing, anyway. I felt like I was in a deep, dark hole. All I could think about was how stupid I'd been. It took all of my focus to ward off a panic attack. Thank God I'm not claustrophobic. I spent my time praying that you would rescue me." She looked at Antonio.

Antonio remembered his dream: the long dark tunnel, and Gabriella reaching out to him from the darkness. He would share that with her later. "So that's the aroma I've been smelling on you!" he said, choosing a lighter note. "I've been trying to put my finger on it all night."

She laughed. "It was so strong inside the cask, I almost felt drunk." Hearing her laughter was enough to set Antonio's heart back on the right track.

*****

He had just finished cleaning up and crawled into bed when he remembered his promise to call his son, Jonathan. Jonathan breathed an audible sigh of relief and promised to call the rest of the family. Antonio's consolation was short-lived, however, when Jonathan delivered some news of his own. "Leah's come down with Covid-19, Dad. We think she got it from one of our servers, who probably got it from a customer. It's no wonder the governor is shutting everything down. I'm worried that the twins will get it."

Antonio suddenly felt his heart in his throat. His twin grandchildren, Randal and Christina, were only five months old. "How is she doing?"

"She's running a fever of a hundred and two. Her breathing is labored. I think she's going to be okay, though. I've shut the brewery down. I have to be here to take care of the kids. I'm sleeping on the floor in the nursery. I can't call upon Aunt Alessia or Grandmother Elena. They've got their hands full. And we can't risk giving this to Matthew … it could kill him. Besides, I should be in quarantine myself."

"You feeling okay?"

"So far. I do have one piece of good news to tell you, though. Teodora has come up from Healdsburg to help her mom. Alessia was about to crack under the pressure. She's been in much better spirits since she arrived. And they actually seem to be getting along," Jonathan chuckled.

Antonio smiled. It had been like World War III in their household when Teodora was a teenager.

"That's great. Listen, I wish I were there to help you right now. I'm hoping to be home in a few days, depending on when I can get a flight. I'll call as soon as I know something."

*****

Antonio saw the rays of the sun coming through the shutters, casting their symmetrical pattern on the floor. It brought his mind back to the present. He rolled out of bed and threw on yesterday's muddy jeans. He headed for the kitchen, hoping someone had made some much-needed coffee. Angelica was leaning on the counter, drinking a steaming mug. "Do you parade around shirtless in front of all your cousins?" she asked with a laugh. "Or is this show just for me?"

Antonio could feel himself turning candy-apple red. She'd always had that effect on him. "Cut me some slack," he said. "Rough night."

"More like a rough week, I'd say." She turned half-way serious. "Listen, cousin. I've got to ask. Are you going to marry this girl or not? I'll never forgive you if you let her get away."

"You did hear we're engaged, didn't you?"

"Yeah, and I also heard you're going back to Seattle. Are you stupid, or just a little slow?"

"It's not that simple, *cugina*. They need me at home. I've got my ..."

"Yeah, yeah," she cut him off. "I've heard about your reasons. Just don't come crying to me when she finds some Italian stallion while you're half a world away, unable to return during this pandemic."

"Thanks for your advice," he said, as he poured a cup of coffee. "I'm just trying to do what's right. You're not making it any easier."

She had said what she wanted to, and just stared at him over the rim of her coffee cup as she took a sip. He studied her eyes which were the color of the sunlight on the ocean. Unusual for an Italian. He felt like she was dissecting his every thought and emotion.

"Umberto and I are leaving in a few hours, now that the world is safe again." She smiled. "We need to see if we can find anything at the coop before we go into hibernation. At least we'll have plenty of wine, cheese and bread," she laughed. "Mamà loaded us up with a lifetime supply of cheese, and Umberto has become quite an accomplished bread baker." In a moment, her lips turned from a smile to a frown. "I'm not sure when I'll see you again, *cugino*. But just so you'll know, I'm only saying these things because I love you. I think Gabriella is pretty damn special." She kissed him on the cheek and rushed from the room.

Chapter Fifty-seven

Tuesday afternoon

U mberto and Angelica were on the road by mid-morning. The house felt quiet and uneasily peaceful. Antonio could see Chiara was missing them already. "I don't know when I'm going to see my grandchildren and great-grandchild again," she lamented with a frown. Sylvio was smart. He just gave her a close embrace. Then she busied herself by preparing lunch, her modus operandi whenever she didn't want to face her emotions.

General Marcello Bianchi showed up about half past one. "Sorry, I'm late. I got involved with interrogating our truck driver, Salvo, and his cohort, Maurizio. A waste of time. I doubt we'll get a damn thing out of them. They're too afraid. Can't say I blame them. They know that there's no place that they're safe. Not even in prison."

Chiara set a plate in front of him with some leftover pasta with a Sugo Pomodoro, a simple tomato sauce. *"Mangia!"* she said. He nodded and smiled, took a few bites, then continued his story. "Chia's working on Ettore. She's as good of an interrogator as I have but I doubt she'll have any luck with him either." He indulged in another bite, drank a sip of wine, and wiped his chin. "I called the hospital. Alida is expected to recover fully. The bullet cracked her skull, as you suspected. She has a concussion but it appears there's no serious brain damage. They're transferring her to Firenze for an MRI to be certain. I reminded them to lock her to the stretcher bed. They said I should be able to interview her as early as tomorrow."

"You better put a suicide watch on her," Gabriella said.

"Already have. The hospital wasn't happy with me insisting on having an officer on duty there. They've got him wearing one of those space suits."

"Did your forensic duo find anything interesting with the truck or Mercedes?" Antonio asked.

"No. I didn't think we would, but wanted to double-check anyway. I brought in some bomb-sniffing dogs to make sure they hadn't been transporting any explosives along with the small arms. Nothing."

Antonio nodded. That was a smart move. Marcello was always thorough.

"I sent Marina Gallo, Barbieri, and Corporal Garza to check out the villa and winery more thoroughly, and take barrel samples. That wine issue is not nearly as significant as the murder and arms movement, but it was the thing that brought your brother, Andrea, here in the first place." He looked at Gabriella. "If there was fraud going on, and they were trying to cover it up, it helps to establish motive. The hardest part is going to be putting together murder charges on Alida and Zampari … if he even makes it. He's still touch and go. We have both of them on kidnapping, and her on weapons trafficking, and we know they threatened to kill both of you, but pinning the murder of your brother and Bria on them is another story since those were done by Salvo and Maurizio. We still don't know who shot the wine chemist.

"You also have Zampari on the murder of Marianna Bellini," Antonio said. "Even though Donato did it, Zampari admitted it was on his orders."

"You're right," Marcello acknowledged. "How could I have forgotten? Too many twists and turns in this case, and not enough sleep."

"Also, when Alida had the drop on me, she told us that she was the one calling the shots," Antonio said. "She claimed to have had Zampari under her thumb."

"Not enough," the General replied, as he twisted his fork with some more pasta against the side of his bowl. "I want to pin the murders on her and put her away for life. Her stepfather, too. That will be more difficult unless we can get her or Zampari to cooperate."

"What about their cell phones?" Gabriella asked.

"On it … we have the phones from everyone involved. Chia and Amara Bertoli are working on them. They think they'll have a preliminary report ready for me by late this afternoon. As brazen as Alida and her family were, we might get lucky."

Antonio and Gabriella spent another hour with Marcello, answering detailed questions as he took notes. He then asked for written statements, which took another hour. If they had not been experienced at such things, it would have taken far longer. While they worked on those, he talked individually to Sylvio and Giulia and had them write their statements as well. He followed that up with a call to Umberto for the same. He wanted everyone's observations. He already had an appointment with the senior magistrate for all of Tuscany tomorrow, and wanted to leave no stone unturned. He was expecting to be up most of the night writing up all final case reports himself. As additional evidence came to light, he would file it as addendums.

As if that were not enough, *Zia* Frankie and *Zio* Pasquale followed her out the door, doling out kisses and generous hugs. "What are you two doing here?" Antonio asked. He was surprised to see them. They had returned home to Positano less than two weeks ago, after coming up to help when Raphael was missing.

"We've closed the hotel for now," Frankie answered. "We didn't have a single booking and it looks like things are going to be shut down any day now. We decided we'd rather shelter with family than alone in Positano. It was Sofia's idea."

Frankie, real name Francesca, was the youngest of the three sisters. Antonio had always thought she radiated the sun of the Amalfi Coast where their small hotel sat perched precariously half-way up the hillside of Positano.

The final event that improved Antonio's mood was seeing *Zio* Nicolo walk out the door with no cane and hardly a limp to show for his gunshot wound. They embraced. Nicolo was much more than an uncle to Antonio. He was closer than a brother. Antonio's mother, Elena, was the oldest sibling—the only one born before the great war. Nicolo, the youngest, had arrived late in life, born less than five years before Antonio. They had been through so much together.

They had let Nicolo and Sofia know that they were on their way. Sofia had insisted that they stay for dinner. They had done their best to decline, claiming exhaustion, but she wouldn't hear of it. Now, she locked arms with Antonio and escorted him into the house, promising they would dine early.

*****

Sofia and Frankie retreated to the kitchen to put the finishing touches on dinner. Antonio usually liked to be in the middle of it, but Gabriella had a different idea. "How long until dinner?" she asked Sofia.

"We should be ready to eat at seven."

"Do you mind if I kidnap Antonio a while?"

"Of course not!" Sofia said, understanding written all over her face. "I'm sure you want to spend every last minute together."

"*Grazie*, Sofia. We'll help clean up after dinner," Gabriella said.

"No, you won't! Nice try though."

Gabriella smiled a thank you. She took Antonio's hand and led him through the vineyard. "We won't go far," she said. "I just wanted to talk alone." Antonio had no idea what to expect. His insecurities kicked in for a moment, but one look in her face told him he had nothing to worry about. She looked radiant in the blue light which followed the golden hour. He noticed that the light had returned to her eyes. He hadn't noticed it was gone until now. She put her arms around him and gave him a tender kiss.

"Marry me," she said.

"I plan to."

"No. I don't mean later. Marry me now."

"Now?"

"Tomorrow."

"How are we going to pull that off with everything shut down? Who'd perform the ceremony?"

"Damn you! Stop being so practical." She punched him in the chest. "Remember when you were writing your statement this afternoon and I disappeared?"

"Yeah. You said you needed some fresh air."

"I did. While I was out there, I called Father Bruno and asked him if he could come tomorrow."

Antonio thought of this man he'd met just weeks ago, but had come to hold in such high regard. "He said yes?"

"He did. An enthusiastic yes. He said it would be the greatest honor of his life."

"But you know I still need to go home for a time. My family. My business ..."

"I know." She put her arms around him. "At least it would give us one night together before you go."

"Kind of like a soldier getting married before he goes off to war."

"Yes. Sounds romantic, doesn't it?"

He pulled her close. His senses came alive. Every fiber of his being wanted to be with her. He stepped back. "Where?"

"Right here. If they will let us."

"We better go talk to them."

"Is that a yes?"

He looked deeply in those dark brown eyes. "You really think I could ever say no to you?"

Chapter Fifty-nine
Wednesday afternoon

Butterflies fluttered in Antonio's stomach as he stood before the arbor on the terrazza, sweating bullets beneath the dark suit he had borrowed from Nicolo. Father Bruno, tall, lanky, and handsome, stood on his left. Nicolo, to his right, serving as his best man. He had shaved for the first time since his gunshot wound. He looked twenty years younger.

Antonio scanned the faces smiling back at him expectantly. The wedding had been planned for late afternoon to allow those traveling to make the drive. He was amazed how many were here on such short notice, one day before the country was to go into total lockdown.

The phone tree had kicked into action moments after they talked to Nicolo and Sofia. As soon as Chiara and Sylvio got the word, they called their three girls. They, in turn, called their own children, many of whom sat in front of him now. In the front row, Sofia sat next to Giulia. Leonardo sat next to Giulia, holding hands with Chia. Then came Raphael with his girlfriend, Serafina, her head on his tall shoulder. On the opposite side sat Gaia, Gabriella's intrepid mother-in-law. Gabriella's brother, Alessandro, had also been able to make it. Gabriella's only regret was that it was too long of a trip, and too risky, for her parents from Marche. In the row behind them sat Marcello, who had come straight from his meeting with the magistrate. Marina Gallo sat next to him as his date, which had Antonio second-guessing his detective skills. He had not seen a single clue that they had feelings for one another. Today, a five-year-old detective could figure it out.

Sofia had appointed herself wedding coordinator the moment they asked about having it in their home. She and the family worked far into the evening and throughout the day making things ready; preparing food, cleaning the terrazza, borrowing chairs from neighbors. Giulia had managed to pull together some music, thanks to the ease of modern technology.

Antonio had gone into near-panic when he realized he had no ring to give to Gabriella. When Sofia found out, she took his hand. "Come with me," she'd said. She led him to her room, opened her jewelry box, and pulled something out. "Here." She placed a beautiful ring in his hand. It looked familiar. "This was *Nonna* Valentina's," she explained. "*Nonna* made us promise not to bury her with it. She had hoped one day it might be needed."

How did she know? Antonio wondered. He looked up toward heaven and whispered a thank you.

His wandering mind snapped to attention when Giulia pressed a button on her phone and the music changed. Serena emerged first, smiling ear-to-ear, with her hair in a twist atop her head. She was wearing a pale blue dress and carrying a bouquet of just-picked daffodils, the only flowers they could come up with this time of year. She looked so mature.

Next to arrive was Francesco, Gabriella's father-in-law—a second father to her. He stepped around the corner, looking like he'd never been prouder in his life. But he became just another face in the crowd the moment Gabriella appeared and took her place beside him. She stole Antonio's breath away. She wore a beautiful white wedding dress that he had known nothing about. He found out later it was Sofia's, and had been tucked away in a trunk for almost forty years.

Gabriella's face looked like the morning sun. He noticed those strong cheekbones which always reminded him a little of Sofia Loren, but in his eyes, she was even more beautiful. For a brief moment, his mind flashed back to his first wedding, an event in a large church with hundreds of people. He thought about Randi, so young and beautiful with baby's breath in her blond hair, with the slightest of red highlights. These two women couldn't be more different from one another. And yet both were a perfect match for him. He made eye contact with those deep brown eyes—dancing with joy—and tears welled up in his own.

~~~~ **FRIDAY, MARCH 13** ~~~~

Chapter Sixty

Friday afternoon

Antonio leaned on the railing, along with a few others, taking in the island, which grew ever larger in front of him. The sea brought his senses to life, along with memories of his youth. Being raised in Seal Beach, California, had instilled in him a love for the ocean with its many moods. He could smell the salty air mixed with other aromas. He'd often heard that as you approach the French Isle of Corsica you could smell the fragrance of the *maquis* carried on the breeze from the mountains. He picked up subtle hints of eucalyptus, juniper, and wild herbs. There was one scent he couldn't identify which he assumed to be that of the *immortelle*, the aromatic yellow shrub which he knew to be everywhere on the island. He had only seen it in photographs.

Antonio's great-grandfather, Antoine Cortese, had come from Corsica. He had immigrated to America just prior to the First Great War. Though the island is part of France, it wasn't always so. The Corsicans are fiercely independent, and many have Italian surnames. Thus, the name Cortese. When Antonio's father was born, he was given the name Anthony, the American version of Antoine. Antonio's mother, Elena, chose to continue the tradition but decided upon the Italian variation, Antonio.

Antonio had never been to Corsica, but knew he had relatives there. He hoped to meet them someday, but not today.

He had boarded the ferry in Livorno, on the Tuscan coast. It would land in Bastia, near the northern tip of the island. It was the only option he'd been able to find for escaping at this point. In Bastia he would change ferries for one taking him to Toulon, on the south coast of France. Landing in Nice had been another option. But returning to the city where Randi and Christina had taken their final breaths was more than he could deal with at this time. From Toulon he would catch a train to Paris for a late-night flight. France was beginning to shut down, like Italy. But after hours of near-fruitless searching online, he'd been able to procure a coach ticket from Paris to New York's JFK. He would have a six-hour layover, then fly from there to Seattle.

It had turned into a gentle day after the morning storm moved on to the east. It was probably raining in Tuscany about now. He watched the breeze play across the water, licking up tiny whitecaps, which glinted in the sunlight that shone on the Tyrrhenian Sea. It was not enough to rock the large vessel. It drove most of the other passengers inside, except for him and another man who glanced at him and nodded. He looked vaguely familiar.

As they got closer to the island, the water became shallower and smoother. He was mesmerized by the color as it turned more and more turquoise. It added to the dream-like state his mind was in, barely comprehending the events of the last few days.

At least I'm returning home in one piece, he mused. Even his hand was getting better. He laughed when he thought about how three of his family members had gone out of their way to congratulate him for staying out of the hospital. He was grateful for that, but far more so that God had heard his pleas and protected Gabriella. He tried to focus on that and other positives, because, though his body was in one piece, inside, his emotions were still tearing him in two. Every happy thought was countered by sadness, and every feeling of thankfulness by misgivings. Leaving had been impossibly difficult.

He thought back to the wedding, and the celebration afterward. It had ended early so everyone could travel home before the midnight deadline, shutting the country down. He smiled as he thought about his cousin, Angelica, planting a kiss on him as she was leaving and whispering in his ear, "I knew you'd listen to me."

The early departure of the guests had not been a disappointment to Antonio, who was secretly desperate to be alone with Gabriella. Nicolo and Sofia allowed Serena to stay with them another night so they could spend their wedding night alone. The night had exceeded all he imagined it would be. He thought of Gabriella's seemingly ageless body wrapped about him, neither able to sleep after their burst of passion, in which they released all of their tensions. After a time, they had made love again … gently, slowly, savoring every moment. Afterward, he had slept more peacefully than he had in years.

The following morning, fate—or God—had smiled upon them. He'd spent hours searching online until it became clear that he would not be able to get out of the country that day. He managed to make the ferry reservations for today, and the two of them had a second glorious night together. He thought of how her body trembled as his fingers unbuttoned her blouse.

They had slept-in late this morning until a call from Marcello woke them. He was calling to give them an update. Their bodies had remained entwined as they put the call on speaker and listened to the mostly good report. The sobering news was that Captain Zampari had died overnight. The intestinal damage from the gunshot wound had been more than his system could handle. Antonio hoped he had made his peace with God after all the evil he'd done.

One item of good news, which surprised them both, was that Marianna's son, Jacopo Bellini, had chosen to return home and take over the family wine business. Whatever his reasoning, it felt right. He had even chosen to keep Marianna's dogs and breed them for future generations.

The best news was that Alida had turned into a cooperative witness. The text logs on her phone had reinforced their case to a point that her conviction was a foregone conclusion. When the magistrate spelled out her options of life in prison, or a lesser sentence if she gave up her stepfather, she chose the latter.

Antonio recalled Marcello's exact words. "I don't think she has the same fear of Lorenzo Tarantino that drove the others to silence. She's convinced herself that he loves her too much to have her killed, even if she betrays him." Antonio wondered if that were true. Marcello had gone on to explain, "General Peluso is working with a General Matera in Apulia. He is confident he is uncompromised. Search warrants have been procured and they are planning to raid several locations today where she told us that weapons are likely to be found. They've probably already begun. It could be a major haul. As much as I hate to admit it, this wouldn't be the case if Gabriella hadn't gone out on a limb to find justice for her brother and Bria."

*****

Antonio's thoughts returned to Gabriella. She'd gone silent again after Marcello's call, barely saying a word all morning. He was left to wonder: was it the reality of him leaving that was heavy on her mind? Outwardly, she supported the decision, but she'd made it perfectly clear that she didn't have to like it. He assumed other things were weighing on her as well. She was probably re-processing the loss of Andrea and Bria, as well as some of the choices she'd made in her efforts to bring their killers to justice. He knew the smartest thing was to give her space. He'd half-expected the silence to continue on their drive to Livorno, but she'd surprised him with another reversal. She even broached the subject of a honeymoon.

Prior to Covid-19 turning the world upside down, Nicolo and Sofia had been planning a sabbatical and dream trip. They had reserved a large sailing yacht and planned to travel from the south of France to Portofino, then Cinque Terre, then to Corsica and Sardinia. From there they would make their way south along the Amalfi Coast, at least as far as Positano, maybe even Sicily. They had invited Antonio, Gabriella, and Serena to join them for any or all of it. Other family would join them for portions of the journey. The boat had four cabins and a well-outfitted galley.

"I hope we can take them up on it," Gabriella said, with a hopeful glance his way. "We could take some time to ourselves—just the two of us—in various ports along the way. It would be perfect!" Antonio was all for it and told her so. But it was hard for him to embrace her enthusiasm. It felt like an impossible dream right now. At least it gave them something to look forward to after the difficult days which lay in front of them.

*****

Antonio's thoughts had just turned to the difficult goodbye at the ferry landing, when the vibrato sound of the ferry engines changed, distracting his mind. It began to slow as it neared the quay. He was thankful to escape these painful reflections.

He looked to his right and noticed that the other man leaning against the rail was staring at him. He gave a slight nod, with a knowing smile. Antonio nodded in return, then turned to watch the approaching ferry landing. The ferry reversed its engines for final docking.

Antonio took the handle of his single piece of luggage, preparing to move toward the ramp where he would offload. Straight away he felt a tap on his shoulder and turned. "*Mi scuzi, signor.* I think I may know who you are. Is your name Antonio? Antonio Cortese?"

Antonio eyed the man suspiciously, wondering if he posed a threat. He didn't think so. "*Si.* And you are?"

"I'm a *Capitan* with the Corsican *Gendarmerie.* I'm returning from an investigative trip which took me to the Cinque Terre. I was forced to return early when the lockdown prevented me from completing a joint investigation I was working with the Carabinieri. When I saw you, I couldn't believe my eyes. I've seen your photograph … on a family genealogy website. I was doing some family research. My name is Ruggiero … Ruggiero Cortese. I believe we may be third cousins."

Antonio stared in disbelief. The family resemblance was unmistakable.

About the Story:

This story, and the characters within, are fictional. However, there are elements within the story that have a basis in fact.

In a few respects, Antonio's character is based upon my own life. My family and I owned and operated an Italian restaurant, Frankie's Pizza and Pasta, in Redmond, Washington, for 24 years. I used that experience as a restaurateur and chef to bring rich detail to the cooking and meal scenes. During those years, I also gained a great deal of knowledge about wine, especially Italian wines, which allowed me to approach that subject with authenticity. In addition, my wife and I have made several trips to Italy and Tuscany. Thus, we have first-hand knowledge of most of the places described in the book. I am also a cyclist and a gardener, which I believe allowed me to present those scenes with authenticity.

This particular story is set mainly in Montepulciano, one of my favorite hill towns in Tuscany. I have tried to portray it as accurately as possible, including a few tidbits about its history. In the story, the *consorzio* references a real organization, a "consortium" of wineries which includes the vast majority of the producers of the superb wine known as Vino Nobile di Montepulciano (as well as the less noble, easier drinking, Rosso di Montepulciano). I hope I did not disrespect them by suggesting that any of their member wineries might involve themselves in fraudulent winemaking practices. This is strictly a work of fiction. However, there is a basis in fact regarding the event known as Brunellogate. It was a true and highly controversial event which did, indeed, damage the reputation of many fine Brunello wines for a time.

In the book, I reference an acronym known as DOCG, with little explanation. It stands for *Denominazione di Origine Controllata e Garantita*, which translates as "Denomination of Controlled and Guaranteed Origin". It is a classification system governing Italian wine production to guarantee quality. There is a less stringent classification known as DOC. The addition of the G puts it at a level with higher standards. These rules govern the types of grapes which can be used in a particular wine, as well as the geography of where those grapes must be grown.

Now, regarding the mafia. I have once again utilized a mafia clan in my story. I have done extensive research regarding the Mafia who operate in Italy. Prior to this, I had naively thought (and hoped) that the Mafia was slowly becoming a thing of the past. It appears that I was quite wrong.

The *Sacro Corona Unita,* who are a part of my story, are a real mafia clan who operate primarily in the southern Italian region of Apulia (the heel of the boot, Puglia in the Italian spelling). They are often referred to as the Fourth Mafia, after the more prominent mafia clans of 'Ndrangheta from Calabria, the Camorra from Campania, and the Cosa Nostra of Sicily. Small arms trafficking is one of their major crimes.

As in my past books, I make reference to a major terrorist event which took the lives of Antonio's wife and daughter. Though their characters are fictional, sadly, the terror attack on which I based their death was a real event. On the evening of July 14, 2016, a 19-ton cargo truck was deliberately driven into crowds of people celebrating Bastille Day on the Promenade des Anglais in Nice, France, resulting in the deaths of 86 people and the injury of 458 others. The driver was a Tunisian, living in France. The attack ended following an exchange of gunfire, during which the terrorist, Lahouaiej-Bouhlel, was shot and killed by police. The Islamic State claimed responsibility for the attack, saying he answered its "calls to target citizens of coalition nations that fight the Islamic State".

I hope you enjoyed this book. Look for more Antonio Cortese adventures to come.

Frank Curtiss

About the Author

Author Frank Curtiss is a retired Italian restaurant owner. *Death in Abundance* is the third title in the *Antonio Cortese Mystery* series. His first two novels, *Deception in Siena*, and *Missing in Firenze* have received excellent reviews.

Frank also authored and published a cookbook, *Frankie at Home in the Kitchen*. It is available as an eBook on Amazon and we're hoping to have physical copies available again soon.

Frank and is wife Rhonda owned a popular Italian restaurant, Frankie's Pizza & Pasta, in Redmond, Washington, for 24 years. When the property owners sold to a developer, they chose to retire from the restaurant business. It was at that time that Frank decided to pursue his dream of becoming a writer.

Frank has a passion for all things Italian: the food, wine, people, and place. During their restaurant years they were able to travel to Italy on several occasions. It was natural for him to use Italy as the primary setting for his novels.

Speaking of his writing, Frank says, "As an author, I've drawn upon my lifetime of experiences as a restaurateur, chef, wine connoisseur, cyclist, gardener, traveler, photographer, and artist. My wife and I have also experienced some very difficult losses in our lives. I believe this has enabled me to develop believable characters of great depth and complexity. I hope you enjoy my books."

Frank and Rhonda grew up in southern California. They moved to Washington State in 1979, and currently reside in Redmond, Washington. They have two adult sons, both married. They currently have the joy of raising a teenage granddaughter.

Made in the USA
Monee, IL
13 August 2024

63821699R00206